Maimouna flashed ̶ ̶ ̶ ̶ ̶ ̶ ̶ ̶
umph.

"You'll come with us now. We will show you
what Bardo is really concerned with!" The woman
smiled bleakly. "You'll wish you had never found
out."

"We're going to be sent to an ice-cap," pouted
Maimouna.

"Far from it! Your particular Bardo skills are far
too . . . let's say, *protective*, of us all. We will go to
what is blithely called the Procyon Embassy. We
will open some more closed doors for you!"

"That hotel," said the man, "happens to be one of
the three Command Control Centres for the defence of this whole damn planet. The others, of
course, are in Kazakhstan and Lhasa."

"For the defence of—?"

"There aren't any charming alien friends out in
space. Space isn't friendly at all. You'll see."

Also by Ian Watson in VGSF

THE JONAH KIT

THE MIRACLE VISITORS
(VGSF Classic)

THE EMBEDDING
(VGSF Classic)

THE FLIES OF MEMORY

STALIN'S TEARDROPS

THE MARTIAN INCA

IAN WATSON

ALIEN EMBASSY

VGSF

First published in Great Britain 1977
by Victor Gollancz Ltd

First VGSF edition published 1993
by Victor Gollancz
A Cassell imprint
Villiers House, 41/47 Strand, London WC2N 5JE

© Ian Watson 1977

A catalogue record for this book is
available from the British Library

ISBN 0 575 05607 X

Printed and bound in Great Britain
by Cox & Wyman Ltd, Reading

For Marjorie Brunner

If all knowledge were within a man, and ignorance were wholly absent, that man would be consumed and cease to be. So ignorance is desirable, inasmuch as by that means he continues to exist . . .

Jalaluddin Rumi
Discourses

PROLOGUE

'Come in, Rajit,' the Teacher called; and the boy in the turban followed the echo of his knuckles into the room.

(This must have been how it happened . . .)

On one of the white plaster walls an emerald lizard poised, the membrane of its throat trembling convulsively. The table bore crockery, school exercise books, a bronze statuette of a Tibetan god copulating with a highly gymnastic partner, and a large box. A louvre window intersected the rows of palms and the flowering tree outside, producing a chequerboard effect. One of the two cane chairs was occupied by the African Teacher, the other by a Chinese whose olive green tunic and customary holster (which may or may not have contained a pistol) showed him to be a Dobdob, one of the police wing of the Space Communications Administration, Bardo, which also handled all the world's internal affairs.

'I hear you'd like to be a lama when you're older, Rajit?'

The boy nodded firmly.

'More than anything!'

'Why's that?' A pucker of amusement creased the face of the Chinese.

'To see India one day—' the boy blurted out.

The Chinese cut him off angrily.

'Do you feel confined, here in Africa? Here is the same as everywhere else – part of human society. If you're a lama, what do you think you'll be preaching about? Tourism?' He made the last word sound obscene, which it was. 'What sort of people travel the world nowadays?'

'Some sailors do.'

'Oh yes – carrying essential supplies! That's just because everywhere isn't self-sufficient. Even the biggest of the sail-barges only need a few husband and wife teams to crew them—'

'A computer trims the sails, I know.'

'The barge is their world, not the ports they call at.'

Rajit flushed.

'But *you* travel, sir. There's nothing wrong with travel if you're really contributing something.'

'You're forthright, at least! Bardo officials travel, right enough – to co-ordinate the world and see that everyone is fed and cared for and correctly educated. Perhaps to find candidates for starflight, if we're lucky . . .'

'I only want to visit places . . . to contribute. Like you, sir. Only slowly, as a lama.'

'Quite! The trick of being a lama is just that. To move gently from place to place, to teach the people social ecology. To repeat the good news of how the human body-field can be used to contact our star friends, without squeezing the world dry to build rocket-ships and other paraphernalia. The lama proves by his own example that there's no need for people to waste energy that way. He doesn't wander from town to town because he's been allotted some sort of magic carpet, but because he's the perfect compass needle to point the true way. That way always points *right here* – wherever he is, in a little village like your Bagamoyo or a big far-off city like Bombay.'

'I agree, sir.'

'But you'd still like to see Bombay? Well, honesty's a fine thing, Rajit. At the same time, the really honest man also knows when to tell a lie. He knows when it's more *true* to tell a lie. Sometimes we have to tell little lies and play games, don't we? He who doesn't know how to do this is a fool. No one would want him for a lama.'

The Chinese smiled.

'You'll be a lama if you study hard – and learn to tell a lie convincingly, for the sake of pointing the way. In fact, you can even start right now. I have a little service to ask of you confidentially.'

'I won't tell a soul, whatever it is,' Rajit promised fervently.

A stray mosquito had blown into the room along with Rajit. It flew about now, trailing legs like loose threads, whining ever so faintly but persistently. The lizard made a rush across the plaster and froze above the Dobdob's head, a green flame.

'You see that box on the table? Inside there's a coco-de-mer. Yes, a real one. It's quite heavy. Take it down to the shore. *Secretly.* I want you to dump that coco as though it had been washed up by the tide – but nowhere *too* conspicuous. Then get rid of the box. Smash it up. Now, there's a girl in this village called Lila.'

'Yes, we're good friends.'

'So I've been told. I want you to make sure she finds that coco. By herself, though; on her own – that's essential. I'll leave it up to your own ingenuity to arrange. Point her the right way without her realizing it; and keep the other children out of the way. After she finds it—'

Rajit listened carefully to every word.

Outside, a dog barked in the hot dust, and the blue jacaranda bloomed.

ONE

When I was just eleven years old and my breasts were freshly budding I found a coco-de-mer washed ashore. It was tangled up in damp seaweed, though strangely it was quite dry itself. Cocos are huge, double coconuts. Because they resemble a woman's parted thighs and vulva, they've always been powerful ritual objects. The ocean had brought this one all the way from the Seychelles Islands, for me! Forgetting my sandals in the excitement of being singled out by fate (for I firmly believed I was destined for Bardo even then, though it was to be six years before the Dobdobs came to confirm it) I ran barefoot through the Bagamoyo streets, staggering under its weight, to show the prodigy to my friends. The Bardo Building – the former mosque – contained an ebony carving of a coco-de-mer, which we children had to dust and polish; but we'd never seen a real one. They're only found in the Seychelles. The southern equatorial current generally bears them all the other way: to India and Sri Lanka, where they've been treasured for centuries.

Yussuf, Rajit, cousin Rose and Timothy crowded round.

The black, polished double shell stood as high as my kneecap on the dusty road. The central cleft where the shell divided was smooth and milky white. Symbol of human love and joy – and more than that, the gateway to the stars.

Our own thin, lanky, domestic coconut palms spiked the blue sky everywhere. Their clusters of nuts were only a fraction of the size of my coco: little skullfuls of milk. Tattered parasols of leaves drooped from the tops of their knobbly, banded trunks, providing the only shade for our village, apart from a few corrugated awnings along the shops, and an arcade outside the dispensary where patients could squat and gossip.

Dun, humpbacked cattle with tight, ribbed hides grazed right down on to the beach under the shade of these palms, nibbling seaweed at the high tide line.

'*Mer* means *sea* in French,' Rajit said knowingly. (All those

12

facts crammed into his turban along with reams of oily black hair.)

'They never spoke French in India,' Yussuf protested.

'People always performed a ceremonial when they found a new coco!' Rajit said. 'We must do the same. Out at the tombs. That's the proper place!'

'She ought to take it straight home,' mumbled Timothy the albino. He was scared of the old ruined Arab graveyard. Scared of spooks, since he looked like one himself. His skin was mottled pink and ivory, and his flesh had a poachy texture like thick sour milk. He was a sickly boy. We all know that he'd probably die in his early twenties, since albinos only live a little while. Rajit took an unkind advantage of his appearance in our games. Timothy was the perfect ghost. However, we were children, we didn't care, and Timothy still followed us round sheepishly, grateful not to be excluded. Tears sprang to his eyes as he begged us not to go to the tombs, and we told ourselves that it was just the sunlight hurting them.

Cousin Rose and I were both black and glossy as polished ebony. We wore our hair plaited in tight corn rows. Our mothers spent hours unwinding and retying them every weekend – a whole morning of fidget and chatter, during which we heard (for example) how Bibi Mwezi had poured boiling water over the contracapsule in her arm in her anxiety to conceive a child, and how she put up with the worsening pain for weeks till Mboya, the Barefoot Doctor, was hard put to it to save her whole arm from amputation. Or we heard the tale of how the baobab tree gets its strange shape – for a baobab looks as though it's growing upside down, with its crown buried in the soil and its roots poking in the air. That tree is somebody whose head got stuck in the 'Divine Ground' by experimenting with Tantra, the yoga of love, without proper knowledge or safeguards. This was a cautionary tale put about by the lamas, and I mention it mainly to illustrate how we behaved with Timothy – because a huge baobab loomed over the Arab tombs and one day the tale suggested a game to Rajit. He uprooted a large stone to make a hole in the ground, and forced Timothy to stand on his hands, with his head hidden down the hole, while we stood round laughing at this white baobab tree with legs wagging in the air. Other times, we collected the fallen baobab pods, smooth as the heads of babies, with the lightest down of hair, to crack them open for their sweet sherbet.

The graveyard sang with heat and insects. It was just after noon. For centuries now the old pillar tombs had been rotting back into their natural state of coral. Pockmarks gnawed the blocks and columns; their plaster mouldings had nearly all fallen off. Most of the lime and gypsum mortar had washed loose during the past four hundred and fifty years, although there were still a few geometric friezes and even an unbroken blue and white Chinese bowl inset high up at the top of one pillar just underneath the turban-like knob. It bore the Chinese character for 'long life' (according to Rajit). All other inset plates and bowls had long since fallen out or been stolen.

I carried my coco-de-mer up to the base of one tomb and propped it against the carved coral.

'Whose tomb is it, Yussuf?'

Yussuf, who could read Arabic, squinted up at the remains of the squiggly dotted script.

'It says, that this is the tomb of the Muslims . . . He is as-Sultan Shonvi la-Haji . . . He died in the year something after the Flight of the Prophet. He must have been a salt trader, Sultan Shonvi. The salt boss. That's what it means.'

I tried to visualize the bearded Arab in his flowing robes and jewels. The slaves, the sacks of salt on their backs. Whipcracks. Laden dhows in the now silted-up creek. Before the Europeans came to this part of Africa. Then went home again. Before Americans brought sacks of grey dust from the seas of the Moon, and bags of red sand from the Martian deserts, at incredible cost. And abandoned the whole enterprise. Before the human race discovered the true way to the stars through the sexual union of Man and Woman.

We were all so young then. Even Rajit, with the first soft bristles on his chin, was merely cruelly innocent when he made us carry out the masquerade that afternoon among the graves. He insisted that Timothy and I should act out the copulation of Black Kali and White Shiva. Kali the Destroyer stands for the ravages of time, Shiva for the eternal spirit of creativity. Thus, though Shiva is slain, a white corpse, he still has an erection, even in death. Kali rides upon his body, her four arms

14

brandishing weapons, her red tongue sticking out in scorn. She's supposed to do so in a graveyard, by night.

After dark the graveyard was always full of great scuttling crabs marching up from the sea, and the baobab tree glowed ghostly in the starlight. Sighs of wind through its branches sounded like lost souls to take possession of you.

However, the sun was shining down on us right then, from overhead. Ants were tunnelling through the bones of the long-dead Salt Boss, turning them into flutes and trumpets; and the hum and buzz of insects round about us sounded like music played on them, filtering up above the ground.

'You'll have to take your clothes off, both of you,' ordered Rajit. 'Timothy must lie down with his eyes wide open. He's dead. He's the white corpse of Shiva. He has to be *virile*, of course.'

'How can he be?' wondered cousin Rose. 'There's nothing to excite you when you're dead.'

'But Timothy isn't really dead, he's only pretend-dead! Anyway, it has to be this way because Kali on top of Shiva means that you're leaving your physical body behind – by means of the sexuality of the body. Right, Lila? It's just a symbol for Bardo flight. So Timothy has to be virile just by thinking about it. He isn't to touch himself, because he's dead. He can't move, see?'

'Tim will get awfully sunburnt. You know that his mother won't let him take his clothes off to swim, in case his skin peels,' said Yussuf.

'That's the salt water, not the sun!'

The only occasion when I'd seen Tim naked, he had looked like a great fat maggot, his flesh as spongy as white bread, with pink blotches as big as saucers. I loathed the prospect of touching his naked body with my own; no doubt Rajit was aware of this – and it added to his sadistic glee. Both Rajit and Yussuf had proved their newly-acquired virility recently, standing in the surf, squeezing their own white seed into the foam. But could Timothy produce anything? To be sure, he had a contracapsule implanted in his arm, just as they did, but the Barefoot Doctor might only have given him one as a kindness, to save him from the scorn of his peers. So, despite my repugnance, I was curious.

As we stood arguing a giant green mantis sprang on to a knob of the Salt Boss's tomb and glared at us – ten centimetres long with saw teeth on its open arms ready to snap shut like an animal trap; with globe eyes and very little brain behind them. A Female; and she was pregnant. Her swollen egg-case slumped beneath her angel's wings. A green Kali had come to watch over our little ceremony. Her arrival settled the matter.

Timothy stripped off awkwardly and laid his blotchy body down by the tomb. It was a beached gasping fish's body. We all felt at once guilty, fascinated, excited.

'Open your eyes,' said Rajit. 'Dead Shiva's eyes must stare.'

'But what at?' Tears welled in Timothy's eyes.

'At Kali, obviously. Now take your things off, Lila. Don't squat on him till he's virile, though. He has to do it by thought power.'

'I can't!' said Timothy.

I slipped off my java-print frock and handed it to Rose.

'Let's use the coco to help him!' giggled Rajit. 'Concentrate on the magic coco, Tim!'

Rajit picked up the heavy coco and deposited it on Timothy's thighs, while I straddled them, pinning him down. Then Rajit pressed my hands down on the coco and began rocking it to and fro as though the coco shell was making love to the albino. He slapped and rubbed Timothy's flesh against the groove in the coco. It was like a sea-slug smacking concrete.

Poor Tim stared blindly at me through a film of tears, while I rocked to and fro, clutching my coco, dreaming of space travel.

'He's wet himself!' said Rose.

I scrambled clear and snatched my precious coco free. Tim swung over on his side to escape our gaze, and blubbered quietly.

Rose threw my dress back at me brusquely and knelt by the crying boy, stroking his wispy ginger curls, as slick with sweat as a bawling baby's skull.

'We didn't mean to hurt you, Tim. It's only a game,' she crooned.

None of us were looking at each other any more. We were ashamed. I stumbled when I stepped into my frock and tore the cotton on a toenail.

Back home, my mother greeted the advent of the coco with such delight that I might already have been accepted by Bardo for the space programme. She called the neighbours in for bowls of coconut beer, and sent a message to Teacher Makindi, who soon arrived to take a drink. He seemed to see the coco as something of an omen too. Naturally we all believed it after that. Whereupon my aunt (Rose's mother) grew jealous. 'Hush, girl, it's just a lucky find, it doesn't mean anything. You're only eleven years old.' But I tapped the tiny bump of the capsule in my arm.

'I'm a woman,' I said, and drank my beer down. The fermented coconut juice buzzed in my throat.

'I'm a womb-man,' I sang. 'My womb is Space!'

· After a while my head swam. I was already swimming through the psychic space inside me, out to fabled Procyon and far Barnard's Star.

TWO

Our little group fell apart after the cemetery masquerade.
A wedge had been driven between us. Timothy avoided us
utterly now, a solitary ghost of a boy who'd used up his whole
life's energy bearing the weight of my coco that day. He sat
dully in school, dozing and lazy. He deliberately made his
skin more repulsive by sitting out in the brightest sunshine till
he was a kind of walking chrysalis, except that no butterfly
would ever emerge from it, only the same white grub.

Rose and I no longer had our hair corn-rowed together. My
aunt let Rose's hair grow into a bush. My mother filled up the
lonely gap of Saturday mornings more satisfyingly by entertain-
ing Teacher Makindi, who continued calling round at our home
to show me mandala prints during these hours of hair dressing,
paying court to my mother on the side.

Before long, Teacher Makindi was coming round constantly.
When I was there, he spoke about Astromancy, about Psychic
Spaceflight, and about Bardo, while Mother looked on proudly
and hopefully. If I happened to be out of the house when he
came visiting, Mother looked equally exhilarated on my return.

Our school lessons took up the five weekday mornings. Afternoons were for swimming, playing Go with pebbles on the
beach, fishing or helping in the fields. Saturday – Restday –
we could do what we liked, but every Sunday morning we had
extra classes in the Bardo Building, the old mosque, on the
significance of Bardo and Social Ecology – on outer space and
the inner workings of the world, which had now joined hands.
On successive Sundays, week in, week out, we learnt from
Makindi or from a visiting Barefoot lama precisely how the
Social Ecology of Earth is sustained by our new knowledge of
the stars and why the proper organization to administer the
Earth's affairs is Bardo.

Rajit, his sights set on being a lama, did well in Social
Ecology. As he grew into adolescence, he gave up pranks and

masquerades. His eyes were firmly fixed on the dusty road downcoast to Dar es Salaam, whence the computer-rigged sail-barges set out with their cargoes of sisal fibre, copper and salted eland carcasses, for the Persian Gulf and India. Dar es Salaam was the lama training centre for all East Africa.

Bardo – and Astromancy. That was my best lesson. The word Bardo actually stands for *Bureau of Astromancy Research and Development Organization.* Two hundred years ago, in the Bad Old Days, they had had rocketships and dreamt of colonizing the stars. The Earth was becoming a desert while they shipped dust back from dead worlds.

Then, in the far north of People's India, where Tantra, the yoga of sexual ecstasy, had kept a toehold through all the revolutions of the time, the woman known to us as Comrade Tara Dakini found herself for the first time in human history in full true contact with a Rakshasa, one of the alien intelligences inhabiting the moon of the second planet of Barnard's Star; and the human race passed suddenly from one mode of science to another. The foundation of our knowledge shifted; our present world was born. Society shifted abruptly too: towards loving mutuality and stability. So we learnt. So the Teacher and the lamas told us.

Teacher Makindi was thin, sleek and svelte in his blue tunic. Always encouraging and helpful, he kept remote from me at heart, however. I never quite ceased being in school, even at home when he visited (and later still, when he became my step-father).

'Astromancy,' he taught me one Saturday morning at home, while my hair was being done, reiterating the previous Sunday's lecture given by a lama passing through Bagamoyo on his preaching circuit, 'means communication with the stars by psychic means, just as necromancy means communication with the dead, in graveyards, when people believed in such things—'

He smiled a private smile as though he knew all about our game among the graves. And Mother tugged my hair even tighter, exposing scalp as though preparing my skull for electrodes for my Bardo test, years in advance.

Bardo. It was once a Tibetan word, before the Bureau took it over. There was an ancient Tibetan religious book called the *Bardo Thödol,* the so-called *Book of the Dead,* a title which

19

should really be translated as 'Liberation by Hearing on the After-Death Plane'. In the old days the Tibetan lamas used to read this book over corpses to guide departed souls to new bodies for reincarnation (or so they thought). However, the book's real value lay in the mental disciplines it contained for projecting the human mind beyond the body.

'There's a lot of confusion in that book, as in all religious texts,' smiled Makindi. 'No one before the time of Comrade Tara Dakini realized that all religions and mythologies were simply interstellar messages from our friends out there, gone astray. All that nonsense about life after death! Let Men make a hell of the Earth, because there's a heaven elsewhere! We could never have true social ecology as long as that philosophy prevailed. No, Lila, when the body dies, the brain melts like a jellyfish in the sunshine. Consciousness melts too. You linger in the minds of other people for a while, in what you've made and done. You carry on socially. But individually? What is an "individual"? Are you an individual when you're asleep? You have no consciousness of yourself then. There's really very little individual consciousness, as such. It's an illusion.'

The human race briefly hoped that Comrade Tara Dakini was indeed in contact with the souls of dead humans, that alien worlds were truly spirit abodes, as the ancient Tibetans believed. They were wrong. That was the last great illusion of humanity. With its passing, the old world passed. True aliens inhabited those alien worlds – and the psychic 'Bardo plane' happened to be the uniquely logical way for alien worlds to communicate with one another, not the way of the radio telescope. Indeed, a technological approach to Space dealt death to a culture, sooner or later, the aliens told humanity.

The only true way was the way of the body-field. The human 'body-field'! How Makindi enthused about it – as indeed did each lama who passed through our village. And rightly so.

Religions had always more or less acknowledged the existence of a body-field – a field of energy associated with each living organism. Why else did Christianity have its saints with haloes? Why else did the head of Buddha, in meditation, wear a bright corona? In the East the body-field had been charted for several millennia by various means: in highly abstract mandalas and other cosmic 'circuit diagrams', or, more practically, in acupuncture charts. But the superstitious masses doted on fakirs and miracles, while real holy men simply yearned for union with the great blank of nirvana.

In the West the body-field was largely ignored by religion, and by science . . . Until an American called Cleve Backster wired up a lie detector to the leaf of a rubber plant on a whim one day, and discovered that all living matter, even an individual sperm or a single living cell, possesses 'primary perception' – an extended sensitivity field. Until a Russian called Kirlian photographed – electrically – the aura of his own body, and found it to be emitting flares of light corresponding to the ancient Chinese acupuncture points. Until leaves were filmed electrically, and seen to have a body-field that remained intact for a while even if the leaf was mutilated; proving that there was an energy body as well as a physical body. Given proper guidance and enough energy, the body-field could be beamed far from the body itself. Here at last the Eastern religions pruned their magic and mysticism, and the Western technologies found common ground.

The 'astral-plane' – jeered at for years by Western science – was found at last to be the plane of the stars, indeed. Guides were waiting patiently, guides who had long been projecting their own, better-organized body-fields towards the human race, only to be taken for Gods or Devils, or phantoms of the afterlife – the very mistake made by those reincarnation-minded Tibetans who wrote the *Book of the Dead*. 'The Book of Life' it should have been called, instead!

'Can you lend me this *Book of the Dead*, even if it is a bit wrong? I'd like to read it.'

He shook his head, regretfully.

'I've only read a summary myself. You see, though it's a great classic it's also a profoundly misleading book. There are so many wrong notions in it. It took long enough to disentangle the sense from the nonsense! Bardo don't want people confusing themselves again. Besides, somebody might try to put it into practice all on his own. You know how much some people want to be accepted for Bardo travel.' (I knew!) 'But the *Book of the Dead* ignores a lot of the practical side – for instance the tantric yoga you need to free the body's energy, to fuel the Bardo journey. The *Book of the Dead* is only one wheel of

Bardo. A truck can race along on one wheel for a while, but then it topples over! Tantric yoga is only one wheel too. Raising that kind of energy in private is really dangerous. You need to study mandala diagrams to train your mind, you need computers to monitor your brain waves – oh so much else.'

'Comrade Tara Dakini must have been either a very clever woman, or very lucky, to fit it all together by herself!'

'Well, the Rakshasas helped her . . . They set up the first mental embassy here on Earth, and of course they showed us how to fit our jigsaw pieces together. Part of one Eastern religion here, part of another mental discipline there.'

'A mental embassy? What does it *look* like? I can't imagine.'

'Oh, just a building, like any other,' he chuckled. 'I've seen photographs of the Procyon Embassy. It's a converted hotel, on Miami Beach. Barnard's Star use the Potala Palace in Tibet. The Yidags of Epsilon Indi use a Russian monastery near the old space centre in Kazakhstan. But the main thing is that you need a very special cast of mind to be just right for Bardo and not one tenth of one per cent of human beings have it.'

'I know. I mustn't feel disappointed—'

However, Makindi and my mother exchanged a glance. I knew what they believed. Perhaps their love for one another was so cemented by this hope that they needed to believe it, true or not.

I walked out into the blinding streets to be alone.

Astromancy. For me, the world held another world cradled in its arms.

Romance.

I wasn't thinking of the erotic aspect of star flight, the need to take a love partner. I was imagining what it must be like to brush against such a being as a Rakshasa with one's mind. Those fiery, mercurial shape-shifters, those flying denizens of cloud-cities soaked in the ruddy orange glow of an alien sunlight! How did they manifest themselves in Lhasa? Was it as a blazing light or pillar of fire? The Rakshasas had been exploring our galaxy for ten thousand years on the Bardo plane, they said. After ten millennia they had still only reached five hundred light years out from Barnard's Star. It would take so much time to chart the whole galaxy and meet all the strange beings in it. A hundred thousand years might be too short. Yet free time was what we had now. That was the uniquely precious gift of Bardo. Breathing space!

Sunlight boomed on the white street, cleaving a line of darkness under the rippling tin awnings, where an old man sat at his sewing table running off white linen tunic tops. His foot danced on the pedal; danced in the same spot all the time, as the whole world danced joyfully nowadays, not moving anywhere. As I passed him, he grinned dreamily and broken-toothedly.

A bicycle lay on its side outside an open door. The ribbed track of its tyres uncoiled down the street like a very long sloughed snakeskin. A hen trod this path pedantically till a dog ran barking out of the house and scuttled it away in a clucking of affronted feathers. This was the pace of human life today. And this pace was exactly the same in Nairobi, New York, Moscow, Peking. We had saved ourselves. All space and time was ours.

There were still many large cities, true; but they were no longer the tumours of the twentieth century, as depicted in our school history book. That culture reached its breaking point because of its mad urge to conquer space with machines, and subdue the Earth the same way – as though Nature wasn't alive, a friend, and each plant did not have its own vital animated body-field but was a *thing* that needed poisons and chemicals to make it grow.

Science had its proper place in life today: the computer-rigging systems on the transocean sail-barges, or the solar energy panels for power, or the contracapsules in our arms limiting population to a sane level – all of them developed in the twentieth century, to be sure, but only as puny 'alternatives' to the main cancer of growth.

We were surely very different souls now from the main mass of greedy, selfish competitors then – more like their Chinese, in fact, who had helped inaugurate the New Way while the West went bankrupt and the alien guides at last made contact. Even their Chinese had had to discard their own false growth ideals, learnt from the West – though it was easier for them to reassert the cosmic forces that had always subtly moulded the human soul and tied it to the stars, without our knowing it. They had traditions on their side.

23

Very difficult for us now to understand the minds of twentieth century men — their blind thrust, like so many moles ramming themselves down dark tunnels in pursuit of wealth, power, spaceflight, super-highways, hectic travel, packaged electronic amusements! Our school history book, issued by Bardo, only stated the bare facts, the better to condemn the Bad Old Days . . .

At least we knew our *own* minds. Nothing that *they* had wanted then, did we want now. And truly we had given up nothing, but rather gained a sane and healthy world; and friendship with star peoples.

Calmness was a quality that I doubt they understood, those men and women of the previous 'civilization'. We were calm now — but vibrant as well, like living plants rooted in the earth, each with its own scintillating aura. We had seen enough Kirlian photos of these in school. Each static vegetable was really a galaxy of light and energy. If we were static, we also sang with life.

THREE

Rajit came up to me in the street one day, carrying a glass and rubber mask with a pipe like a chimney sticking out of it.

'It's called a snorkel. You can see underwater.' He stood fidgeting. 'My uncle found it in one of the old beach hotels. Do you want to try it? Out on the island with me?'

Our fishermen never used anything like this. It was a genuine plaything from the age of waste. The breathing tube was even made of plastic. So his uncle had found it in one of the abandoned tourist hotels? In such perfect condition after all these years? I didn't really believe him. But as there was no other explanation, after a while I just had to believe him.

Rajit had shot up tall and lanky since the cemetery days. He was many centimetres taller than me now, with fuzzy adolescent beard.

'We can sail out with old man Mkwepu tomorrow. I already asked him. There's a whole different reality underwater. You can almost feel what Bardo flight is like.'

I felt slightly repelled by the plastic tube. The whole world was once almost ruined by things like it: frivolities and trash by the cubic kilometre, using up resources uselessly. However, the mask was here and now, not two centuries ago – and I was curious to see what Rajit really wanted on the island. Evidently he felt it was time for more grown-up games than cemetery masquerades.

On Saturday morning, therefore, we helped Mkwepu to load his nets and sisal fish baskets into the outrigger – a home-made job like all small fishing boats, marks of the adze notching the wood everywhere inside. Mkwepu had painted a yantra mandala on the prow for luck; the nest of interlocking triangles, four pointing upward and three downward, which stood for male and female forces respectively, with a dot in the centre that was the reputed entry-point to Bardo Space – when you learned to enter it! (I was already preparing myself to learn, though. Staring at yantras and other mandalas by the hour, till they printed themselves on my mind's eye like new brain circuits ... Mkwepu's painted yantra was crudely drawn, compared with the beautiful prints Makindi showed me, but it still had a hypnotic effect.)

The old man agreed merrily to maroon us on Sinda Island for the day, and we set sail for the fish shoals out there. Rajit had brought some palm wine, sweet coffee cakes and a pawpaw to feed us. He played a wooden flute as we sailed, tootling a glittering jagged melody that teased and excited.

'We're sailing on the surface of reality,' he proclaimed importantly, taking the pipe from his lips to point at the foam sprinting past the prow. 'Soon you'll know what's underneath it all.'

'I bet,' I laughed.

For a long time we seemed very close to the shore, then suddenly we crossed some visual dividing line and we were a vast distance away. The mainland shrank to a green line pasted along the sea horizon.

Apart from birds and crabs Sinda was deserted. Landcrabs as big as skulls scuttled among the spiky scrub. Speckled yellow weaver birds flitted through the tangle. Sooty gulls stamped up and down the beach at the tide line. Otherwise, only Rajit and I. Sea currents forked turbulently round the island some way offshore, leaving a hundred metres of slack inshore water rippling calmly back towards the beach.

When we undressed, it was so different from the last childish time in the cemetery. My breasts were little black pears now, with cusps like horns of the quarter-moon. Rajit was gangly to the point of emaciation, bones poking through his flesh in far too many places. Unpinning his turban, he sent it snaking up the shore. Unpeeling his hairnet, he let the glossy black rope cascade down. He looked like mad, skinny Kali in some frantic Calcutta oleograph. Little white camouflage crabs, thumbnail size, dived sideways into their steep tunnels; parts of the beach flickered and swallowed themselves.

The mask made my breathing sound like snoring. My words boomed and misted the face-plate. If Rajit looked strange with his hair let down, how strange did I look with a single blue plastic antler rearing from my head like a visible snake of Kundalini!

I paddled out into the shallows, ducked my head, and thrust forward. Before long, as promised, I was floating in the sky of an alien world I'd never seen before . . .

Corals branched and bloomed beneath: scarlet fans, purple tusks, violet dishes forming curious, tiered cities. Yellow brains squatted in fields of bristling urchins. The jet-black quills of the urchins waved softly in a liquid breeze, yet there was nothing soft or fleshy about the life, though bodies wore a soft jelly bloom, a velvet gel. This was a world where minerals had taken on static, garish life: a silicon planet with porous brain-masses and fungoid domes as its Thinkers, presiding over strange cities, vividly bright, midway between life and stone.

Tiny iridescent fish, more like darting flocks of birds, flashed through the cities, wings flickering and bubble-eyes staring. The cities seemed to be projecting these flickering motes of softer life through their skies as signals from one part to another. Would the cloud cities of the Rakshasa world, the forests of Asura, the Yidag bottle-beings seem any stranger?

Abruptly, towers, tusks, tiers and brains all halted on one final sprawling lip. The world fell sheer away. I hung above a deep down precipice.

Down. So far down. In the abyss, out of focus, amorphous shapes lumbered and blundered. The Deep was crowded with them. Yet, too, they were invisible. They were just the blacknesses of the deep resisting light.

Was this the way the space between the stars would look? Not an emptiness that impeded nothing, but something heavy as lead whose fabric clung to the traveller instead of letting him pass? Something with its own fierce gravity very different from the gravity of worlds? Compared with this, did planets possess any true gravity at all – or was gravity just a force of repulsion exerted on them by the heaviness of space?

I hung mesmerized, scared to my wits' end, staring downwards. Drifting further outwards. Then a delta-shaped *something* flapped up towards me out of that stiff nothingness, detaching itself from its background, taking on colour. A fat

27

rubbery sheet of matter congealed, and flew at me till it was brilliant blue, with yellow eyes glowing from all parts of it.

Not eyes. No. Spots all over its skin.

And then I recognized it.

Its two actual eyes stared up at me. Its tail flicked a whip that could kill me.

Thrashing my way back to the shallows, away from the sting-ray, I found Rajit floating on his back, hair spread around him like a veil.

When he stood up, the hair clung sleek and lank to his body, tracing lines of force from head to loins, and he was a Siddha, a man of power of ancient days. His gaze was harsh and commanding. His smile, shy and hungry. We walked up the beach together and he passed the bottle of palm wine to me in such a formal, ceremonial way. A nervous gush of words from him, endearments, flattery, compliments? None of that. He *said* nothing. He only *did*, after I had drunk. And it was better that way. It was more shocking, alien and mysterious – yet something expected, too, something that lay in wait, had always lain in wait. We made love on the beach with fierce concentration like silent strangers, unlocking the sealed doors in our hearts and bodies. We shocked awake the hidden selves within ourselves.

The next year was the year that the Dobdobs came for me.

FOUR

A purge, taught Makindi, is a time when society gets rid of the poison in its bloodstream. Not by a blood-letting, however; that kind of wound takes too many years to heal. Society itself is wounded. Isolation is the proper cure. Putting the disease on ice. So the purged elements of the old world – the scientists against mankind, the false philosophers – were sent to live out the remainder of their days harmlessly in various quarantine areas which were cold but bracing, with a certain purity of landscape. Dobdobs had needed guns *then*, to guard the social enemies. But who would compel a Dobdob to draw his gun nowadays? Who would refuse the honour of being chosen for Bardo, even if it meant never seeing home or family again? Not I, not anyone!

A Dobdob team flew in to Bagamoyo by helicopter, the roaring chatter and the flashing blades thrilling us all. The once-monthly coastal bus, with its solar roof panels drinking in the African sun, was speed enough for our world at any other time – and the dhows calling in at sisal harvest. Aircraft were only for emergencies, disasters – and for the business of the Space Administration.

There were three men in the team: the pilot, a tall, rangy Caucasian with blue eyes and straw-coloured hair; and two Asians – one with a merry, expansive face, chubby cheeks, full lips, protruding eyes, features slapped together like pats of butter; the other with an older, harder face, a clever commanding face.

Makindi gestured Rajit to help the Dobdobs carry their equipment. My stepfather took one metal case, while Rajit struggled with the other, which proved heavier than he expected. Rajit ground to a halt in the sand; the blue-eyed Dobdob hefted the burden instead.

We were to take the tests in the schoolhouse. Myself, my cousin Rose, and another more distant cousin from Kigongoni village, a few kilometres inland. Makindi and Mboya, the Barefoot Doctor, recommended suitable candidates on the basis of perception and memory tests, basic metabolic rhythm, half a dozen other factors.

Soon, the merry Dobdob called me into Makindi's office and sat me down in a cane chair before the table. The room was dim, the louvres shut to a bright grating casting soft rainbows on the far wall. He chattered soothingly. There was no question of 'passing' or 'failing'. The hunt for a body-field suitable for Bardo travel was more like the search for a rare blood group ...

'I'm not nervous,' I said. 'Really I'm not.'

'Why not? Most people are.'

'I just don't feel nervous, that's all.'

'You're the girl who found the coco?'

'Yes.'

'So that's why you're not worried?'

'I suppose so.'

The other Dobdob laughed quietly, in the midst of tuning his testing machines.

'I know that only a tiny number of people have the Bardo power in any useful form, and it's all pure chance who they are; even so—'

The merry Dobdob let me ramble on.

And yet, if I hadn't found the coco, would I ever have been so eager to imprint Makindi's mandalas on my mind? Ask anybody how Bardo made its choice of star travellers, and you would surely get the answer that every child on Earth had a chance. Yet at the same time the chance only happened on rare occasions: whereupon it was an honour, a privilege, a rare achievement. It was a privilege shared with everyone, however. So we felt no sense of resentment, or any inequality.

The other Dobdob had checked his apparatus by now. Electrodes lay plugged into it, and earphones, and a kind of mask reminiscent of the snorkel (but opaque), and beside them a case of silver needles.

Delicately, the second man fixed the tiny electrodes to my scalp with dabs of paste, using touch alone to find the right spots, measuring my skull by the breadth of his own fingers, his eyes half-shut even in that dim light.

He would play recordings of mantras through the earphones. How much did I know about mantras?

I repeated what Makindi and the lamas had taught. Every single atom in the universe is a pattern of particles which themselves are simply interference patterns between primitive energy vibrations. The mantra sounds, devised in ancient India, mimic these basic vibrations. They are the root 'noises' from which reality is made. To utter mantras the right way, enough times, aligns the mind with basic universal rhythms.

'Naturally I haven't ever heard any mantras,' I hastened to add. It would be playing with fire . . . Awakening forces that the untrained mind could not control.

The Dobdob touched his silver acupuncture needles.

'We have to measure the main chakras of the body which resonate with the different mantra sounds. Tell me about the chakras, Lila.'

The energy centres of the human body. 'Wheels.' Eastern medicine discovered them first. Western medicine finally accepted them two centuries ago – as East and West converged into one world. Kundalini, life energy of the body, rises through each successive chakra to the brain, thence out into the cosmos.

'We shall have to raise your kundalini force a little way to be able to measure it. If you aren't accepted today, you must promise faithfully never to try to raise it on your own, using your memories of this test.'

I promised.

Playing with fire.

'Now, the mask—'

It was a stereoscope, for showing three-dimensional pictures. It would project a yantra mandala in depth before my eyes. The Dobdob held up a card.

'This yantra. Do you know it?'

I saw a dark walled square with four gateways. Inside the square, white lotus petals were arranged around a jet-black circle. At the centre of the circle blazed a white dot set within four white triangles pointing downwards. Of course I knew it. I had known it for years, thanks to Makindi. It was the Kali Yantra. The Yantra of Female Energy.

The mask incorporated a retinascope, to shine pencils of light into the blind spots of my eyes where the millions of nerve fibres bunch together and open directly into the brain. Just as the spots of light at the heart of a yantra – the bindu dots – open, through a point, into infinity, so these blind spots in the retina are its special bindu dots, where the outer world of superficial realities passes through from sight into true vision, to the world of thought within.

The Dobdob chose needles and sterilized them in alcohol. He asked me to strip to the waist.

'The topmost chakra of all, in the brain, is called *Sahasrara.* Actually, Sahara might be a better word – because from there on is a vast immeasurable desert where you can easily get lost and die. The alien worlds are as distant as any oasis on Earth. This isn't the *easy* way to the stars, remember. It's just the true and natural way.'

The test began. I heard a dog bark outside, then I was muffled in the earphones, blinded by the darkness of the mask.

Lines of light shone out before my eyes, a cone of down-pointing triangles containing within them . . . blackness. They surrounded a blind black disc, like the sun in full eclipse – with a corona of white lotus petals and a seed of light at the heart of it, as though a hole was bored through whatever eclipsed the sun. That black sun gobbled light. The triangles confined the darkness, though. They wove an internal fence of light. In my deafness, I heard . . . the mantra. At first, indistinguishable from the soft pounding of air on my eardrums insulated by the ear-phone muffs. But then, in that thudding silence:

HUM . . . HUM . . . HUM . . .

Throbbing. Intensifying. Laying down resonances in my mind between past, present, future, till all time was one, and I was in all time.

HUM, hummed each bright white corona petal as I rotated round that black sun from prominence to prominence, half in time, half in eternity.

My navel glowed. An acupuncture needle must be there now. Or not there, perhaps – but somewhere else, communicating with the navel along the invisible, immaterial nerves of the body-field. A soft jewel of flame burnt painlessly yet insistently at that point in my body where my flesh folded into itself, and

32

my body imagined an umbilical cord, pulsing with hot fluid, connecting me to the universal womb that I floated in, just as the bright-petalled black star floated, fenced by triangles, within a dark, walled courtyard.

The petals of the corona took on a bluish tinge as the heavy darkness leaked outwards, becoming lilac, violet, purple. When they became black, the black sun disappeared as a separate entity. And I floated above a funnel of bright triangles which had ceased to be a cone of fences, barring access and exit, and had become an inverted pyramid of *steps* – a funnel leading downwards.

The mantra changed to a brassy clanging.

TRAM! TRAM! TRAM!

The funnel oscillated dizzily. First it was a funnel, then a pyramid. It collapsed through its own dimensions, sickening me. One moment I was balanced on the bindu point itself, then it was deep below me and I was falling down down down. A pyramid pushed me up again.

Between my breasts, a second warmth was glowing. It calmed these wild gyrations. I couldn't see the pyramid any more, only the deep funnel, the steps of light leading down to the central point of light. Only, it was not *down now*, it was *out*. Out of myself, out of the world!

'*HRIH! HRIH! HRIH!*' came a strident keening in my ears, like the wail of a beast caught in a snare. And my throat burned.

The fire in my navel had faded. I no longer knew where my legs were, couldn't place them. The whole top part of my body was drifting upwards out of them . . .

So this was how it felt, when the Energy Body detached itself! I felt like a centaur, my Subtle Body rearing out of my Matter Body like the human out of the horse!

My throat burned incandescently. '*HRIH! HRIH!*' I shrilled, with flaring, whinnying nostrils. The sound was me; I was the sound. Earphones? No earphones. This was the seed-sound of my own existence. I even knew which nostril this scream of breath was rushing out through: it was my left nostril, not my right.

With a lurch, with a snap, one of my energy legs kicked

loose; and the outermost of the five triangles sprang past me, jumped behind me – while the four remaining triangles swelled to fill all space. The bright dot dilated, became a disc . . .

The *HRIH!* wail died to a buzzing. Triangles and bindu disc disappeared. Only after-images danced.

Something – somebody – was pulling the earphones from my ears. Someone was speaking. Someone was lifting a mask from my eyes. A world reappeared: a room ghostly with dissolving geometries of mist, phantom dots and triangles.

The Dobdobs pulled charts from the test machine. Their scrutiny stretched out interminably while I sat neglected, not knowing whether to button my dress.

Finally the merry one glanced up and grinned.

'Congratulations, Lila. You'll fly to the stars.'

FIVE

There was barely a couple of hours to say goodbye – during which time the Dobdobs were busy testing first Rose and then my other cousin, with negative results – but I felt that haste was best. I was a sort of prodigy now, a village miracle. Yet I was also something slightly frightening. I sensed this from people's anxious congratulations as they packed my mother's house to accept bowls of beer. I was going to travel to the stars, so that our village could stay as it was: immobile and secure. There was recoil in their good wishes – the equal and opposite reaction to my own impending flight.

My aunt, Rose's mother, came to kiss me goodbye. This quick visit seemed to herald a reconciliation between herself and my mother. They embraced one another, united in fellowship of loss and gain, for what they lost in me they gained in each other; and they seemed happy to have it that way. The jealousy which had marked the years since I'd found the coco withered away. Soon, Rose would be visiting my mother's house again, taking over the place that I'd held in her heart. Rose didn't come, herself. Was she crying at home in disappointment? I would have been, in her position. Rajit had been accepted as a student at the lamasery, but that was ordinary news; he would have to stay in Bagamoyo for another three weeks before catching the bus southwards.

At the end of this hectic interval, Makindi came home with the blond Dobdob; he kissed me perfunctorily on the forehead and surrendered custody of me.

Everyone crowded out to watch the helicopter take off, and wave frantically. At it, not at me. They'd already forgotten me.

The palm trees, which had always borne their crowns so high, sank into the ground and became green starfish with black urchin shadows on a tawny cloth of earth. Landscape became a model of itself, a toy, from the air. People could lose the scale of things that way. The world became a map they could doodle on. No single field or tree was vital. More world was always unfolding – available, expendable. I could see how easily mobility brought a sense of careless exploitation.

We flew away from the coastline at an angle, following the red strip of murram road as it cut through the lush green tangle round a small river, then through a couple of villages stippled by coconut palms. Tawny cows the size of dung beetles grazed among them. We were out over sisal plantations then: kilometres of green spikes forming a geometric grid across red earth.

I sat with the pilot. He said his name was Sam – Sam Shaw – and he was from America. The two Dobdob testers sat behind, talking to each other in what I guessed was Chinese.

'That's right,' Sam nodded, when I asked. 'Liu's from China. The boss.'

'And the other man?'

'Yongden's a Tibetan. But don't trouble yourself with their names. They're both based in Africa, so you'll not be seeing them again. I'll only be with you, myself, till I can escort you to the Bardo Centre out in Florida. You'll like Florida. Warm seas, palm trees. More buildings and cities than here – more intensive agriculture. Oranges! You can smell them way off . . .'

'Cities?'

'Oh yes. Miami still houses close on quarter of a million people. That's excluding the Bardo Centre. And it'll go on housing them, since they service the Centre with power and supplies. That's not the biggest city in the world, either! Still, the decentralization policy's worked pretty well, particularly on old sores like the Asian cities and the American megalopolises. We're nearly down to optimum for human habitation everywhere – spreading people back across the countryside. City dwellers no longer feel they're something special. Japan was one hell of a problem; but the Siberian and Australian emigration helped . . . We're picking up some other trainees on the way. You can make some friends on the flight.'

'Do you come from Florida, Sam?'

'Oh, places are just places,' he said, shrugging. 'Any place is okay.'

We flew for fifteen minutes, till some white towers hove into view, rising from low, knobbly, ravined hills, isolated in the midst of barren scrub. As we climbed higher, swinging towards them, the city itself – Dar es Salaam – appeared: a long fringe of red and white roofs around a blue bay beyond, where the sea curved back behind the hills.

'Here's the training campus. I guess your father and your Barefoot Doctor both trained here. We're just landing a while to drop off Liu and Yongden.'

As we flew closer, the buildings looked more time-worn, less glittering. Walls wore a spiderweb of cracks where stucco was peeling. Roads had potholes. Roofing over walkways between the buildings had rusted through. Missing paving stones exposed stretches of red, rutted mud. What did it matter if the road had potholes, now that it was only used for walking? It was hardly important if people got a little wet between buildings; they wouldn't melt.

Men and women in variously coloured tunics strolled along the walkways to glass louvred classrooms. A squad were tilling gardens which stretched downhill from the classrooms to a sewage farm, beside which a hen range sported hundreds of birds – the brown earth surging, churning and fluttering. The white skyscrapers seemed inappropriate – such pompous, greedy buildings. I felt glad they were peeling, becoming realistic. They should be used, but not pampered.

Sam dropped the helicopter to a landing on a potholed tarmac square between two teaching blocks. As the rotors winnowed to a halt, Liu – the Chinese – tapped me on the shoulder.

'Ridiculously far from the city, stupidly luxurious, don't you agree?' (I did.) 'In time of famine they thought to build up a poor country thus. In their minds every country was a pyramid. So here was where a tiny percentage of children could be trained to become bits of the bottom of the bigger pyramid reaching up to the Moon and Mars high over the heads of the wretched.'

Yongden patted me more gaily as he hopped down from the cab. 'Service, not privilege,' he grinned. Liu handed out the cases of test equipment, which Yongden hauled over to the nearest doorway where a barrow waited. Sam's finger was already pressing the ignition switch as Liu himself scrambled out and ducked away. The blades spun, blurring into a solid airy disc and skittering red grit away across faded car-parking

37

lines; then the helicopter leapt into the air in a grasshopper spring.

We weren't going to fly over the city, but direct to the airport west of it. I must have looked disappointed, since Sam tapped the fuel gauge and reminded me: 'Every litre of gas has to come three thousand kilometres by dhow – and you'll be travelling light years soon, Lila.'

So we sped over bush with tall branching cactuses and baobabs where tiny boys herded more dun humpbacked cattle. A dozen factories fringed another pockmarked road, their tin roofs painted with the words *CHAI, KATANI, VIATU*. Tea, Sisal, Shoes. Beyond was an airfield, empty except for the little silver jet waiting for us on the runway. A wire fence kept cattle from straying on to it. Plovers and whimbrels wheeled away in fright from shallow rain ponds in the grass at our approach.

A solitary African Dobdob emerged from the glass-topped control tower to greet us.

'Little black girl in search of the stars, is it?' he said, a hint of venom in his voice. He rubbed his neck ponderously. 'So what *really* selected you out of all the others? Do *you* know? Real genuine mystics used to work all their lives long to perform a few miracles – like walking on fire, or stopping their hearts for half an hour. Nowadays a slip of a girl just walks in, to the whole damn universe! Who knows? Who knows anything?'

'I suppose you wanted to be a Bardo flier?' I asked him sympathetically. He only scowled.

'Now, look,' Sam interrupted angrily. 'You're part of the adventure too, and don't forget it. Every human being is.'

The African Dobdob gestured at all the birds, now settling on to the water again.

'What kind of adventure is *this*? Look at all the air traffic here!'

Sam lost his temper with the man – and quite right too, I thought.

'Would you prefer the sky full of planes – burning fuel and spewing smoke and carrying people nowhere for no good reason? What's the matter with you, man? Is the weather too hot for you here? Would you like somewhere cooler, where you can spend all day shovelling snow off your airstrip? No? Well, here's something to worry about for now – our flight plan.'

Sam thrust a sheet of paper at the man. 'Kano, Dakar, Miami. So will you please clear us for take-off? Control some air traffic for us, huh?'

'Okay, I'm sorry. I apologize. Have a good flight, black girl.' The man grinned wryly. 'Follow your star.'

'I shall!'

'A good flight is an efficient flight,' Sam said sanctimoniously, shepherding me inside the jet as the Dobdob tramped back to his control tower.

Only a few seats were free. Most were stacked with cartons labelled MEDICAL SUPPLIES/BARDO MIAMI/AIRMAIL. It seemed an incredible distance to airlift medical supplies, unless there was some plague raging out of control in America.

'No, it's nothing of the sort,' Sam retorted. He was still angry. None of my business, his tone said. He chose me a seat by the window, bent over to fasten a seat belt.

'It's about five hours to Kano in Nigeria. We'll stay the night there, pick up passengers in the morning. When we're airborne I'll come back and fix something to eat.' He went into the pilot's cabin and began warming the engines up; however, the door hadn't fully closed behind him, so I could hear his voice intermittently through the jet noise.

'Flight MIA-65 to Dar Air Control. Request take-off clearance—'

And we climbed upward, westward, towards jagged hills and a fat reddening sun. Crimson light soaked the few clouds stretched out thin across the land, and went on soaking them in the most prolonged sunset I'd ever seen. We were chasing the sun across the world.

'Liu?' I heard Sam saying into the radio after a time. I couldn't catch all of it. 'A bad apple rots the barrel, Liu. You can't *have* a Dobdob spreading resentment . . . So, maybe he does need more responsibility. Give him the chance to know the facts. The defence facts, right. If he won't co-operate then, he'll have to be put on ice . . .'

I stared out of the window, wondering what *that* meant, but too delighted by the sunset-streaked bush to worry about it. Trees were dots with shadows spiking to the eastward like swarms of spermatozoa swimming over that rumpled magenta ground.

39

'Heck,' exclaimed Sam, when he finally swung out of his pilot's seat and noticed the open door. 'It was pure sour grapes. The man at the airfield, I mean . . . I'm envious of you myself. Imagine travelling all the way to the stars without using a litre of fuel! That's repaying society a million-fold.'

The plane flew on, automatically. In a tiny galley down the aisle – inviting me to help, but actually just to watch him – Sam cooked some savoury rolls of skimmed soyamilk wafers from the Florida soyafields. Taking a dozen dry brittle sheets, he soaked them in a broth of prawn extract, wrapped them in cloth, steamed them, then rolled the mass out in a long pipe and sliced it into four. They were called Yuba rolls. He seemed proud of his cooking.

After we'd eaten, the sun finally escaped ahead of us; and a yellow gibbous moon hung on its side in the sky – that distracting lantern now so wisely ignored by man. Our big, close moon might have been set in the sky deliberately and maliciously to lure us away from our true destiny: hung up there for technological man to howl at like a pack of jackals. I stared at it till I dozed. A barren ball of rock; the wrong way to the stars.

Sam shook me awake, and retreated back into the cockpit, closing the door firmly this time. We were coming in to Kano, and I was befuddled by my early, abridged sleep.

I glimpsed airfield lights before we landed, but these were promptly switched off. We went outside, into hot air so dry and dusty that it made my eyes sore. The half-moonlight disclosed a vast flatness with the bumps of two hills, or perhaps two pyramids or palaces, in the distance. Nearby, a dark building towered many storeys, though only the two lower floors had any lights in them.

Sam coughed and spat on the ground. Rubbing my flipflops to and fro, I found just how gritty the surface was: slippery with sand but with no tang of salt.

We waited.

'Over there's where we sleep. The high building. Luxury hotel once. International airport this, crossroads of Africa.' I could forgive Sam's sarcastic puritanism. He wasn't actually trying to spoil the journey for me. It was just that his job involved travelling all the time – and everyone knew that travelling like this, in expensive machines, was all wrong. He must have felt like a sort of volunteer criminal.

At last two buttons of light growled towards us; a tanker lorry.

The Arab driver climbed down and unloaded a fat pipe from clips along the tanker; I saw more cartons marked 'medical supplies' heaped on the passenger seat.

Sam signed some papers for the fuel to take us on to Dakar, then we set off to walk across half a kilometre of rock-hard soil or gritty concrete to our hotel.

Morning sunrise glared through uncurtained glass. My hotel bedroom looked even starker in the daylight than it had done in the glow of a hurricane lamp the night before. The adjacent bathroom had no water on tap, only a pitcher standing in the dusty bath, with a septic can beside a dry toilet bowl where a ginger centipede lay shrivelled.

Outside, the city of Kano was sheer desolation.

Kilometres of baked earth gradually becoming dunes, and a road running south from the hotel around a wasteland of rubble, beyond which mud-yellow walls enclosed white buildings like blocks of salt. The two camel-like humps I'd seen the night before rose from within the walls themselves – hills like two breasts, only no milk flowed from them. All was dry.

A few white-robed figures rode camels and chalky horses down the road towards the distant city gates, and other people were stooping that way on foot with burdens on their backs: ants under pellets of dung. Someone was herding goats below, but what they grazed on was a mystery. Ribbons of smoke rose from a tent camp outside the city walls.

The sprawling emptiness gradually offered up more buildings, people and animals as I watched; but only sparsely. Kano doled out details grain by grain.

The airport to the west was far huger than Dar airfield, and equally deserted, encroached upon not by birds and grass but by sand dunes.

After I'd washed, in brackish water, Sam banged on the door and came in.

'What's wrong out there, Sam? Why's there a city in a

desert? I thought that everyone had enough. The land's starving!'

'No, it's stabilized now. We're holding it stable. They're provided for. You mightn't believe it, but so many people lived here once, their shit alone made the soil bear double and treble – vegetables, nuts, millet, henna, you name it. The world's biggest piggeries fed on their scraps and leftovers. Then the desert moved south . . . And what happened? They still sent a ship to Mars, to bring back bags of dust while this sand was choking a million souls to death! Whole peoples trekked south to escape. What did they do then? They drew a line on the map and said, so far, no further. So-called economists told them that ten million had to die, so that other millions could live. They fixed that line just north of here. They laid it out with electric fences and minefields – and all the time the great tourist jets were still landing out there, carrying tourists north and south! It's okay now. It may not look it, but it is. Come along and meet our passengers and we can get airborne. Two Hausa boys, going to Miami with you.'

'Hausa?'

'Local language. Don't worry, they speak Arabic and English too. You shouldn't have trouble communicating. They're a couple of chatterboxes.'

The two boys were identical twins. Which made it nearly impossible to tell which of them was Hamidou, and which was Abdoulaye. I soon thought of them as a sort of composite: Hamidou-A and Abdoulaye-H, with each partner alternately in the ascendant. This seemed to be how they thought of themselves. Their heads were thin and equine, with features that slanted down acutely towards pronounced jutting little chins, and large open nostrils. Their eyes shone large and glossy with thick fluttering lashes above tiny bumps of cheekbones. Their skin was blacker than black; it shone as though buffed and polished by all the wind-borne sand.

They chattered away to each other and to me indiscriminately in Hausa, Arabic and English, depending upon who was saying what to whom, switching languages in mid-stream, tuning me in and tuning me out of a triangle of talk where only two corners were real at any one moment. Good-humouredly, without malice or awkwardness, they simultaneously included and excluded me. It wasn't so much 'hard to follow them', as downright impossible – or else perfectly simple! You were either with them; or not. Either there, or not-there, with no in-between stage – and many times I found myself marooned out at an unreal, non-existent point.

As identical twins, early attention had been lavished on them. Apparently Bardo was carrying out a research programme on the theory that since identical twins possess heightened empathy for each other's moods, this in itself might 'tune' their Energy Bodies to a higher pitch than ordinarily happens. They might educate themselves spontaneously to the cast of mind that Bardo was searching for; become more intensely aware of the shape of their inner being, because they saw it reflected directly in another person, and at the same time could detach themselves from Self because there was another, independent Self.

'They gave us tests years ago,' boasted Abdoulaye-H.

'When we were just little boys,' added his twin. (Hamidou-A had a small pimple on his left cheek; one of his brother's long, tapering fingernails had snapped off short . . .)

'Our Teacher gave us yantras to visualize in different rooms.'

'Though they can't tell for sure if you're suitable till you're past puberty.'

'I know that,' I said.

'Your thinking's not properly conceptual before. Conceptual's the highest level of thought. You know what's real, but you know what's possible too.'

'You can spin the Real from the web of possibilities.'

'Since the mind's a spinning reel,' laughed Abdoulaye-H. (Broken fingernail.)

The country we flew over was badly bruised and battered: a pitted ochre wasteland with flimsy interruptions of savannah that always died back to dust. Drab, wretched country.

'It's not till adolescence, you see, that all the world's given facts really become free variables—'

'—all capable of being isolated and recombined and permutated in n number of lattices!'

'Network analysis of n-dimensional space—' chattered Hamidou-A, poking my elbow. (Pimple on cheek.)

43

'—composes the mandalas of mature ideas!' his twin continued.

'Have you learnt Boolean algebra, Lila?'

'I didn't have time,' I said. Actually, I learnt very little about mathematics in school in Bagamoyo. It all seemed so rarified and abstract, what the twins were chanting on about. Trying to impress me? I don't think so. They were at once too natural and too detached to bother.

'Yantras and mandalas are really quasi-Boolean lattices for use in our brain computer, you see—'

'—to switch us over to the Bardo plane!'

'It's a bare world hereabouts. An abstract world. One thinks in abstractions, it's second nature,' apologized Abdoulaye-H. 'I know there are many ways to Bardo. One way isn't better than any other. So long as your mind and body-field get organized. We're just algebraically inclined.' I began to warm to them. On the whole they seemed kindly disposed, for all their mutual intoxication and apparent bumptiousness and their mathematics. In fact, they were a little simple, even charming. Remarkably innocent, for children of desolation. Perhaps because their world, as they said, had always been pure and abstract.

'Can you actually read each other's minds?' I asked.

'We're a conjoint set,' giggled Hamidou-A. 'So we cap each other's minds!'

'Then we cap each other's jokes!'

Which I didn't understand a word of; and the next moment they were prattling away in Arabic and Hausa alternately to each other, and I was left far out at a loose point in space.

Fierce thermals rose above the baking ground; and we flew through a number of air pockets. The twins' chatter had the same effect: lifting me up then abruptly dropping me.

Finally, we crossed dense patchworks of fields and glassy marshes, and suddenly there was the sea: bars of spume wrinkling a surface of blue tin. A peninsula shaped like a giraffe's head bore a dense white city out into the ocean, the neck curving around a bay where breakwaters enclosed ranks of quays. Several of the large trans-ocean sail-barges lay at anchor, canvas furled on their five masts.

This was the biggest city I'd yet seen. It looked alive, organic, well-balanced – unlike Kano, battered by the Sahara. Tall buildings scaled down to shanty suburbs, then to farms; we touched down and taxied between millet and groundnut fields.

Sam told us that this was Yoff Airport, Dakar; but we were only staying for half an hour, to pick up some fuel and another passenger, a Wolof girl.

'Wolof's the local language,' I said breezily to the twins. It seemed a fair guess. Sam nodded.

'She's called Maimouna.'

When we climbed out to stretch our legs, the air was hot and wet as Bagamoyo's, which seemed to astonish and distress the twins.

'Are you meant to breathe it?' gasped one. (Fingernail.)

'Or drink it?' his brother spluttered.

We followed Sam round the jet, kicking our legs out exaggeratedly to flex them. Two other jets were parked unattended on the tarmac, and a trio of helicopters. Beyond the perimeter fence, some way off, women walked by with baskets on their heads, while trucks of farm produce – some solar-powered, others drawn by bullocks – trundled by at various speeds towards the centre of Dakar. I caught a faint reek of fish from an articulated truck driving the other way. But there was nowhere in particular for us to go; we were fenced in. All we could really taste of Senegal was the thick air. How barren plane travel actually was. I felt sorry for Sam; I admired him for putting up with a life in the sky, for the sake of the smooth running of Bardo's affairs.

Maimouna's skin was milk chocolate. Her lips pouted, her eyes were sullen – or sultry, I suppose. Her head was shaved bald and her eyebrows plucked to match. She was a wooden carving of Beauty. Her pout seemed to be an inbuilt part of her features. In other respects she had about as much facial mobility as a carving. She seemed all image; as though she thought it vulgar to be less than an ideal image of herself.

Suspended from her pierced ear-lobes hung yellow glass globes encased in filigree wire nets, which bobbed about like miniature fishing floats. Personally, I thought these made her

45

look as old-fashioned as though she had her lips pierced and great wooden plugs stuck in them; but obviously she thought highly of them.

When the twins danced up to her irreverently, and clicked them with their fingernails, and cried, 'Ping!' 'Pong!' she looked highly offended.

'Why don't you two boys wear something, so people can tell you apart!' I laughed. 'One of you could get your left ear pierced, and the other your right.'

'We could wear half a tunic each!' one twin said, giggling.

'And half a hat!'

'And half a set of chromosomes!'

Maimouna just shrugged and marched on board the jet.

Back inside, after refuelling, I found her sitting in the seat where I'd been, by the window. I sat down beside her.

'Do you speak English?' I asked her, a little irritably. Then, for good measure, '*Unasema Kiswahili?*'

She looked cool. 'Maimouna speaks English, French, Wolof and Chinese. Actually, I had hoped to be sent to Lhasa to communicate with the Rakshasas. You see, I had a Chinese Teacher, so I took the trouble to learn his language. Of course, you don't speak Chinese, so you'll never see Lhasa, will you?'

'How do you know I don't speak Chinese?'

She said something to me in Chinese and smiled faintly.

'It's a complex language, dear.'

'Are you from the coast? I'm from the other coast – the other side of Africa! I've been watching the whole continent go by—'

'I'm sorry, do *you* want to sit by the window? Did Maimouna take your seat perhaps?'

From across the aisle, Hamidou-A poked me in the ribs.

'Watch out. First class bitchsnob.'

'Why should I care about the view?' I said. 'I'm not a sightseer. Are you?'

'All that you mean is, it's all ocean from now on.' She yawned. 'Quite monotonous and dreary.'

Sam finished piling cartons into the rear seats and scrambled back to the cabin, stopping to tell Maimouna to fasten her seat belt. We others already had.

46

'No point in wearing the thing, till one's ready for take-off, surely?'

'Just be co-operative, will you?' Sam said, leaning over to buckle her in.

'Maimouna *always* co-operates,' the girl purred. 'A selfish attitude absolutely ruins one for Bardo flight.'

'How fortunate for you, having a Chinese Teacher,' I said sarcastically. 'What a pity it's all been wasted, as they don't speak Chinese in Miami.'

Closing her eyes, she ignored me.

Soon we were flying out over sea, more sea, then more sea again.

Later, Sam announced: 'There's a hurricane building up in the Gulf of Mexico. Miami airport's closing, so we're going to land at the Cape.'

'Cape Canaveral?'

'The space port?'

'That damned place,' scowled Sam.

SIX

And so, on a fitful evening, with a storm brewing and red sunlight lancing low from brawling, accelerated clouds, we flew in over the abandoned launching sites. It was a flat, abstract place criss-crossed polygon-style by broad roads linking the launch pads, which looked very much like a set of gargantuan yantra mandalas pointed at the stars. As though the old space administration had built the right shapes, but done the wrong things with them! If they only could have unlocked the powers residing in the shapes they paved the earth with!

A few steel gantries still stood erect; and one gantry in particular still held a tall rocketship in its clasp, unlaunched these twenty decades: a magnificent penis-lingam. How almost right, yet how utterly wrong!

'See,' cried the Hausa twins, 'it's a *stupa*!'

Yes, it looked like that too: the spire from an Indian temple, hugely magnified. And of course the spire of an Indian temple is intended as a penis-lingam.

'An American *stupa*! Stupendous!' laughed Abdoulaye-H.

'What a shame they were in such a *stupor* that they didn't realize what it was!'

'*Stupid* astronauts.'

The black mass of storm clouds was piling up fast. Raindrops smeared across the windows. As we landed, on what must have been the longest runway in the world, fat bobbles blurred the glass; against the boiling darkness of the horizon I could still see a monolithic building, half a kilometre high at least, that seemed to suck the storm towards it, condensing the darkness into a solid block.

We slept in a small hospital, through the storm-tossed night. Dawn came mauve and violet, and only tatters of raincloud were scudding seawards now.

After Sam had fixed breakfast of red beans on flapjacks, dolloped with syrup, we helped transfer the cargo of cartons from the plane to a small bus – Maimouna carrying fewer than the rest of us, scrutinizing the place names of origin on the labels with a knowledgeable air, as though it mattered. Then we drove off across the empty spaceport, bound for our true port of embarkation – where ecstasy, not hydrazine, would be our rocket fuel to the stars.

'Why couldn't we fly on to Miami?' complained Maimouna. 'It just so happens they were driving some more fuel in from Orlando overnight for your convenience, but the lorry skidded. Driver broke his arm. So the plane'll have to wait refuelling. Hell, but I hate this place. It insults the human spirit.'

The monolith we'd seen the night before continued to dwarf us for a long time. Sam said it consisted of one single enormous room, the hugest room that man had ever made. It even had its own weather. Its own clouds and lightning inside. They had assembled spaceships in it.

Leaving the spaceport, we drove along the centre of a six-lane highway, of which only the middle lanes were in good repair, overhauling occasional trailer-trucks loaded with fruit and vegetables, looking like mobile greenhouses with their overhead solar power panels. There was more traffic on an adjacent railway line; several trains passed, mainly hauling lumber, plumes of coal-smoke pouring from their funnels. Inland were rolling hills of orange groves, but hereabouts was a flat, well-irrigated landscape with people of all races – blacks, amerindians, whites, all dressed in similar blue dungarees – working in fields of soya and sweetcorn, celery and radish.

We passed through beachside cities of peeling palaces and overgrown gardens, where fishermen were repairing nets, caulking hulls and sewing sails under the lazy bend of palms. Processing factories vented rich smells of fish and fruit. VERO BEACH MULLETT MEAL. PALM BEACH PELLETED CITRUS PULP. FORT MERLE SOYAMILK SKIMMERY. DANIA DRIED BEAN PRODUCTS. Florida was noticeably more thickly populated than my own part of Africa, and all the passing towns gave the sense of having been far more crowded once – without, however, having become 'ghosts' of their former selves. It was the frills and extravagances – the decayed amusement parks, hotels and such – that had been shut away and left to crumble or overgrow; just as the superhighway had been reduced to a simple road. The backbone of life remained – with a new spirit to it, witnessed by the billboards over the canals and waterways of Fort Lauderdale extolling social ecology and the way of Bardo ...

Male and Female contain within each other the Mandala of the Universe!

To bring about a little change for a while isn't enough; it must be permanent!

After Enlightenment, Chopping Wood and Carrying Water!
Our Alien Friends help us Find Ourselves!

Finally we arrived at Miami, a substantial city as Sam had said – though similarly thinned out and repaced – and Miami Beach, Bardo headquarters for the Western World.

Fifteen kilometres of white palaces fronted the ocean, linked to the mainland city by causeways, for in reality this 'beach' was a long island. We pulled up at a checkpoint, manned by four armed Dobdobs, with grey bombs clipped to their belts, and machine-guns, their steel helmets decorated with the yantra sign. Yet the fierceness of their naked weapons was fairly well belied by what they were actually doing. Two were sitting playing Go under a sun awning outside their slit-windowed concrete hut. A third was dangling a fishing line in the bay. Only the fourth man, who had been scanning birds in the lagoon with a pair of binoculars, paid attention to us.

'Big smelly guns,' sniffed Abdoulaye-H, nevertheless, as Sam handed over a wad of papers to this man – including my own Bardo test charts, I noticed. The Dobdob took them away into the concrete hut.

'Don't get the wrong idea about these guards,' Sam explained to the Hausa boy. 'They're really a cross between data processors, keeping an eye on who's coming and going, and an honour guard for the Procyon Embassy. See, that's it, over there where the flag is. You need a little bit of ceremonial for star guests.' He pointed out a distant hotel, with antennae on its roof and a fluttering green banner.

'If it's a *mental* embassy,' asked Maimouna innocently, 'why should you need real guns and a real flag?'

'For us,' laughed Sam. 'For human beings. Seeing's believing. Still, it's amazing what people *will* believe! In the early days I hear there were even accusations that this place was some sort of luxury brothel for the world's new controllers.'

'What is a brothel?' asked the other Hausa boy.

Maimouna uttered a sleek laugh, and told him. 'Of course,' she added, 'people who thought that sort of thing would all have been purged, wouldn't they, Sam? But that's all ancient history – the camps in Antarctica are all closed down now, aren't they?' I wasn't sure whether she was simply showing off her knowledge again – or probing Sam. After what I'd heard Sam say over the radio to Liu – *if he won't co-operate, he'll have to be put on ice* – I felt like probing too.

Sam just shrugged and remarked: 'You see, the flag's green because Asura is a forest world.'

It was early afternoon. As we waited at the checkpoint, a convoy of slow battery-driven drop-side trucks, laden with cabbages, milk churns, plucked chickens and crates of eggs, drew up behind us, driven by men and women in blue dungarees. The two Dobdobs who had been playing Go got up and went to attend to them. A long barge which had been moving across the bay moored alongside one of the palaces to start loading refuse from a chute.

Then the Dobdob came back from the hut with our documents and four plastic cards, two white ones and two red, which he handed over to Sam, to pass on to us.

My card, a red one, had LILA MAKINDI embossed above a long number in computer type; the back of the card had several metallic strips across it.

'That's a coded identity card giving your body-field profile from the tests. Your Bardo tunics'll have a special pocket for them,' Sam said. 'Keep them safe till then.'

Shutting my eyes, I ran my fingers along the bumps, to see if I could read my name by touch; Maimouna's voice purred in my ear.

'Computers don't read credit cards with their fingers, my dear. All the data's printed magnetically.'

'Computers think by Boolean algebra,' Hamidou-A chipped in. 'They think yantra thoughts!'

The steel pole rose up and Sam drove the bus out along Broad Causeway. An old sign half way along had been overprinted with the slogan: *Ecstasy is Mental Rocket Fuel!*

'It's a sort of *credit* card,' said Maimouna. 'In the old days people used to buy things with little bits of plastic like these. Of

51

course, that sort of credit's all gone – but in a sense the world still exists on credit, doesn't it, Sam? Mental credit from our friends in space, wouldn't you say?'

'Amazing,' was all Sam said. 'This was all one big mangrove swamp once, and now the Asurans of the star Procyon are here.'

'In a manner of speaking,' teased the Wolof girl. 'Mentally.'

A second, more heavily armed checkpoint held us up briefly on the far side of Broad Causeway, while our 'credit' cards were run through a machine. Then we were let into a wire-fenced parking space. Exit gates led to various hotels. Sam drew up beside a gate giving directly on to marble steps, at the top of which glass doors revolved.

'Your first briefing's in just two hours. We should have been here last night. Go on through. You're expected.'

As he spoke, a tall Asian woman Dobdob came through the revolving door and stood waiting. Sam bundled us out un-ceremoniously and we walked through the gate and up the steps.

The woman led us into a large, lavish lobby. Green and gold tiles checkered the floor; glass galaxies of chandeliers hung from a high ceiling. Fuchsias and tree-ferns grew lushly in terracotta urns. Fat red carp circled lazily in a pool, in the centre of which stood a bronze Tibetan god, with water sprinkling from a cudgel in his left hand. His right hand supported a bronze woman copulating acrobatically with him, with one leg looped right around his waist.

While the woman Dobdob was at a desk with our cards, we wandered round this jungle of a hall examining the various paintings, reliefs and carvings of love-making.

One carving, on a plinth, was of a man and woman so com-pletely and contortedly wrapped around one another that they'd become a perfect, cubic block of limbs. Had it not been for the red paint on the woman's body, and the white paint on the man's, there'd have been no way of knowing whose arms and legs were whose. Impossible contortions! We all stared at this one, wondering . . .

The woman called us back and returned our cards, along with various lists and timetables.

'The hotel has a beach out front. You're free to use it in your spare time. Otherwise you're restricted to this building. For organization reasons. Don't worry, you have plenty to do. Commencing at sixteen-thirty. You'll see from the timetable that you're due in the lecture room on the third floor along with the rest of the new intake. The hotel manager will welcome you, on behalf of us all.' Her eyes drifted to Maimouna's glass ear-globes, disapprovingly. 'Jewellery. We don't allow the wearing of jewellery. It gets in the way of the helmets and interferes with the body-field—'

'It's all right, they unclip.'

'It is *not* all right! The function of art is to be an effective focus for the mind. Not a distraction, a frivolity. All the artwork that you can see here is *effective*. How on earth can you focus on something stuck away on your ears?'

'I do think about them!' protested Maimouna. 'Each little glass globe is a world. The wires form yantras round the world, protecting it from harm. Do you see?'

The woman nodded doubtfully.

'I take them off every night and think how awful it would be if there wasn't a yantra like a fence around the world. What's inside the glass? There's a little spider locked in one and a fly in the other. In preserving fluid. Ancient enemies! Only my skull keeps them apart. My head and my brain. And the wire yantras. They're symbolic, you see, not decorative.'

'Well, keep your lucky charms, if you must – in your room!'

Maimouna flicked a glass globe and looked smug, as though she had proved something to herself. But frankly, a yantra wasn't a fence around the world at all! It was a means of reaching *out* – to other worlds. So I found her explanation ridiculous.

I had been allocated a bright, soft, elegant bedroom with a narrow single bed in it. Our rooms were for rest, not love. (Indeed, I read, it was forbidden to make love privately – or with anybody but an assigned Bardo partner.) On the wall hung a gay print of love-making, though. A man with a curly moustache and a woman with breasts like grapefruit, he and she both plump and languid, gazed in a hypnotic trance into each other's eyes. They were decked in jewellery: rings, bangles, combs and beads. Obviously before the time of Bardo! Air-conditioning vents bore faded labels, 'OUT OF USE', and the windows now had glass louvres to angle in the breeze. A white telephone hung by the bed. To use it, you had to push your credit card into a slot.

I found clothes laid out waiting on the bed – lightweight red cotton trousers with a draw-string waistband, and a red cotton blouse with a pocket containing notebook and pencil, and a smaller, empty pocket on which my name was stencilled, for my credit card.

Down on the third floor, fifty young people of all races sat in the lecture room, girls dressed in red, boys in white. Everyone wore close-cropped hair, though only one boy, with skin like orange peel and protruding ears, had gone to Maimouna's extreme and shaved his skull entirely bare, to fit a Bardo helmet.

The hotel manager, a red-haired blustery man, rapped his knuckles on a rostrum.

'I'll try to keep this brief,' he said – rather inaccurately, as it turned out. 'I welcome you all to Miami – from Hawaii, Scandinavia, Africa, Brazil, wherever your first home was. From now on your home is here. Bardo is the most important business the human race has ever involved itself in. I take it you'll all agree to that! Bardo holds the world steady *and* reaches to the stars. That's because *we* work with human beings, not machines. Sure, we use machines too, as boosters, but they're not the main thing. The human mind is the main thing. The human body-field. We'll only survive by using *that*. Rakshasas tell us that the total lifespan of some planetary cultures – *dead* cultures – they've come across is just a few years, from growth spurt to collapse. They only know two worlds to date, besides themselves, that made it past the hurdle. The most important of them, for your purposes, is Asura. Someone tell me about the Asurans, then! Come on, don't be shy!'

'They're trees,' said one voice.

'They're birds,' said another.

'Actually, they're symbionts,' Maimouna's voice announced haughtily. 'Birds *and* trees coexisting symbiotically. Which means they depend on each other. The birds feed on the sap of the trees, for which in turn they provide higher brain functions. The two together form temporary higher-order beings—'

'Right! Actually, it's an island world, Asura, with a million islands, each with its own little clump of interlinked trees. It just *looks* like a forest world, with a whole maze of straits and creeks all over the place, as there's no actual big sea or lake anywhere. Each island has its own little tree-clump. The trees provide a primary vegetable nervous system. The birds chip in with higher consciousness. Bird and tree plug into each other and depend on each other. Long ago, before symbiosis, the trees were busily soaking up solar radiation, becoming like great biological radar dishes, and the birds' brains were growing big by figuring out the star patterns they navigated by. When symbiosis finally came, the brainy birds were able to apply analytical reason to the cosmic radiations which the trees were able to read on a primary, instinctual level.

'On the wing, in isolation, a bird operates more instinctually than rationally, of course. It's only by "plugging in" to the trees, by merging, that you get the full Asuran individual – bird *plus* tree. Still, each bird-personality flies off from its tree with a magnificent sense of emotional, social belonging. Those Asurans really *know* society, biologically. They're never submerged by the symbiosis – only enhanced.

'Asura would be midway between the orbits of Earth and Mars, if it was in our own solar system. Only, Procyon is a hotter star than Sol, so the temperature averages out the same as Earth ... Why is it called "Asura"? Just wait till you hear the sound of the wind through those leaves, and the wingbeats overhead! It's a beautiful world, Asura – and most of all in the social-ecological sense. The sheer harmony of feeding, mating, navigation, meditation – of sun-drinking and star-watching. It's all in balance.'

Our first three months would mainly be taken up by physical and mental exercises, and lectures. In the mornings: lectures on ways of charting the body-field – from Chinese acupuncture, through Tibetan 'mental map' mandalas, to Kirlian high-voltage aura photography and the Backster Effect of 'primary perception' in all living cells – as well as Maths and Physics, particularly the general theory of the Action-at-a-Distance Cosmos, which allowed us to beam our body-field to the stars at the speed of thought. In the afternoons: physical activities – body-field co-ordination, yoga and sexual exercises.

After the first few weeks in this 'Orientation Unit', each of us would be allocated a partner who had already flown to

Asura, whereupon we would go to live in what they called the 'Initiation Unit', another hotel. After about two more months, we should be ready to make our first mental journey to the stars, from the Procyon Embassy building itself.

The three hundred hotels of Miami Beach housed approximately three thousand Bardo trainees, we learnt. Which posed huge organizational problems. This was why we were not to stray away from our own hotel. Inside the hotel, we were not to enter any areas of the building marked by red swastika warning signs on the doors.

'So: work hard. Train hard. Remember, we need round-the-clock vigilance at the Procyon Embassy. Our contact with them must never be lost—'

And so the hotel manager's speech subsided.

'Any questions, queries, problems?' The three melted into one, because everything was still a question, a query, or a problem.

'Obviously not right now,' he laughed. 'Well, the bigger questions sort themselves out as time goes by. Any immediate difficulties, ask at the desk or phone down from your room.'

Maimouna nudged me in the crowd, afterwards.

'Why do Bardo need so many trainees? Three thousand people training just to keep in touch with one world! In the old days there were only a couple of hundred astronauts, ever.'

'That wasn't mental travel. It takes a lot of psychic energy. You have to rest up between flights. Flights are shorter—'

'They've been training people for years and years. What's the urgency? Is Bardo flight so exhausting that they need these sort of numbers? I tell you, the manager was scared of something – something about Bardo.'

'Nonsense.'

'Scared, my dear, as my fly is scared of my spider. I *know*. My Chinese Teacher laid his hands on my skull when I was ten years old. He stared into my eyes and said he saw the spider in my left eye and the fly in my right eye, and I'd always know them when I met them in my life. If Bardo spins mind webs into space, Lila, why was our manager sweating like a trapped fly?'

Hamidou-A butted in. 'That fly and spider – it's just an image of the two sides of your own brain, Maimouna, to help

56

you concentrate on integrating them. Didn't you realize? Fly must learn to trust the spider. Spider must learn not to want to eat the fly.'

'The left side of your brain analyses,' echoed his brother. 'It spins webs of analysis. The right side intuits. It flies into the beyond. Your Chinese Teacher was just taking your own personality into account with his fly and spider story – trading on your sly, suspicious nature, to make the best he could of you.'

'You're always spinning webs for people, to prove how clever you are.'

'Take care you don't catch yourself in your own web!'

SEVEN

During the first month, we attended lectures on the field phenomenon we'd be using to make our almost instantaneous transition to Asura: Action at a Distance.

Our instructor, an Indian from Arizona, showed us a time-lapse film of a seed germinating, sprouting, becoming a full-grown plant, flowering and dying. Then he ran the film backwards. The plant grew back into the seed again.

Next he showed a film of a waterfall falling *up* a cliff face, instead of down. Then another film, of stones and dust flying together to form a solid boulder – at which we all laughed, it looked so silly.

'That's a natural reaction – laughter,' commented the Indian. 'Time always flows in one direction only. So rivers never run backwards, and rubble never reorganizes itself into a boulder after you've dynamited it. Time flies forward like an arrow. It stands to reason, eh?

'It so happens that it isn't reasonable at all! According to modern physics, events should *always* be reversible, theoretically. Consider the universe, overall. The universe is a unit. There isn't anything that *isn't* in the universe. Consequently all parts must be connected to all other parts. Strictly, there can't be any "parts" at all! So what is it that links "near" to "far"? What is it that links this single unit, the universe? Please consider a source of energy anywhere in the universe. Waves radiate outwards from this source at the speed of light. Radio waves, X-rays, visible light, whatever. We call all these energies "retarded" waves, because they arrive somewhere else later than they set off, whether it's a minute later or a million years later. Obviously it stands to reason that something should arrive later than it leaves. The effect has to follow the cause.

'Just you try to prove it! According to Maxwell's fundamental equations for electro-magnetic fields, the opposite case is equally possible. "Advanced" waves can also exist, which travel back through time to converge on their so-called "point of origin". As these must be in equal and opposite reaction to the emission of the retarded waves, we can call on Newton's Third Law to back us up here—'

The Indian drew diagrams of radiating arrows and squiggly lines, and chalked up formulas which we scribbled down in our notebooks to study later and be asked questions on.

'All this is theory. But does any waterfall actually flow back to its source? Does starlight ever really fly backwards through time to a star to arrive at the same time as it radiates it? Plainly not – *to our eyes*. Yet this has to be the case for the universe as a whole, or it simply couldn't hold together in one single unit. It has to act upon itself at a distance in this way. When a "retarded" wave reaches Procyon from Sol, Procyon reacts with an "advanced" wave which travels back through time, to arrive at Sol just as the original retarded wave is setting out. This is happening all the time, everywhere. The whole universe constantly and simultaneously interacts with every single event, every single charge. Only thus is it a "universe".

'Whenever any event occurs – no matter how humble, just a single electric charge being jiggled – waves radiate outwards and forwards in time to the furthest reaches of the universe, and simultaneously converge from these far reaches. That's the underlying fabric of Reality – the glue, the universal binding medium. That's the cosmic field.

'It's this field through which the Bardo flier transmits his thoughts. You perceive an arrow of time. You live your lives by it. Yet cosmically there's no such thing – and all matter, your brains and bodies included, being simply bundles of charges, this is how your thought patterns can interact with the thoughts of the Asurans—'

From a Dobdob Instructor called Ramon Fernandez, a Spanish American, we learnt more details about the peculiar beings who inhabited Procyon IV – those strange composites of Bird and Tree, the Asurans.

At first it was hard to really *feel*, at gut level, how one kind of life-form, a Tree – however well endowed with 'primary perception' and however sensitive to cosmic rhythms – could possibly link up with another kind of life-form, a Bird – however brainy it was – to form an integrated, higher-order being. Quite hard for us human beings to conceive – at least until we had ourselves experienced depth hypnosis and a number of consciousness-altering drugs and discovered how composite and often contradictory our own identities actually were; how many different states and subsystems of consciousness actually clustered in our own brains, not always even compatible with each other! We weren't quite the solid, connected individuals we imagined ourselves! In a sense, Asura reflected outwardly what was going on constantly inside our own heads . . .

Each tree had one specialized feeding tube close to its fruiting body, at the most complex node of its vegetable sensory system. Here the birds roosted, plugging in to feed and to tap the tree's body-field.

Usually each symbiosis only lasted a single day. At nightfall, the higher aerial consciousness of the bird detached itself from the chthonic senses of the tree to seek out a different base and form a new, and equally temporary, Asuran. Temporary, and unlikely to be repeated twice – yet at the same time there was a genuine world-wide continuity of awareness between all these separate individuals who came into being and dissolved again, so that experience and knowledge were diffused right across the planet; and handed down, too, cumulatively from generation to generation.

Certain birds roosted longer than usual in specific 'contact' trees these days, playing the role of Bardo communicators. These had undertaken the 'compact of stability', as it was called . . .

In the numerical sense the population was fairly small. In the mental sense, though, it was huge since there were so many possible permutations of Bird and Tree, and constant variety was the rule rather than the exception. Obviously there was no need to 'increase and multiply' the sheer numbers of the population in order to broaden the range of individuals!

Psychologically, because of the constant plugging in and unplugging, the Asurans had achieved the detachment of mind sought for by generations of Earth mystics; while they remained at the same time perfectly connected social beings – unlike the mass of Earth's mystics in the past.

The trees had always functioned as mighty radiation absorbers: the bands of chloroplast stroma in the leaves photosynthesizing adenosine triphosphate, phosphoroglyceric acid, fatty acids and amino acids. But it was the crucial adaptation of the leaves to 'night sight' – to radiations on radio and other wavebands from the stars, stimulated by bird-curiosity – that led the Asurans to key in to the Bardo plane. The Rakshasas actually made the breakthrough to Asura. They were the great initiators. That was 10,000 Earth years ago. Even then the Asurans were already very advanced in their understanding of the structure of the cosmos and the binding of space-time, because of their unique union of tree-receiver and bird consciousness.

We also learnt something – in brief – about the two other alien races, the Rakshasas and the Yidags; though these weren't to be our speciality.

Rakshasas looked like inflatable balloon versions of the sting ray that I'd seen off Sinda, with squidlike 'arms' around their mouths. Their world was a moon orbiting the second gas-giant planet of Barnard's Star – which filled their sky with vivid swirls of orange, red and yellow. This accounted for the 'firemist' effect. Actually their world was very cold indeed.

The gravity of their moon was too weak to hold its atmosphere. This constantly leaked into space. Fortunately for the existence of life on Rakshasa, the lost atmospheric gases all gathered in a tight band around the gas-giant, which happened to coincide perfectly with the orbit of the moon itself. Thus the moon scooped its atmosphere back from space as quickly as it lost it. Apparently this was the case with Saturn's moon Titan, in our own solar system . . .

The weak gravity allowed the Rakshasas to pulse-jet about freely among the slender, spiring mountains of their moon; and even to escape from their world by inflating their body sacs to the utmost and soaring out into the band of atmosphere around the whole orbital path. Using their own bodies as spacecraft – at least within the confines of the doughnut band – they learn to navigate right around the gas-giant, becoming living satellites, though ones which had to return to their world for nourishment.

They discovered how to use the whole gaseous doughnut as a huge natural antenna – three million kilometres from edge to edge, nine million kilometres in length. Modulating it by storing within their own bodies the ionized gases produced by the charged field of the gas-giant's magnetosphere, they succeeded in producing a highly sensitive receiver-transmitter ...

By contrast, Yidags were the real 'fire-beings'. These were massive, static, metallic-crystal 'jugs' inhabiting a blazing hot planet closest to its sun, almost naked to raw space.

They drank in sunlight by day and stored it through the nights like so many organic batteries. Communication was by laser pulses in the deep infra-red. They even reproduced by this means – patiently building up new crystal forms of their kind by interference patterns of their laser beams falling upon the fluorosilicone pools. These beings were information analysts extraordinary; and their 'consciousness' didn't so much dawn at 'birth' as accrue gradually as each bottle-being was slowly built towards maturity and began to accept more load in the 'circuitry' of Yidag society. For the Yidags were methodically transforming the very surface of their world into an analytical, thinking nexus ...

Oddly, it was the Asurans from their sylvan watery world who made the breakthrough to Yidag on the Bardo plane, rather than the Rakshasas. The perpetual switching-in and switching-out pattern of life on Asura let the Bird-Trees appreciate more readily the world view of Yidag, where 'individuals' were only nodes in an evolving planetary network.

EIGHT

'So what's the secret link between the three worlds?' Maimouna demanded one day as we piled out of class on to the beach.

Was there one? Each world seemed very different from the next. Mineral creatures, shape-shifting tar balloons, birds in trees. Boiling, freezing, mild.

The three worlds were all very stable, very patient, compared with what Earth had once been. I couldn't see how the Asurans or Rakshasas could ever have built up a technology, as we know it, given their basic lack of raw materials. Was technology the devil, then? No, since the Yidags had built a technology – albeit an organic one. But the Yidags couldn't move about their world, except by proxy. Still, the Asurans were always flying about from place to place . . . Maybe the fateful combination that wrecked up-and-coming civilizations was inorganic technology *plus* mobility *plus* intense individualism. Maybe this combination was almost inevitable for mammalian cultures, whether they evolved from proto-rats or proto-apes or proto-bears or whatever. Significantly, none of the aliens were mammals of any sort . . .

The surf washed ashore, tossing weed and shells from the Atlantic. Fenced groins divided our beach into strips. Other intakes of students sat chattering in the sun beyond the fences, in separate compounds.

'They're distinctly *simple* worlds!' said Maimouna, contemptuously. 'I mean, really simple-minded. I'll say that for a start. Particularly our precious Asura!'

'Come along,' Hamidou-A protested, 'we're just starting to find out about it. You're so impatient. That's the whole trouble with us humans – wanting everything at once. Maybe that's our carnivore sickness: the primal hunt syndrome. If we hurry now, we're likely to trip up! It might take ten million years to spread the A.D. network through this galaxy alone, never mind to other galaxies. So what? That's just a wink of the eye, cosmically.'

'It's a lot of time too,' I said. 'I can't help wondering whether civilizations will ever get round to visiting each other physically during it, in actual starships?'

'What's the point? We already visit them, they visit us. Why build a tin can costing half the world's resources? Who would want to be shut up in it for years?'

Inspired, Maimouna clapped her hands. 'Something out there must be building "tin cans", though! It's bound to happen some time. Not every mobile technical culture absolutely has to destroy itself. Perhaps some forms of life can't ever travel the Bardo way. Not all human beings can. Maybe that's what Bardo is frightened of! Maybe the Rakshasas or Yidags have found out that things in tin cans are heading our way! Or maybe our "friends" just don't want *us* making tin cans, which is why they showed us a faster, easier way – to keep us away from them! To keep us out of the universe, while giving us the illusion of belonging!'

'We never could have made tin cans,' objected Abdoulaye-H. 'The sort of world that made spaceships was already collapsing, even as it conquered the Moon – if you can call it conquering.'

'Answer this, then! Bardo flight is practically instantaneous, right? Yet it's taken the Rakshasas ten thousand years to push out a few hundred light years. Why is it taking so long? What is Bardo having to push against? What force is *against* us?'

The Hausa boy sighed. 'It's easy for us to visit the three established worlds, compared with what their own fliers are doing – leaping out into nowhere, catching a toehold on nothing.'

'So you accept a wait of five or ten million years before we can ever cross this galaxy? My dear boy, what were we human beings ten million years ago? Nothing like what we are now! What will we be as far as that in the future? Completely different creatures, because of evolution. It's just stupid thinking of us, the human race, as any part of the future. We won't be. We can't be. I don't know how you imagine we can be.'

'It's my opinion that Bardo *is* a way of evolution for the human race from now on—'

64

'Nonsense. How can it be? Evolution is genetics, not inter-stellar communications. At the present rate of progress, we'll disappear as a species long before there's any galactic civiliza-tion. It's too tragic. Don't you see, the human race will never know the universe *because of* Bardo.'

'I'd say that the next evolutionary step involves learning *alien* information and incorporating it,' Abdoulaye-H said. 'Genetics is simply information transfer, basically. Look at the Yidags – there's a beautiful example of a society which is com-pletely conscious of how information makes new individuals—'

'Oh, aren't they a beautiful textbook example! They might have been specially invented for the purpose! That's what I mean about how simple-minded these three alien worlds are. They're so stripped down – like a set of equations!'

'They succeeded,' said Abdoulaye-H with a shrug. 'The other cultures all went smash.'

'So we're told.'

'Anyway, I like them. They're clear, logical worlds. Not a mess.'

The warm sea rolled in, line after line of bubbling foam soaking the Miami sand, percolating back. Except for the pre-sence of the hotels, it could have been a million, or a billion years ago. And the year was only 2170. The Hausa boys were right. Humanity had been in existence in a civilized state on this planet for such a tiny number of years. Maimouna would just have to curb her impatience.

For exercises in training the mind and body-field we were driven out to the Villa Vizcaya, a few kilometres south through Miami City.

Miami was modestly bustling with service facilities for the Centre. I noticed a number of one-time 'banks' and 'air-line' offices, with their names still stuck above their glass windows in a sort of comic indictment, though Dobdobs were plainly working inside on various kinds of records and administration as we passed, and the real names of the buildings were sten-cilled, more discreetly, across the doors. A certain 'Chase Man-hattan Bank' was actually the 'South-Eastern States Contracap Agency' . . .

Villa Vizcaya was a palace with formal gardens built by an

eccentric rich man two hundred and fifty years earlier, in the style of an even earlier period: Italian Renaissance. Our Dobdob Instructor was a mellow, oval-faced Persian called Shotai. His skin had the lambent, amber tone of a peach. He led us through to a large geometrical water-garden flanked by orange trees and low white walls. Statues faced one another on plinths. Red and yellow roses sprouted between lines of box hedge, punctuated by bushes. A tall, *stupa*-like fountain bubbled into an emerald pond inside low lotus-petal walls. Pathways and watercourses wove a kind of yantra design around it, a life-size yantra of which any visitor immediately became part. Set at the centre of the design, the fountain was its bindu point. It was the vanishing point of a garden of the mind.

Shotai injected me with a perception-enhancing drug called MMDA – a synthetic compound from one of the essential oils of nutmeg, which stimulates intense eidetic displays, not of past experiences, but of the Now, the Present, and strengthens the powers on concentrating on these and organizing them. It had none of the somewhat disorienting effects of the 'mind-dividing' drugs we'd been given earlier, in preparation for Asura, to show us how composite our own minds actually are. It was really a very old and natural drug in a new form. Nutmeg had been known to the ancient Hindu scriptures. The Persian Dobdob told me to stand stock still and concentrate all my attention on fixing every tree, every branch of every tree, every spray of leaves on every branch, in my mind's eye. Then I must memorize the roses, the hedges, the watercourses, the statues.

For one whole hour at least I didn't move, but only stared.

When I thought that I knew the garden perfectly, I shut my eyes and *saw* it, eidetically. The image remained sharp and clear. I spent half an hour *seeing* it, this way.

Then, step by step, I began erasing what I saw.

Erasing details at first, not specific items. Texture, richness of colour, length, breadth, depth: I drained away the garden's qualities one by one. Roses lost their hue. Trees became monochrome. Clusters of leaves, amorphous.

The garden was now a child's grey charcoal sketch. Next, I began erasing the items themselves.

This proved much more difficult. Shapes fought to remain

66

in being – while I tried to retract the trees into the earth, to make bare ground, empty channels, a dry fountain.

Finally, I willed even the fountain into a mere line, standing upright, alone in flat-land.

This line I urged to diminish to a point.

It shrank slowly, in my field of consciousness. It became one-dimensional.

And I asked myself, as Shotai had told me to, what is the nature of a point? What sort of unique 'being' does a point possess? From our point of view here on Earth, all the stars were points because they were so far away. If I could make an earthly garden retreat to a point source, how could I make a point, on the other hand, turn into a star – the star Procyon? That was the task of Bardo flight.

I could only do so by entering the point, by becoming the point in my own mind.

I didn't succeed on the first day, nor the second! (I'm capsuling things, you see.) It took me till the fifth day to reduce the garden to bare bones, and till the seventh to reduce it all to a flat plane with a single upright line.

Then, on the eighth day, the line receded to a point. And this was the seed point from which the whole universe of stars and gardens springs . . .

I was doing well.

Later, we spent days in the Vizcaya gardens identifying ourselves with the shrubbery, instead of abolishing it.

On these occasions I had to squat before a cone shrub on a velvet lawn. Fiercely and mutely, aided by another essential oil of nutmeg derivative, I had to force *my* existence to be *its* existence.

No longer was I flesh and blood, but root and branch, leaf and sap. No longer did I have legs, but roots. No longer fingers, but stalks. No longer blood, but chlorophyll. No longer two eyes, but a thousand leaves catching the light.

The whole purpose of this exercise was to prepare me to feel that I was a tree, growing on Asura.

This was actually a far more difficult exercise than the other one. But the moment when it succeeded was more dramatic! After staring for several afternoons at the same shrub, my attention lapsed briefly. I was distracted by the flicker of sun-light on some egret's wing, flying seawards. When I looked at the shrub again, I was looking at myself. I was looking at a human body, out of my thousand leaves!

I gasped in surprise.

And Shotai the Persian was by me in a moment.

'There!' he urged. 'You *saw*!' I nodded at him dumbly, though there was only that shrub there again before my eyes, and the blood was pounding through my own human body.

After more such afternoons, I felt that I could simultaneous-ly be present at two points in space; possess two viewpoints ...

In the hotel, after this success, I was fitted with a Bardo helmet. While I concentrated on recalling my experiences of the garden and the shrub, the helmet measured my brain waves, feeding them to a computer. The Dobdob neurologist in charge told me that we all have actual physical maps inscribed in our brains, in an area called the hippocampus. I thought of it, fancifully – and perhaps not so inaccurately! – as a field of horses all galloping off on journeys in different directions at different speeds. The placing of objects in space maps on to columns of cells in the hippocampus. The mapping process and the map-reading process for recovering the information use the electrical theta rhythm of the hippocampus. This was what he was measuring. When I finally flew on the Bardo plane, a computer would monitor the 'map' of my journey via my helmet.

And so we moved out of the Orientation Unit, to another hotel further south where we were teamed with our Bardo partners.

The Hausa twins were paired with a freckled Irish redhead and a raven-haired amerindian. Maimouna took a young Japanese lover.

And I met Ahmed Klimt, descendant of some central Euro-pean guestworker who had emigrated to the once oil-rich Arab Confederacy long ago.

NINE

Klimt was small, tough, wiry. At nineteen, he had already made several mental flights to Procyon. His skin was swarthy as dried meat polished by the sun. When he took off his white tunic to practise asana positions with me, there was hardly any flesh on his frame, only corded muscles rippling and oozing like snakes. The dark pupils of his eyes bored holes in me as I undressed, as though he was trying out a 'reduction to a void' exercise upon my own body! I felt his gaze dissolve my skin, my flesh, my fat cells. It dried up the fluid parts of me, reduced me to a piece of coral, an empty honeycomb. What he desired was not me; but only to penetrate *beyond* me, into the space within my body and beyond it.

I could never 'like' him. Still he was charged with magic power. His presence warped my feelings into a perverse intoxication.

We were both naked now, apart from electroencephalograph skullcaps, and an adhesive pad fixed to my belly and wired to the cap. Klimt's skin was mottled with tiny moles on the thighs and shoulders, like flecks of gravel that had buried themselves at high velocity. It took me a minute or two to realize that the contracap was missing from the proper place on his arm. A faint scar was the only trace left of it.

'You haven't got a contraceptive . . .'

'You'll lose your capsule too, as soon as it's time for your first real flight.'

'The contracaps alter the hormonal messages, Lila,' interrupted the voice of our Dobdob instructor from the observation room. 'That's how they work. But they throw the body-field out of balance. For our purposes, we have to remove them. The body channels have to be clear. After you've practised the basic sexual asanas together for a fortnight or so to tune your bodies to each other, we'll excise your capsule—'

'Isn't there a risk of me getting pregnant, as soon as I start flying?'

69

'Oh, it can take some people years to conceive. You don't automatically become pregnant the moment you're off contraceptives. Still, maybe *now* you see why we need so many Bardo fliers. There's what you might call an occupational hazard involved.' Her voice was brisk and hearty. 'Actually, the whole Virginia Beach area south of here is set aside for precisely this contingency. It's a really beautiful educational environment.'

'But ... abortion. Surely?'

'No, Lila, abortion is out of the question. It would ruin the balance of your body-field. Take you two or three years to recover, if at all. If you get pregnant, the child has to be born. Of course, this would seem terribly unfair in the outside world, with the population under such strict control. As though you had an indefinite number of free birth permits—'

Yes, indeed, I remembered Bibi Mwezi's scalded arm. There would be resentment.

'We have to be discreet. Not that the children suffer on account of it. Far from it!'

'So you're probably a father, Ahmed?'

'How should I know? I never asked. What on earth does *that* matter, compared with starflight? We're wasting time, Lila.'

'I don't suppose the aliens have this problem, do they?'

'Hardly, given their biology! But *we* have to work with the bodies we have. Let's work!'

We pulled the helmets down from the lightweight, hypermobile booms swinging above us, and slipped them over our heads, clicking them on to the skullcaps. We were using helmets without face masks for these practice runs, to damp the full kundalini effect. Mantra to listen to, but no yantra to watch. The helmet sat on me weightlessly, barely noticeable, apart from its blanketing silence. If I moved, it floated with me, light as down.

Klimt was elegant, gymnastic and tireless in his love-making. Dare I say 'tender', too? For him, tenderness was simply perfect smoothness of performance. He didn't exactly confirm the existence of my body by his love-making! Rather, he denied it, dissolving my flesh into nerves, my nerves into energy.

So, then, his limbs entangled with mine. He corrected my

posture gently with flat palms. With fingernails and tip of tongue he traced the outline of my subtle body – that other body within my body, my energy body – searching the chakras in my navel, my throat. Finally, he entered me.

The Bardo helmet hummed in my ears, singing the seed-sound:

HUM, HUM, HUM—

My brain vibrated with it, breathing *HUM* like air. My two hemispheres were like lungs drawing the rhythm into all the energy conduits of my body. Automatically I fell into the proper breathing pattern. I was conscious of the entry and exit of my breath, but it was no longer just air: it was *prana*, the breath of being. I breathed from my deep abdomen like a baby. Kundalini power began uncoiling at the root of my spine, a flow of soft molten metal, lava from a volcano, spreading upwards.

She was a fierce, intoxicating Other Creature living in me, this Kundalini. Yet she was also my own unknown root self. I hailed her: Greetings, Being of Fire and Energy! Greetings, Creature of Destruction and Delight!

TRAM, TRAM, TRAM, my lover throbbed. Kundalini rose higher through my belly. Then the mantra sound stopped.

A slurred, slowed-down voice began ordering me to do something in a strange language.

'*Mulabhanda! Mu-la-bhan-da!*' the voice insisted urgently – sluggishly, time was so drawn out.

I heard the word three times before I understood it. Then I remembered. 'Bandhas' are the muscle contractions of yoga. 'Mulabhanda' is the anal contraction, which prevents ejaculation, and stops the rise of Kundalini. She was telling me to send my Kundalini down again. This was only an exercise, and I was already half lost in it!

So the creature of fire and joy, destruction and delight, came to a halt and began sinking slowly down my spine again.

Time speeded up.

Klimt uncoiled himself sleekly from me.

We lifted our helmets and they drifted up towards the ceiling on the booms and hung there. Our skullcaps and my belly pad came loose with faint *plops* and we laid them on the matting like bedraggled baby octopuses.

When I tried to stand up, my body turned to rubber; sparks flashed before my eyes, and Klimt supported me, with a faint grin.

'You need a shower. Then food; then sleep,' he said functionally.

In the anteroom, needles of icy water revived me. Soon after, I was eating ravenously with Klimt in the hotel refectory. I tried to talk to him about his home in North Africa, then about the likelihood of our having a baby (a possibility I was still trying to come to terms with) but I had to give up both these topics. He hadn't the slightest interest in either his origins or his potential offspring. I could just see him as a growing boy, wrapped in some white burnous, rushing out into the blank rippling desert at dawn, willing it to be the Bardo plane; reducing palm trees to lines, reducing himself to a one-dimensional person! A fanatic, from way back.

Yet Ahmed Klimt was the first person I had met who had actually flown to the stars. Maybe star flight had this effect on one. Being so utterly remote from Earth in one's mind might cause a sort of madness, for all I knew. It might make you feel that the real world was only something glassy and transparent, which on closer inspection would dissolve into a void.

Five weeks passed, and I was ready to fly . . .

The Procyon Embassy had once been called Morningside Palace Hotel. Now, over it, a forked green banner rippled in a strong breeze, a dragon's tongue of flame. For an eye, the dragon wore a yantra.

Klimt and I handed over our credit cards to the armed Dob-dob guards on the door, and they were fed through a desk console before being returned to us.

'What does the Asuran ambassador look like, Klimt? Do you see a tree growing in the middle of a room, or a whirl of light, or what?'

'For heaven's sake, you don't see them *here* on Earth. How literal you are! We only see Asura through *their* eyes when we fly there. We need an Asuran receiver.'

'They don't need a human receiver, to be here, you said.'

'They're far more sophisticated than we are. They've been at it for tens of thousands of years. They can hang loose.'

He waved his hand grandly. 'They could be anywhere, hanging in the air, if they wanted. We just wouldn't see them. Or hardly see them.'

I thought about all the ghosts and devils that people had reported seeing since the dawn of records. Were those all half-glimpsed star-fliers? If so, why couldn't we see an Asuran here, if not in the flesh, at least as some kind of manifestation?

'Guarding them gives the impression they're all safely locked up in their embassy!' laughed Klimt. 'Anyway, they say that "hanging loose", as we call it, is a terrible drain on energy. I suppose that's why it takes so long to push the sphere of Bardo flight further out.'

A Dobdob led us to an elevator. We were whisked to the very top floor.

Here, we received our pre-flight briefing in an anteroom with a small window, beyond which could be seen all the paraphernalia of space flight control: a big room with technicians at desk consoles; a glass-panel map of the world the length of one wall, criss-crossed by zigzagging lines; and cabinets with tape drums whirling, halting, whirling on. Actually, the mesh of security wire in the glass as well as the sheer thickness of the glass itself lent the scene a foggy, grainy, indistinct appearance.

The Dobdob cautioned us once more about 'hook rays'. The Tibetan *Book of the Dead* constantly warns about the false attraction of other starlight, while in transit. Light from strange stars can lead you astray.

After this statutory warning, he went on:

'It's very important that you stack everything in your mind for debriefing afterwards. You're taking part in a debate of great scientific importance. If some of it sounds, well, queer or idiotic . . . believe me, just hang on to every scrap of it. You'll be recorded during the flight, of course, but we need to double-check.

'You'll be discussing "boundaries" basically – the logical structure of boundaries. It's a basic problem of knowledge, this. It poses the question of how much we can ever really know about ourselves, and, as a correlate, how much we can ever expect to know about the universe at large. A philosopher once asked: "How can you imagine a mind observing the *whole* of itself? If this mind was entirely taken up with observation what exactly would it be observing?" Well, if we're ever to understand the cosmos we have to solve this riddle – because mind and the universe have at least one thing in common: they are both complete, unique systems.

'A universe has no boundary *except itself*. On the other hand, the universe might have boundaries built into itself internally, just as we do, so that it *can* be a universe – the one and only. Just as the mind can't inspect the whole of itself, neither can the universe – in spite of the binding glue of Action-at-a-Distance. What sort of boundaries has it got, though? Likewise, what sort of built-in boundaries has our own *knowledge* of it got? Are there "alternatives" to the universe that we know? Are there alternative universes within the overall framework of the universe, which we could gain access to?

'Essentially, a boundary includes something inside itself – while excluding everything that isn't inside it. But this very fact implies that there's something positive and definite which gets excluded! So, can knowledge ever leak across such a boundary?

'The Asurans are ideally set up to understand this, right down at gut level. Bird in the tree. Bird on the wing. Bird in another tree. They include themselves in a larger entity; then they exclude themselves by flying off to form another alternative being with a new mental perspective. And yet they carry over some continuity.

'We need to find out from them whether "our" universe – the one we know – is only a partial one. A sub-set of a larger universe. We need to find out whether an "alien" universe can partially share our own frame of reference – and, if so, what type of boundary we might have with it. In other words, how "leaky" is this bounded universe of ours?

'The Asurans are very cute at boundary-crossing, given the kind of biological make-up and consciousness they have. So kindly discuss "boundaries" with them, for all you're worth! Even if you do feel you'd rather discuss something superficially more exciting on an alien planet.'

This was mainly addressed to me. Klimt's expression indicated that he knew it all already.

Beyond the glass panel, tapes spun on cabinets, technicians turned dials, flipped switches, scribbled notes on printouts, as the Dobdob opened the padded door for us.

So we entered the Contact Room to explore each other's bodies – and thus explore the universe.

TEN

We held each other in dark silence. Then the sri yantra mandala glowed before my eyes. The mantra *HUM!* entered my ears. And we entered one another. The Kundalini rose with a firm, fierce glow. *TRAM! TRAM!* drummed the next mantra. We passed the second triangle.

HRIH! HRIH! came a shrilling in my heart.

RAM! RAM! went a gonging in my brain. Triangles fell away.

OM! OM! boomed the greatest mantra of all; and the central bindu point exploded. It novaed out around me, sucking me down into the blaze of stars. Stars swept past me, forming into a great ring – a torus of light from which 'hook rays' of silver and saffron and sapphire light beckoned, each photon promising to expand into a separate star, a world, a haven. The whole galaxy condensed into this ring of light, through the centre of which I flew, from one darkness towards another darkness; and the faster I flew, the further behind me the ring of light shrank – as though I was flying right out of the galaxy – till it became a mere hoop in empty space, left far behind me: a presence which I did not so much see with my bodily eyes as sense with the pineal eye within my brain – with my third eye awakened! The sum of all the stars there were shrank behind me till they made up one large star, and then a single intense point-source of light – the only point of light in existence. I still seemed to be fleeing from it! Yet at the very instant that I fled away from it the fastest, because it was the only point that existed suddenly I found that every way led towards it. Abruptly it lay ahead of me rather than behind. So it became my destination – the only way that I could go.

The point novaed out again, engulfing me in light. In daylight. The daylight of another sun.

I was roosting in a tree. All its branches rose to the same

height, supporting a stiff array of interlocking leaves, all canted towards the late afternoon sun. Not the sun of Earth. The sun of Procyon.

I was a green bloom at the tree's tip, my wing-furled body a lozenge of bright viridian feathers, perfectly contained in my roosting node.

I was practically a winged brain. Crop, gullet, stomach and intestines had all atrophied as my brain enlarged. My food, rich sap, I soaked up entirely from my tree. Once a year my tiny reproductive organs swelled with oestrus, calling me to the Great Intermix. Each Asuran dusk, until recently, I also flew to the Little Intermix. After millennia my wings still beat strongly, though I no longer had legs or feet, and could only land in the crown of a tree, like an egg in an eggcup.

What sort of creature was I? A Tree-Bird. A Whole Being, undivided. Yet one that must divide so that I might become, by way of the Intermix, a new and different Whole Being. With something of the old. Whereby I shared my wings down the millennia with all Asuran history, and right across this world with all the many other Identities I had been, and would be once again when this present compact of stability was over for me and my duty done to the 'humans' . . .

With my hooded eyes half shut against the diminishing solar glare, I hunched like so many other green-skulled flowers pressing out the sapience of the trees beneath, all around our world.

Green islands rose from the green sea every few hundred wingbeats. Green water interrupted green land. There was no continuity between the sea and the land, except for our wingbeats. Land-life existed by exclusion of sea-chemistry; land-life looked to the burning sun. Our world was all frontiers and boundaries, interlacing one another. Inclusions and exclusions were everywhere.

Asura, whispered the rising pre-dusk breeze, brushing the canted flanges of my leaves.

The sun sank faster, swelling into a yolksac as it rested on the horizon – the broken egg of day, dripping underneath the curve of Asura.

Yet the egg of day never really broke. Yolk only spilled into the hard white shell of others' days, elsewhere around the world. In the same way, the Intermix spilled the yolk of my previous Identity into the unbroken shell of a future Identity.

A fellow Asuran sat on this same island as me, a few wing-beats away, keeping the compact of stability too. He was the Speaker, the Answerer, while I was the receiver of the human pair that nestled in my mind, the Questioner. Indeed I *was* the human pair. I *was* Lila . . . an Asuran Lila.

As the sun went, my leaves canted back to begin the nightly starwatch.

Perhaps human 'sleep' was a sort of Intermix? Not really. Human beings always woke up exactly the same people as before. How disappointing for them. They had my pity.

Or rather, they believed they were the same people – while they were not even that . . .

Asura, Asura— Overhead, the first wings were beating to the Intermix.

Together, Klimt and I were absorbed in this Asuran 'receiver' who was a full Asuran only by virtue of being two-in-one . . .

'One and one is one,' I chirped at our Tree-Bird neighbour. Or sang. Or said. I don't know. Yet I conveyed a meaning.

'Our name,' sang Klimt (who had been here before), 'is *Cags Kyu-ma*, I believe. Greetings.' Words heard in my head; his voice lacked echo and timbre.

'Greetings. Our own name is *Nammk'a Dbyins*. "Nammk'a" names the tree-nest. "Dbyins" names our free variable, the flying bird. But *Cags Sgro-ma* is your name now. Your free variable "Kyu-ma" flew away to the Intermix. Now the free variable "Sgro-ma" sits on the tree-nest, heeding the compact of stability.' And the Asuran added, enigmatically, 'Numbers build nests, as well as birds. Rational numbers as well as irrational ones.'

'It's talking about mathematics,' Klimt's voice whispered. 'Irrational numbers are numbers like "pi" – the ratio of the circumference of a circle to its diameter, you know.'

'Roughly twenty-two over seven,' I said; I knew that much!

'Very important number. You couldn't do geometry without it,' commented Klimt. 'It represents a real geometrical relationship. The moment you draw a circle, *pi* exists. Yet it's entirely irrational. There's no rational answer to the sum "twenty-two over seven". You can divide twenty-two by seven for ever but you never get a real definite answer. Or take the square root of two . . . A simple little calculation. No exact solution. Only closer and closer approximations "nesting" around the theoretically perfect answer. It's one of the enigmas of numbers, this! An infinity of possible answers. So infinity is born in the act of thinking about numbers! Mind and infinity are linked in some strange way. Perhaps the infinite even *needs* thought, to bring it into being!'

He posed a question, which I echoed dutifully: a hangover from his last visit, I guessed.

'I still don't see why Number Two is different from Number One twice! You Asurans are only "one" when you're nesting, correct? But that still involves two separate beings – in your case Nammk'a the Tree *plus* Dbyins the Bird. How can two separate entities be the same as one?'

The Asuran sang back, 'Integer Two – that's to say the whole number "two" – is quite different from "two ones" put together. You may find this hard to see, but actually a "number boundary" encloses Integer Two in the same way as it encloses Integer One. A whole infinite universe of fractional numbers, created by thought, nests between numbers One and Two. This universe is a unit of "oneness", bounded by a horizon of "twoness".'

So we were on course. Boundaries and horizons.

'Now consider the number two universe in its own right,' the tree-bird went on. 'That's a larger universe. It includes the number One universe in one sense, since two obviously includes one. But in another sense it excludes the possibility of oneness . . . That's why you human beings interest us. You can only come here when two of you are joined together in the sexual act. That's the only way you can tap enough energy. Perhaps because each of you has a brain with two separate sides to it, and a mind divided into conscious and unconscious. Very crudely speaking, there are two of each of you: that part which forms the personal consciousness at any one time – and all of the inaccessible and unknown remainder. Yet two doesn't become a real number in your minds, because you can't integrate these separate integers. You remain "one plus one" – isolated, partial beings.'

'He's so right, Lila,' sighed Klimt. 'The eternal division. Male and female, Shiva and Shakti, the twin hemispheres of the brain. Conscious and subconscious. We're always twofold. We have to unify these streams of being within ourselves! When we learn how to fuse them, we'll be one step further towards unravelling the universe.'

'Yes, there are boundaries within us,' we admitted aloud. 'We can't ever consciously know our other self.'

'Your understanding of the universe is imprisoned compared with ours, you see,' replied Nammk'a Dbyins. 'You never really think in Integer-Two terms, as an Asuran does naturally. You exist by division. The boundary within defeats you. We exist by union. Let me make it plain that these Real Numbers – One, Two, Three and Beyond – all correspond to *real* configurations of the Hyperuniverse, perceptible to beings operating on these number levels. All matter is a wave effect, is it not? Waves oscillate in multi-dimensional space. Yet your minds aren't yet organized to conceive multi-dimensional space. Ours are better organized for this—'

'But I'm told our scientists understand mathematics for imaginary dimensions,' said Klimt.

(The Hausa twins would have a field-day thrashing this out, I thought. Frankly, I was feeling more and more restless.)

'*Imaginary* dimensions?' chirped the Asuran. 'Imaginary? Ah, but that's where you're wrong. There's nothing imaginary about these other dimensions. They really exist. Your minds simply aren't equipped to see them around you. Ours can see more of them than yours can. The whole destiny of Asura – and indeed we hope the destiny of other worlds – will be to contact higher-dimensional beings who actually inhabit multiple dimensions. Only this way will the universe be understood. You might call them Gods or Demons, unable to see their actual nature—'

'I want to fly,' I interrupted. To be embodied in a bird, and to have to roost in a tree, talking about numbers, instead of soaring in alien skies above an alien world! Maybe it was an instinct-prompting of my host body, but how I yearned to join

the Dusk Intermix. The beat of great wings whispering, *Asura*
. . . enchanted me.

I exerted my will.

I found I could unfold a wing . . .

'I want to fly
In the sky—' I sang, deliriously.

My wing dangled laxly across the leaves.

Something stopped it, held on to it, pinioned it.

'*You mustn't!*' Klimt's voice roared at me. 'You'll kill us
both if you pull this bird off the tree. Don't you understand,
it becomes two separate, *lesser* beings. Pull them apart and you
pull our minds apart too! Why should they ever reunite?
We'd be lost. Mad, dying. Who wants to fly, anyway, when
there's the whole universe to understand?'

'Me. I want to. That's the excuse I'm always hearing. The
stars are wide open to us thanks to Bardo, so why should we
move an inch! Now that we're here—'

'—only in the mental sense—'

'—we can't move either! What is Bardo, a prison?'

'Look, what did flying ever bring people, but a few handfuls
of dust from the next-door world? You've insulted our host,
moving his wings like a puppet's.'

I gave up. Sadly, I dragged my own arm mentally across the
great leaf, to tuck it by my side; and the wing furled itself again.

'Nammk'a Dbyins?' queried Klimt.

'Let us carry on talking about the nature of numbers and
higher-dimensional beings,' chirped the Asuran, as though
nothing had happened.

We spent what seemed like several hours singing about the
numbers from Nought to Six, their meaning, the nature of
multi-dimensional space, and about boundaries and horizons,
while the stars shone down on our leaves.

By now we were losing power. Asura no longer looked so
sharp. Fog was rising from the sea, drifting over the island.
The stars were dimming in magnitude. The horizon seemed
to shrink, physically drawing closer to us.

'Klimt, it's changing—'

'Yes. It does. Can you imagine how many centuries we'll have to practise mental flying before we can hang loose for days on end, like the Rakshasas in their hunt for new worlds, never mind about other dimensions?'

Slowly the great leaves of the tree rose up round the roosting crown where we were, folding our flower back into a bud.

The leaves crossed. They interlocked. Ranged round us in a yantra shape, they pressed us back through the bindu point again, through the midst of that blazing ring of lurking lights towards the darkness of Earth.

The Kundalini fire died down. I froze. Utterly exhausted and drained, Klimt and I had to be disentangled by the Dobdobs, who massaged us and wrapped us in blankets.

We spent most of the next week debriefing, being checked out physically and psychologically, and limbering up for our next flight, scheduled for eight days ahead. At first my kundalini power seemed asleep – worn out. But by the fourth day my snake was rising briskly once again.

As for my relationship with Klimt, alas . . . How mechanical he seemed compared with when we were flying! I feared he might be furious about my flight of fancy on Asura. (Or should I say my attempted flight? I'd been reprimanded for it by the Dobdobs. But I'd not been grounded or even threatened with grounding – which rather amazed me.) The more I thought about it, the more Klimt seemed like a living proof of something that Nammk'a Dbyins, the wise old tree-bird, had said: that human beings are conscious by virtue of being mainly unconscious. Only up above a certain frontier in our own minds does 'consciousness' exist – in the form of a tiny arc of the whole circle of mental operations (and of course these operations aren't restricted to what goes on in the brain, since the muscles and nerves and body organs 'know' and 'remember' too, otherwise there'd be no body-field). Below this frontier are hidden away the vast majority of our mental processes. What was special about Nammk'a Dbyins, enabling him to spot this flaw in our make-up, was that his own 'arc' of consciousness could take flight independently and leave the rest of its circle behind. It could become the whole rather than the part – even though, in so doing, the free-flying arc of the bird inevitably became *conscious of less* than when it participated in the tree-bird 'circle'...

I began to think of Klimt as a very small free arc. When he joined in a circle with me, mentally and sexually, during Bardo flight he became a bit more communicative – a bit more conscious. He was able to rhapsodize intelligibly about what life meant – about how we must integrate ourselves. But he couldn't bring his extra bit of awareness back with him, except as the memory of a disconnected dream, trotted out in clipped tones to the Dobdobs at debriefing to be taped and filed away. I began to pity him.

We flew again, on schedule. There was more talk from Nammk'a Dbyins about nest of numbers, and boundaries, and horizons in the mind – which I found more exciting this time, by applying the idea not to cosmoses and universes but to the simple problem of how Klimt, my lover (and, I suppose, myself too – though I couldn't really believe it), could be such limited beings in our make-up. This time, I felt that I was genuinely learning something, bringing something back with me.

We returned again, exhausted.

After ten days' duty, they let us rest for a fortnight.

Maimouna and the Hausa twins had also been flying, and were resting up, Maimouna having started flying a few days earlier than I had. Loud and long she gossiped about her own first flights as we sat watching the Atlantic wash in, green over blue; but always she spoke with an edge of sarcasm – a probing edge.

'Those Asurans must be perfectly inexhaustible! Here we are, just look at us, tired out already. No wonder Bardo needs absolutely *thousands* of fliers. Yet a few Asurans cope with it for weeks on end.'

'How do you tire out a tree?' asked Abdoulaye-H peevishly.

'Ah,' said Maimouna, seizing her cue, 'can a tree ever get bored? We're all agreed that Bardo flight's perfectly thrilling. But once you get there... One little island, a few damn trees, the same old birds squawking on and on about numbers and geometry...'

'I had a fascinating talk,' protested Hamidou-A. 'About set theory. What's included in a set, and what's excluded.' Maimouna groaned.

'Me, too,' his brother said. 'We talked about transcendental numbers and uncountable infinite sets, then about the transfinite number for Everything-That-Is, and whether the Whole can ever be equal to the Part. We talked about the Cardinal Number of the Continuum. They're all awfully important for finding out about the logic of the universe. Maybe *universes*, in the plural!'

Maimouna looked supercilious.

'I'll tell you a secret,' I said, boastfully. 'I tried to *fly* my bird. I know it was stupid of me. Really dangerous! But I wanted to *do* something. I tried to fly the bird and I flapped its wing. Klimt made me stop. I might have broken the Bardo link.'

'The Asurans would forgive us,' said Abdoulaye-H. 'We're precious to the aliens. Only the fourth species in the link. The younger brothers.'

'Precious as children. Taking our first steps. Bound to stumble.'

'We can't afford to stumble, can we? Why? Why can't we children stumble?' demanded Maimouna. 'What would happen to us if the Bardo link got broken?'

'A world civilization stumbling is different from a child stumbling. One big stumble and you're done for.'

'Rubbish. I don't see what's so dangerous. Our whole history is a history of stumbling. We're still around. Talking of children, by the way,' she added slyly, 'I'm overdue. I'd say I'm pregnant!'

Maimouna was perfectly right.

ELEVEN

I soon realized that I was pregnant too. Dobdob medics took urine samples and confirmed it. Almost immediately, I was moved to a different hotel further south in the direction of Virginia Beach, the 'crèche' area. From my new bedroom window, the green banner of the Embassy fluttered a full kilometre north of me.

Maimouna had been sent to this hotel too. Appropriately, it was called the Fairchild; everyone in it was pregnant, though nobody would actually give birth there.

'Quite a high casualty rate,' I remarked to Maimouna after my first childbirth-yoga class (which was her fourth, or fifth).

'All that preparation, all that work, and now a silly thing like this!' she said. Her attitude to her pregnancy had soon changed from smugness to resentment. How she loathed finding herself in the same category as a hundred others! 'Why did they have to send us flying at that time of the month? It's easy enough to know when it's safe, by a simple thermometer reading. I thought that's what they were checking on, with all their damned medicals!'

Personally, I felt emotionally positive about what was happening to me – as though I was a living yantra now: a human nest surrounding a central point of vital energy which was growing and burgeoning, to fill me up. The human body is the finest yantra of all, I remembered an instructor telling us.

'No, Maimouna – it's important, being pregnant. It's a sort of Bardo flight into yourself, don't you see? Suddenly there's this boundary actually inside you, and on the other side of it there's something strange and new – a different private universe, yet part of your universe too.'

Maimouna sneered. 'The "little stranger"? I wonder how many times that particular cliché has been uttered since the world began? Aren't we the lucky ones? Blessed with official birth permits after a mere four months' work!'

'You've just made up your mind to hate this thing and sour it for everybody!'

'Lila dear, I've been talking to the others. Hardly anyone flew more than twice. Second time pregnant, same as us. Bardo seem rather *reckless*, squandering their resources like this. Doesn't that strike you as a little odd? What's behind it?'

Maimouna approached me furtively a few days later.

'Come up to my room, Lila, I must show you something.'

In the elevator, she whispered, 'I'm telling you in case any *accidents* happen to me. Such as a sudden miscarriage. Such as my not recovering and never seeing you again—'

Her queer pair of ear-globes lay on the windowsill, spider and fly both trapped: the spider unable to get at the fly to eat it, the fly unable to escape. She scooped them up and clipped them on her ears, as though they would protect her from something.

'You might have bent the wing of an Asuran bird, Lila, but I walked through a red swastika door that someone forgot to lock. That's far worse. I found things—'

'*What?*'

'A microfiche reader. Microphotos of some old books. I copied out some extracts.' She ran into the bathroom and returned with sheets torn out of one of our notebooks. 'This first bit's from an ancient text on Tantric Yoga. Hundreds of years old. It's about what Tantric Yoga is *supposed to be*! Read it. Then tell me what's wrong!'

I read:

If the sexual act is to be a genuine tantrik act it must NEVER end with the emission of semen. This is the meaning of the Sanskrit sentence, 'Bodhicittam notsrjet'. ('*Semen must not be expelled.*') *Semen shall always be retained in the body. This is the whole purpose of the Mulabhanda contraction; to arrest the flow of sperm. The saint Tirumular writes in the text* Tirumantiram: 'Velliyuruki ponvali otame.' *In the Tamil language this means literally,* 'Silver must not flow into Gold.' *Yet this is not a prohibition against Alchemy. Far from it. The Siddha saints were preoccupied with the possibility of transmutation, just as they were preoccupied*

86

with medicine and breath control: they sought to obtain immortality in this life. Here, in fact, Silver is a secret, arcane symbol for human sperm, while Gold is a symbol for a woman's vulva. Yogis who allow ejaculation are consequently termed 'False Silversmiths'. Their efforts are worthless.

'So why am I pregnant? Why are you? Why are so many other people, if there's a perfectly natural, practical way of stopping it – and if ejaculation is the very worst thing that can happen?'

'A lot of these old texts are confused and garbled. We've been told that.'

'A fine reason for locking them away! Read this, now. It's from the actual Tibetan *Book of the Dead* – the *Bardo Thödol* itself.'

O nobly born, – I read – *evil spirits are the Rakshasas, who possess the power of shape-shifting ...*
O nobly born, do not feel attached to the dull green light of the Asura world. That is the karmic path of great jealousy. If you let yourself be caught by its hook-rays, you will fall into the Asura world and bury yourself forever in the intolerable unpleasantness of quarrels and arguments ...
O nobly born, if you are to be reborn as an Asuran, a charming woodland will be seen. Remember your revulsion; by no means enter it. Intolerable jealousy is locked up in those trees.

'The Dobdobs told us that the people who wrote the *Book of the Dead* almost made a breakthrough. They *almost* picked up the star messages intact. Describing Asura as a forest of arguments isn't far wide of the mark!'

'Lila, *think*! It wasn't the Asurans who were trying to contact us all those years ago. It was supposed to be the Rakshasas! Where could all this about Asura have come from?' Maimouna thrust a third sheet of paper into my hand.

'Now, the names, Lila!'

O nobly born, there shall appear to you four jealous deities, guardians of the doors, namely Cags Kyu-ma, Cag Sgro-ma ...

*You must know these to be merely images projected from
your own mind. These shapes come from nowhere else but
your own mind ...*

'Remember what these names stand for? Two parts of a
Being which splits up and never comes together again the same
way twice. The bird flies off its tree to the Intermix and another
bird takes its place. How likely is it that the same couples were
together hundreds of years ago, when the Tibetans were writing
their book? Even swallowing the fact that it's the *wrong* world!'

'Maybe they're common names on Asura? We don't know
many Asuran names.'

'Or words. Or anything. Are you surprised? There's a limit
to how much people can be bothered to invent, to make fools
of other people. "Images in your own mind," it says. "Shapes
from nowhere." That's more like the truth. That's all Asura is
It's a programmed hallucination! So are the other alien worlds.
I told you they were too simple for *real* worlds. A real world
has deserts and seas and forests and mountains and rivers and
bush. A real world is disorderly and complex. Full of variety.'

'Mars isn't. It's mainly deserts and craters.'

'I mean *live* ones, not dead ones. A real live world is giraffes
and donkeys, turtles and tarantulas, anteaters and antelopes. It's
orchids and oranges, bananas and bo trees, cactuses and cucum-
bers. In alien terms! The same richness. It isn't Asura. One
set of trees. One set of birds. Why, by the way, are the Asurans
and Rakshasas described as hostile, venomous, nasty demons?'

'Maybe when they were trying to establish mental contact,
the ancient Tibetans thought the aliens were trying to invade
their minds.'

'That's why they say they're only figments of the imagination? Come along!'

'When you're really scared of something . . . you might
want to pretend it isn't there – like the ostrich pretends'

'Nonsense. None of it hangs together. There are loopholes
as big as—'

She never got to say how big. At that moment two Dobdobs
opened the bedroom door and marched in.

A man and a woman, both of them Asians. I stared at them. I

would never forget that moment. The woman laid her hand on the bedside telephone.

'We were listening. You don't actually have to pick it up to be heard. We have to be careful so close to the heart of Bardo, you see. The moment you put your identity card in that reader to switch it on we had to do something, didn't we? What a shame we couldn't have spoken to you before you involved somebody else. You did that quickly enough! You're quite right about the aliens, of course. They're an invention – a programmed hallucination.'

Maimouna flashed me a look of vindictive triumph.

'You'll come with us now. We will show you what Bardo is really concerned with!' The woman smiled bleakly. 'You'll wish you had never found out.'

'We're going to be sent to an ice-cap,' pouted Maimouna.

'Far from it! Your particular Bardo skills are far too . . . let's say, *protective*, of us all. We will go to what is blithely called the Procyon Embassy. We will open some more closed doors for you!'

'That hotel,' said the man, 'happens to be one of the three Command Control Centres for the defence of this whole damn planet. The others, of course, are in Kazakhstan and Lhasa.'

'For the defence of—?'

'There aren't any charming alien friends out in space. Space isn't friendly at all. You'll see.'

When we reached the Morningside Palace Hotel – the 'Embassy' – they took us down by elevator to the sub-basement. After passing through various red-swastika doors and being checked by guards, we finally entered a huge room closely resembling the Flight Control Room upstairs, except that this one was bigger and more intensively staffed. Dobdobs sat alertly at row on row of desk consoles. The display screen that took up almost the whole wall showed planet Earth as a small globe floating like a balloon in empty space: a simulated alien's eye view of our planet as it might appear from as far away as the Moon. The Dobdobs on duty here were nearly all Caucasians, speaking American or Russian.

We sat at two vacant desks, flanked by our escorts.

'First, we shall show you Earth's defence barrier itself.'

(Defence – against *what*?) The man picked up a phone and spoke to a technician on the first bank of desks. The technician began flicking switches.

As each switch fell, one triangle after another sprang into position around the little globe of the Earth, some pointing upwards and some downwards. Between them they held the planet firmly in their embrace, giving it long spikes like a child's drawing of a star.

'Humans can't travel to the stars by mind power at all. That's one illusion you can discard right now. You *can* interact with near space in one respect, though, thank God! The pattern of human brain rhythms can be magnified and projected out along lines of force around the Earth, related to the planet's magnetic field. What you see up there is a simplification of the field effect. No doubt the general shape is familiar? A yantra mandala, in three dimensions, with Earth's globe inside at the centre. Together with your comrades in Kazakhstan and Lhasa, you weave a protective net around us all.'

A second set of triangles intersected the first; its focal centre was further east . . .

'In Kazakhstan, Russia.'

A third yantra sprang into being, further complicating the latticework. The world poked out as many spines as a sea urchin now.

'There is the Lhasa yantra. That makes up the total defence pattern for the present. When Bardo has enough skilled fliers we shall open a fourth centre in the Hawaiian islands, on Maui. It was always an old superstition in both East and West that you were safe from demons if you could draw a special magical shape and take refuge inside it. In Europe they called it the pentacle. The yantra mandala is the Eastern equivalent.'

'There *is* a demon out there!' the woman declared bluntly. 'If "demon" is the right word! We call it the "Star Beast". We still have very little idea of its real nature – though we know how to protect ourselves from the consequences of its presence! Those consequences are insanity, and death – for everyone on Earth. Our only protection are the fliers of Bardo.'

'If we'd been more advanced technically,' said the man, 'say, if we'd been able to harness the whole energy of the sun, maybe we could have devised weapons in the strictly material, mechanical sense. Sadly, we were about a thousand years below that level of technology. We did have deep space radars, fast computers and high-power war radars, though. Along with an age-old Eastern tradition of mental training – even though this had generally been sneered at by the West. Putting the two spheres of knowledge together, we had enough punch to amplify and beam our mental patterns of deep concentration in a protective mesh around the Earth.

'The history you're taught is true enough, so far as it goes – chaos and mass death at the end of the twentieth century. Very few people outside the high commands ever knew the real cause. It was the approach of the Star Beast.'

'What is a Star Beast?' 'What sort of thing is it?' Maimouna and I both asked at once.

'What indeed! How we would like to know the answer! We can only show you how it looks electronically. We can only show you its edges, its boundaries around our world.' The man phoned again and another technician responded by flicking switches.

Suddenly all the empty space surrounding the 'nest' of Earth was infested by probing, pulsing, amorphous limbs of vivid colour: storms raging across the whole spectrum from red to violet – as though something was testing different frequencies (shown as colours) to penetrate the nest . . .

The woman explained.

'The violent discharges you're seeing are neural wavefronts – huge electromagnetic storms on the same frequencies as human brain rhythms. A "mind storm" is raging out there in near space, trying to think us out of existence. Clearly that isn't all of the Star Beast. It's just that bit affecting us, the bit surrounding us. We estimate that the creature actually stretches across light years. It may embrace dozens of stars and solar systems. That's what we're still trying to find out through our fliers!'

The man took up the story.

'The first sign of its imminent arrival in our vicinity was in 1995. That was the beginning of a kind of global mental breakdown. A brain sickness – pandemic catatonia. Scientists hunted in vain for a virus. They couldn't find one. Some of them attributed the breakdown to population stress. It was dreadful. One million people died in 1995, ten million the next year, forty million the year after.'

The woman produced a folder of photographs. We stared appalled at expressionless, idiot crowds squatting down and dying in the cities and the countryside. People withering like blighted grain. We looked at crowded hospitals, where the doctors may as well have been trying to spoon out the sea. We saw mass graves, lime pits, blazing funeral bonfires. Bodies were lying rotting in the streets. Then, photograph by photograph, she showed us the course of the illness – which struck with unbelievable suddenness. A man would be eating a meal one minute; his hand would freeze in mid-movement, half way to his mouth. He would simply starve to death.

'In every instance,' she told us, 'the same abnormal brain rhythms showed up – the same scrambling of normal brain activity, as though people weren't able to think in synchronization with the real world, or real time, any longer. But it soon became obvious that the onset of illness directly correlated with the Earth's rotation. The proportion of victims even fell away with latitude. Before long, statistically there were enough people succumbing to locate an area in space which somehow corresponded to the illness. When the world's radio telescopes were suitably modified, they could pick up the same broadcasts that our nervous systems were picking up. The source of them was moving closer – a very large source.

'We thought that maybe some entity out there had picked up our early radio broadcasts. Broadcasting ceased, except on an absolute emergency basis. But if it was just radio waves that were attracting it, why should it attack our nervous systems? Now we believe there may be a far more fundamental reason for the Star Beast: one that relates to the whole nature of the universe itself. Had we drawn ourselves to the attention of something huge and ancient in the universe, the way bacteria alert an immune system, sending antibodies hurrying to the affected spot? Look up there—'

On the screen those tendrils, tentacles or wave-fronts pounced and stabbed at tiny Earth . . .

'We're engulfed by it. We're a little alien cell inside its body. How large is it? God knows! Huge, from the first radio telescope estimates. A truly cosmic creature. But how does it think, if it's so large? How does it communicate internally? Conceivably by using tachyons – particles which can only travel faster

than light. Its body might even be made of tachyon particles –
which is why we can never see the thing, only detect its effects.
If it does use tachyons, its thought processes could be instantaneous. In a strange sense they might even be simultaneous
too – as though you could think all the thoughts of your whole
life during one single instant in time, yet with that instant last-
ing for ever. It can't have our time sense at all, our consciousness of an arrow of time. And why should it? The universe as a
whole doesn't obey a time-arrow – as you've already learnt.
For the Star Beast, all events might be occurring perpetually
in a total space-time continuum—'

'On account of Action-at-a-Distance,' Maimouna interposed
pertly, tapping her spider ear-globe as much as to say that
she had always known there must be a Star Beast.

The woman nodded. 'Without the perpetual interplay of advanced and retarded waves produced by every single event
everywhere, we couldn't have a coherent universe. That's why
it is a universe. But let me ask you this. What if the Star Beast
has evolved uniquely to perceive this kind of space-time? If
it has evolved to inhabit the actual reality of the cosmos, rather
than the simple linear world-line we're adapted to? How will
it see us then? Why, as a drastic disturbance of Nature's laws!
A huge statistical bias in favour of retarded events – constant
progression from the past into the future, with no returning.
The Beast transmits advanced waves at our minds, therefore,
to rectify our sense of time – or, alternatively, destroy us.

'The really horrifying possibility is that if the Star Beast
evolved from the actual fabric of space-time itself, then maybe
the Star Beast is a *true* inhabitant of the universe, and our own
sort of life is only a sport, an anomaly, a deviation!'

Up above, the Beast's internal horizons feinted and parried
from all directions at the defence line of the Earth.

'The Star Beast may be nearer to a God than anything else
we can imagine,' the woman murmured, in awe. 'A cosmic
mind, bred from the nature of being itself. And we've brought
this tiger down upon our heads, because of the way our human
minds think! What are *we*, then? Castoffs? Rejects? Faults?
What kind of universe is this, then?'

'At least, damn it, we can hold the Beast at bay!' swore the
man.

TWELVE

They took us up to a large bedroom on the eighth floor, with a swastika stencilled on the door. The room was furnished with two beds. The window was barred. Spread on the floor, outside the shower and toilet cubicle, was a large exercise mat, while a table bore a microfiche reader with a stack of micro-photographed documents beside it. The woman sat down on one of the beds and motioned us to the other, while the man stood with his back to the door.

'Now, our defence depends upon transmitting human thought patterns at the Beast, enormously amplified. The Beast tries to annul these, by responding to them with its own "thoughts". We can broadcast three or four repeats of past flights at it, though that's about the safe limit. That's why we can't automate the system and why we need a lot of individual fliers. But even if we *could* automate, we wouldn't. In the long run passive defence would be pointless. We have to find things out. That's why your Asura conversations are specially important: both the questions you ask and the answers you receive—'

'You said the whole flight's an illusion! Asura's an illusion – a programmed hallucination!'

'So it is. How sane do you think the world would be if everyone knew about that thing roosting overhead, year in and year out? We had to construct this fiction of the friendly alien worlds for public consumption. But we also have to keep it up for the fliers, because it's far better for raising Kundalini energy and getting data from the Beast that you fly open and innocent. So we programme your hippocampus with the "route" to Asura, and the Bardo helmet gives you a nice visual and auditory hallucination of trees and birds – which you accept, because the yantra shapes and mantra sounds effectively hypnotize you.'

'Did we communicate with something alien, or not?'

'Oh yes, Lila. You asked essential questions. The content of the flights may be an illusion – just as the window of that flight control room upstairs is only a videotape screen! – but the formal structure of the flights is real: that's to say, the pattern of your thoughts during the flight, and your whole body-field. Of course, the Star Beast doesn't respond to what you speak to it, as such, but it *has to* respond to the way your thoughts are put together, when we broadcast your thought patterns at it. The answers you get back from the "Asurans" are mainly computer-synthesized. Regularized, so that they don't sound too nonsensical, and come through in human language. There's this feedback filter in the system, then. Still, we *have* learnt to match certain concept areas to certain wavelengths of the Beast with a fair degree of precision. Some of what it "means" does genuinely filter through the conversation. I say "means"! That's better phrased as "its vision of the universe" – in so far as this in any way meshes with ours. That's why analysing the logical structure of barriers, horizons, the whole and the part, or the mathematics of its view of space-time, is so vital!'

'We have to waste time having babies, with this threat hanging over our heads?' complained Maimouna.

'I agree it's unfortunate. But it's unavoidable. The human body-field is pitiably weak, compared with the disruptions that the Beast can produce. We need the strongest possible stimuli to gear it up to peak working; and the really basic root experience of life – stronger even than the birth trauma, which your entry into Bardo space also imitates – is conception itself, the primal journey of egg and seed towards fertilization in the Fallopian tubes, and what happens when they meet—'

'Nobody remembers that!' I protested. 'There isn't any brain then, to do any remembering.'

'The cells remember, Lila. Didn't Backster find that isolated human sperm can sense damage to the mucous membranes of their donor's nose *from fifteen metres away* whenever he sniffs something corrosive? Didn't he find that hens' eggs "faint" when their batch companions are boiled anywhere near them? And what about the experiment where a plant hooked up to a galvanometer successfully identified the "criminal" who had killed another plant in the same room as it, in secret earlier on? That was the first solid scientific evidence of perception *and* memory in the living cell itself. Indeed, how could it be otherwise? How else could the first living matter have organized itself before any proper nervous system had developed?

'So there's knowledge, believe me! We can best call up these biological memories during ovulation. That's when the Kundalini energy rises fiercest, to feed strength and pattern into the coming fusion of the body-fields of sperm and egg – recapitulating the events of the mother's own conception years before. That's when body and brain rhythms are strongest for the radar networks to amplify and project.' She smiled confidingly. 'Really, it's the women fliers who weave the network round the world. Male Kundalini is a feebler thing. The man's body-field can hardly be expected to gear itself up for conception rhythmically once a month!'

'Poor Klimt!' I laughed. 'So proud of his manhood and his body. Doting on every word of that wise old alien bird!'

'Ah, if there were any aliens . . . Technically, the body-field is an electromagnetic field effect in association with a plasma of highly ionized particles permeating and surrounding the whole body. But you can also regard the whole nervous system, including the brain, as an aerial approximately a thousand kilometres long, folded up round itself. *If* there were any skilled or interested alien "transmitters" out there, and *if* there was any way that the jiggled charges of the body-field could be synchronized with the Action-at-a-Distance field effect, it's quite conceivable that you could receive some sort of message from the stars by way of the body-field. In the first years when the Backster Effect was being investigated there was even some evidence of biological communication going on over interstellar distances – which we were intercepting. Plants out in the California desert were recorded picking up pulsed signals – nature unknown – from the direction of Ursa Major.

'Alas, the Star Beast put a stop to any further experiments along these lines. It's the ultimate stifling blanket. And it's that we have to hold at bay, locally, right here. At least we can broadcast human body-field and thought patterns into the skies around the Earth using conventional machine transmitters. It works, thank God, so long as your body-field is at full strength. 'We hope that fertilization won't occur. Yet we're forced to set up prime conditions for it. Such a terrible shame, when high-quality Bardo talent occurs so sparsely—'

'Yes, how *do* you detect us?' Maimouna pressed. And I added:

'We seem to have been expected to pass the tests, years before we took them – even though everybody is supposed to have an equal chance!'

'In the beginning it was by studying the brain rhythms of the Star Beast victims, then filming their body-fields using Kirlian aura photography. Thank God that acupuncture in particular had legitimized traditional Chinese body-field medicine in Western eyes long before the Star Beast came! Or we'd have been lost. Nowadays, the whole thing's tested out by acupuncture, high-voltage aura filming and encephalographs at such an early age that you won't remember it. The Barefoot Doctors are trained to test every child. That's our first screening. Later, the Teachers use aptitude tests to tell how best to develop and enhance a promising body-field: through playing Go, or studying algebra, or dancing Kathakali style, or whatever it is. Even affectation serves its purpose, Maimouna – whatever makes for a formal, energetic cast of mind.'

'It's all decided years ago?'

'The possibles are spotted. They mightn't develop, that's the snag. If we announced who the likely candidates were, this knowledge would be counter-productive. Encourage sloth and complacency. Besides, it would be terribly divisive, socially. All the Teachers and Barefoot Doctors are indoctrinated to keep this secret, with a fairly unbreakable conditioning.'

'So much for equality!' laughed Maimouna harshly.

The man scowled. 'Every human being has the same prospect of going mad and dying, if we don't succeed! I assure you there's democracy in that.'

More gently, the woman said: 'It's necessary, for social stability. The whole fiction of the alien worlds – and everyone having the potential to fly to them. The irony of it is, the more access you have to information, and the nearer you are to the source, the more likely you are to see through it. So, the more strictly you have to be watched. The less you have to do with it, the fewer restrictions there are. It's the opposite of totalitarianism. Here, the élite are strictly supervised – and the ordinary people are blissfully free of the burden. Within obvious social ecological ground rules. Actually, for you to grow up with the right cast of mind, society has to feel itself free and happy, with alien friends.'

'How many Bardo fliers do see through Asura?' asked Maimouna anxiously – still wanting to be special, in some way or other.

'Oh, quite a few,' smiled the woman. 'You'll be joining them . . .'

The old spectre of the ice-cap?

But no.

'In Lhasa,' she went on. And Maimouna grinned hugely, in triumph.

'You'll bear your children there. And work there afterwards. Lhasa is for those who know the truth. There'll be a Rakshasa façade instead. It's the most practical way to programme flights. We'll hypnotize you for the flights. You'll accept the fiction. Only, before and after, you'll know that it's just a façade. The real nightmare will be while you're fully awake. Knowing the Star Beast, and the utter enmity of the universe. It wasn't really so clever of you, finding out, you see.'

Maimouna's smile crumpled; and I shivered too.

Fabled Lhasa . . . yes. Another alien embassy.

Another War Room.

And the horror squeezing the Earth.

We stayed locked behind the red swastika door for a week, spending part of our time in yoga exercises with a Dobdob medic supervising us; and rather more time poring over classified Bardo reports about the strange being enshrouding the Earth.

The first shock of discovery receded. We began to feel excited in a childish way about confronting this mysterious invader, as heroines and champions of the world. Being pregnant seemed a minor problem compared with what we now knew. A baby could make itself. We had to consciously remake ourselves, to take in the enormity of the new knowledge.

Gradually, from deep inside, sprang a *biological* awareness of the sheer rightness of the Defence Facts and the way they were being handled. That yantra nest about the Earth, and our own nests of flesh and blood protecting the budding foetuses within us, synchronized and meshed.

It was Sam Shaw, again, who drove us out to Miami airport. We left at dawn, passing out through the checkpoint on Julia Tuttle Causeway. Maimouna was in a particularly ebullient, effervescent mood. Her callous sophistication seemed to have melted away, and a new Maimouna was emerging – positive and optimistic, full of anticipation. She wore her earglobes ostentatiously that day. Why not? They'd been an image of the true situation all along. A spider did indeed lurk in a web around the world, held in check. The fly of humanity really was restricted and locked in. Yet the sheer spread of that fly's wings held the hungry spider at bay!

By contrast, Sam seemed sulky – calculating how much extra fuel would have to be wasted to fly us to Lhasa (where it seemed he was going *anyway*)?

'We're flying to Maui first,' he finally told Maimouna, in answer to her flood of questions.

'Where they're building the new Bardo centre?'

'I have to ferry some gear there.' He concentrated on his driving.

'Unless there's some *joy*,' insisted Maimouna, 'there's no point to life and we may as well let the Star Beast in! Let's enjoy the journey, can we? Please, Sam.'

'Please do *not* mention the Star Beast in public, ever.'

'We're alone, we're driving along in a jeep!'

'We're out in the *open*, children. There must be no talking about the real purpose of Bardo, do you understand? I was thinking of driving you up to see the new centre on Haleakala Crater. If you can't keep your mouths shut about the most important secret in the world—'

'We'll be quiet as mice,' we chorused.

'What do you think would happen if we did start telling someone?' Maimouna whispered to me mischievously.

Sam overheard it. 'Don't even think it.' He tapped his Dobdob's holster. 'There are standing orders. Valuable as you are, God help me I'd have to stop you.'

Which really soured the drive – though we could hardly believe his threat. The sheer casualness shocked me. The unarguing acceptance. In its way, it was more shocking than the discovery of the Star Beast roosting over us. Because of its casualness, I began to believe it after a while. A little later, I began to agree with his attitude. A simple defence mechanism on my part? Identifying with the viewpoint of the threatener? Maybe. But it did seem to me that it was to the credit of Bardo that they hid the true facts from the world – and hid their hiding of them so skilfully! We wouldn't have had a stable world of Social Ecology otherwise, or the new sense of social joy and joy in the human body. Yes, it *had* to be defended, with a gun if necessary.

Possibly Sam's words were chosen more for their shock effect. The Dobdob's side-arm was almost wholly symbolic. He hadn't actually said that he'd use his gun, only that he'd 'stop' us. I sensed a puritanism in him, a repulsion at what we were doing – a denial of love's body and social joy, that made him bitter and resentful. In his heart of hearts, possibly he did regard Miami Beach as an ancient 'brothel', and he would have much preferred to fight the Star Beast, had it been possible, with bullets and rockets rather than with the fruit of human love. Only, he would never say so. Hence his sharp tongue.

Yet this personality structure gave him his value, too. His sheer rigidity kept everything tightly under control, in his head. He was the most reliable sort of Dobdob to know the Defence Facts and also travel the whole world.

This airport in mid-city was mostly given over to colonies of burrowing owls. Grass between the runways was rutted and tussocked by their quarrying. We took off.

Hours later we landed in darkness on Maui.

We spent the night in a hotel in a town called Kahului, after consuming bowls of a wild goat stew on an arcaded terrace overlooking a bay. A Hawaiian Dobdob, a fat wrestler of a man, dozed on the terrace outside our room all night in a cane rocking chair that creaked and creaked, reminding us that he was still there.

In the morning, Maimouna pleaded that we might drive up into the mountains with Sam. Only later on did it occur to me that the very last thing that scrupulous Sam would have done would be to leave us thirty or forty kilometres out of sight while he drove up to the mountains alone!

A truck stood waiting outside the hotel loaded with the usual scores of cartons labelled MEDICAL SUPPLIES / AIRMAIL / URGENT. Body-field profiles, I assumed. Or Star Beast records. In fact, this *was* a world-wide emergency, as the human bacteria fought back against this cosmic attempt to kill them off.

Personally, I didn't feel very much like a bacterium that morning; I throbbed with life, hilarity and happiness. Kahului was all quick, smiling patios, arcades and fountains. Sugar mills, molasses plants and pineapple canneries vented delicious aromas. Playgrounds were full of beautiful children with brown skins, amber skins, cream skins. Waterfalls of black hair cascaded, there were frizzy heads, and pigtails . . . They could all laugh and play because Bardo had managed to hide the horror in the skies. I'd have died to defend this unique, marvellous world and its cargo of life, that morning.

The vegetation surged, scrambled and erupted. Earth was dense with vines and creepers splaying over factories and homes – ginger, jasmine, hibiscus. Trees with stiltlike aerial roots, with swordleaves. Trees with blooms of velvet, fluff, feathers. Trees with flowers like boiled crab claws. The air sang as much with odours as colours. No wonder the children sang too. The Earth herself sang. Bardo were so right to do what they did.

After driving through sugarcane fields, we began climbing and twisting through sloping horse and cattle pastures towards the highlands. The temperature cooled steadily; soon we were into eucalyptus groves and fern-choked ravines. Some trees wore red pompoms.

At a place called Puu Nianiau the road divided into two carriageways, one lane neglected, with ferny potholes, the other recently patched, up which we rode easily. However, I was starting to feel sick at the change in altitude and had to gulp in great draughts of the cool, aromatic air to get sufficient oxygen. Soon I was shivering; Maimouna sneezed.

'Anoraks behind my seat,' Sam said. 'Pull them on. We'll be at three thousand metres soon.'

As we drove into misty cloud, the sun dimmed to a faint

chalky lamp. Clusters of buildings loomed up, and two great bowl radars canted upwards, spiderwebs sagging with dew. As we pulled up at a checkpoint – a metal shack among ruined, tumbled stone huts – the sun burned through the mists. We had drawn up almost on the edge of a cliff, which plunged deep into queer, distorted terrain from which very tall yellow and purple cones reared their heads.

When the Dobdob on duty handed back our cards, we drove up to one of several geodesic domes. Sam said to stay in the truck while he unloaded. As I was I sitting there, though, an agonizing cramp suddenly knotted the biceps of my right leg, which had been squashed against the seat. Muscles wrapped themselves up in a fiery ball.

I moaned and writhed about like a fish on the end of a spear, then threw the door open and hauled myself out to hop about and massage the leg back to life. I limped away to look down the mysterious cliff, Maimouna in my wake.

The cliff stretched off to right and left in a vast circle. I realized I was actually looking down into a giant, dead volcano. Pastel mists swirled across a jungle floor spiked by those bright cinder obelisks, each one as tall as that abominable Vehicle Assembly Building at the Cape. Everything kept going out of focus down there, there was so much shimmer and distortion.

Exclaiming, Maimouna pointed.

A rainbow had arched between two of those giant pillars which stood as tall as mountains now, bridged by that spectral arc; underneath that luminous archway two alien figures stood, ghouls of painted fog, jerking giant limbs about.

'It's us. It's ourselves. Don't you see?' hissed Maimouna. She clenched her fist and immediately one of the giants clenched its fist back at us.

Already the monsters were breaking up and drifting apart, like disintegrating souls.

'Programmed hallucination,' I whispered back. 'This must be a new alien world Bardo are going to discover. A mist-giant world. They must be testing their machines—'

When Sam came over to take us back to the truck, he said no, this was just a natural phenomenon, but we didn't really believe him. We left that eerie place, where in a few more years other Lilas and Maimounas and Klimts would be making love and believing in the Bardo myth and discussing barriers and boundaries with huge frothing ghosts, and drove back down to the heat and perfume of the lowlands.

In the hotel, I spent half an hour practising yoga. Maimouna wouldn't join in. Seeing herself so hugely enlarged in the crater seemed to have advanced her pregnancy perversely, making her all of a sudden bulky, torpid and querulous.

THIRTEEN

Next day was all westwards over water, water, water: a blue blankness more monotonous than the sky. Sam dozed in the passenger cabin mostly while the jet bored on automatically, sandwiched between one realm of blue and another. At some point we ate a vast meal of cured pork mixed with spiced vegetables and some starchy purple paste. Hours, or minutes later – I couldn't say – we ate it all once again, as ravenously and gluttonously as the first time. And did we eat it yet again? Time vanished down the gullet of these monotonous, endearing feasts. Time solidified; it became fat and flesh. The jet plane was stuck fast in it. Our real journey became the slow increase in our own weight: an increase in body, not in distance . . .

When we reached land again, the coast of China's Fujian Province, mountains rolled over mountains in growing darkness till our jet was squeezing through a flat plane again – this time between black earth and a black sky – in which the stars were just random sparks on our retinas, faults of vision.

We slept, we woke, we slept. All the time we were exhausted.

I dreamt we were flying to the stars. When we arrived at a star after several centuries, it turned out to be only the actual size of one of our jet's windows. Alternatively, we ourselves had expanded enormously during the journey. The whole journey could have been purely and simply a slow process of inflation. We hadn't moved at all, only swollen grossly. My bloated body butted against this star (I *was* the jet plane now); and it stung me, burnt my belly with its fire.

I woke in a sweat, believing I was a Star Beast myself, trying to digest a sun and its worlds. I had awful indigestion. I had to swill down cup after cup of milk to pacify my stomach.

Finally, after a million years, we did land and creep out of the jet, shivering and gasping for air, staring around at huge amorphous star-iced mountains.

Two Tibetan Dobdobs, with great sun-baked faces, purple

cheekbones, fat hooded eyelids and long broad noses like horses', came to take charge of us. We couldn't speak their language, nor they ours. *Any* of ours. Maimouna tried out her Chinese, and gave up. Maybe she spoke the wrong dialect. They took us to a hospital clinic near the airfield, where, putting their fingers to their lips, they led us to two empty beds. We slept quickly, deeply and dreamlessly; the sleeping during the flight had tired us out so much.

Crowing of cocks and clank of utensils woke us. Old women were shuffling about the dormitory in thick blue quilted gowns. Some made tea, others braided each other's hair. They grinned and cackled at us and brought us some tea in porcelain cups with red horses racing round them, their riders wearing long white scarves.

The tea tasted vile. Salty and greasy. As soon as I swallowed some I felt sick and my nausea turned the very air in the room to a thin, trembling greasy jelly. Everyone's face was saturated with that same flavour . . . I yearned for the sweet cakes that Rajit had plied me with on Sinda Island a lifetime ago. Oh for a spoonful of sugar, oh for a dozen spoonfuls! What did I care if I rotted my teeth till they were as black as my skin! I craved sugary night, not this bright oily day.

I stared through the window at the outside world: anywhere, away from the wobbling, unctuous dormitory.

I watched fields of ripe barley, with blue meandering irrigation channels. Feathery willows and poplars formed clumps and avenues. A long road, with a few early morning cyclists on it, led through a ceremonial arch topped with Chinese characters in wood or plastercast. The closer buildings were neat blocks of cement with glinting corrugated roofs. Further away were row on row of dun-coloured tenements looking like muddy escarpments honeycombed with caves. Beyond all, a huge palace – or else a cliff looking very like a palace – towered up, itself dwarfed by the mountains.

Far off, bells donged, setting the jelly trembling again. An old woman with a wall of white teeth touched me on the arm and took my half-full cup away, then brought it back again full, aswirl with fat.

Somehow I reached a washbasin – and retched helplessly.

The vomit only amounted to a few spoonfuls of clear, insipid liquid. Twisting my head to the tap, I sucked in mouthfuls of ice-cold water, rinsing and chewing till the nerves in my teeth ached.

Women gathered round, clucking helpfully. One of them went for assistance, and soon a Barefoot Doctor appeared: a cheery young woman in thick maroon woollen clothes, tough boots of hide, a leather satchel slung over her shoulder. She produced an oxygen pillow with a long rubber tube which she slipped into my nostril. Maimouna tried out her Chinese again, and this time was understood. Presently the Barefoot brought me a big cup of sugared milk and gestured me to drink it all. Slapping her medicine satchel, with a nod at the mountains, she departed, leaving the oxygen pillow with us.

A while later, some food arrived. A mash of grilled barley, tea and butter.

An hour after that, a jeep drew up outside. A Chinese Dobdob walked in to greet us. His face was burnt as dark as anyone's.

This was Feng. He would supervise our new way of life here in Tibet.

I thought unkindly that he deserved his name – with such a wall of ivory teeth jutting from his upper jaw, like sawn-off, polished fangs, overlapping his lower set slightly. Maybe his jaw was deformed? Gaps between individual teeth hardly looked deep enough; teeth fused into a wall instead of forming a fence. *Feng* was surely the best collective name for them!

We left. He drove us along the road I'd been watching, past the hundred-year-old cement buildings, past the thousand-year-old tenement caves.

The Potala Palace – for that was it – rose up vastly: a high ridge where scenery itself turned into architecture, where the two categories were confused. Walls sprouted from different levels of the cliffside, soaring up to different heights, all of them leaning backwards at a slight canting angle to one another, imitating the sloping of a mountain towards a flat, plateau summit. Thus their weight appeared to float upwards towards the thin blue of space, rather than pressing down on the earth. Arrays of deep-cut windows picked out in black made the sun seem to be blazing down from directly overhead, producing dark shadows below the protruding lintels. In fact, the sun was nowhere near overhead. Yet so firmly did these lowering windows insist otherwise, that one couldn't help but search the zenith for a second, somehow more real sun, a truer cosmic sun shining down on the building from an axle of the universe far out in space, from a point dictated by the perspective of the tilted walls.

Golden canopies, or pavilions, were pitched like tents on the plateau-summit: a second world above the world.

The Palace approaches had long since been mechanized. A concrete-lined tunnel bored straight into the hill. Into this we drove, after the obligatory halt at a checkpoint.

A set of thick steel doors was recessed into the rock, and a second set ten metres further in. Thereafter the tunnel was pitch-dark, the only illumination coming from our own head-lights.

After several hundred metres of subterranean roadway, we swung into a domed cave and halted. Various tunnel mouths, swept by our lights, suggested a huge underground complex: an undertaking as vast below, perhaps, as the rearing of the Potala had been overhead. Chinese characters in faint luminous paint peered at us from steel doors and rock walls, faces of alien beasts. This must once have been an atomic bomb shelter for the people of Lhasa. Or else a military shelter, for a whole army.

An elevator came down, lighting up the underground parking space briefly till we stepped inside; then its doors squeezed on the darkness of the cave, and up we sped. The doors re-opened upon a room like a box of giant stone blocks. A hard earthen mound cut through the centre of the floor, poking out of a round gap in the stones as though the room was balanced on this pinnacle.

'That's the top of Mount Potala,' Feng said. 'We call this room the Hinge Room.'

So we entered the Rakshasa Embassy, castle of our confine-ment.

During succeeding months, we practised childbirth yoga on the rooftops with a score of other girls and women in different stages of pregnancy, all of whom had, one way or another, seen through the 'happy myth' of Bardo – and also run up against the occupational hazard of Bardo flight. Gazing down from our lofty elevation upon the wormcast rows of houses and patchworks of fields, we felt ourselves utterly detached from the city. The Potala Palace miniaturized the world below it till we were giantesses scared we might injure it with our huge footprints if we took a careless step over the brink.

The air grew colder as autumn advanced. Icy gales blew, and there was no more exercise on the rooftops. Instead we exercised in the Halls of the Sutras and the Great Funerary Halls within the building. We worked away at polishing gold altar lamps. We dusted porcelain, jade and enamel-ware. We even dug some old bullets out of faded millennium-old frescoes of Lhasa that showed the city full of red-roofed houses and lamaseries, with blue shrubs lining rivers wavy as tresses of curly hair – a city where everyone, labourers and monks alike, seemed to be wearing exactly the same rose-red robes. Here we were, wearing the red tunics of Bardo, almost like them.

'It hasn't changed much,' observed Maimouna, as we patched a bullet hole, wondering who had fired the gun in this palace, and why, and when. Presumably during the upheavals of the year 2000, as the Star Beast came closer to the Earth, and world government had to be forged out of near-anarchy.

Newly-pregnant, or newly-enlightened members joined our group; while others left to have their babies and recommence flight duty. Sometimes we would glimpse the new mothers, slim once more, down one of the passageways. But we were segregated from them, and we heeded the red swastikas now that we understood their urgency.

One day I discovered the actual origin of the word Dobdob. One of the Tibetans told Maimouna and me, in Chinese. Long ago, when all those red-robed monks shown in the frescoes had meditated in the monasteries of Tibet, Dobdobs were policemen-monks who carried cudgels to hit people over the shoulder if they saw their attention wandering or caught them drifting off to sleep . . .

We were all bound by rituals in this timeless stone limbo set above the world: rituals of our own bodies, schedules of gestation.

FOURTEEN

I wake up in my tiny cell bedroom in the back of the Palace (where slaves' or servants' quarters once were) hating my body for its perversities. My nails are turning brittle and cracking. I have to hold them away from the walls wherever I walk these days, in case they catch and splinter. My breasts plump fatter, turning themselves into chocolate hemispheres from which the nipples push like worms from wet soil. Nipples are exceptionally tender and damp to the touch, while breasts themselves grow coarse with all the moisture settling in them, becoming thick granulous membrane-bags full of lumpy sodden sponge. They tug down from my shoulder blades, pulling the skin so taut that my collar bones stand out from deep hollows, giving the upper quarter of my body a ridiculously gaunt appearance.

A hidden, ghost's hand is rubbing me out and drawing me back in again in cruder, darker lines. A thick streak of pure charcoal plunges downward from my navel, a faint signpost.

Down in the Great Hall of the Sutras I polish whatever is smooth and round and golden.

Alone in my cell, I follow the tracks of the foetus within me, amazed. See, here they are upon my belly! Upon my breasts! It's travelling somewhere, inside. Not walking; it hasn't proper feet yet. Yet it leaves dark oozy trails on me, from inside. I'm always one step behind it in trying to anticipate its moves, because I can't see it. Nor can it see me. Yet, still, there are these traces and tracks connecting us. I'm its horizon, its boundary. Nevertheless, it's *it* that curves me round itself. Otherwise I wouldn't be this shape. It curves me. It lays marks on my belly to measure me. But these marks broaden and coarsen as I curve, so that it can't really take my measure. Thus, in a strange way, we enclose one another mutually. Each one of us is the boundary of the other's boundary. Only the most indirect observations are possible.

If the nature of the space that we both occupy, and warp, is a well-nigh insoluble problem, the time scale we share is even more questionable. For my dreams carry me outside time, and there the foetus lies in wait for me. It is actually far older than me – as old as life itself, which it recapitulates. I have only lived eighteen years; whereas it has already straddled a billion years of evolution. So far as my sense of time goes, I feel myself balanced upon its vast (yet tiny!) base like another Potala impaled on the tip of a mountain hidden inside.

I discuss this with Feng, who comes to see me. He nods approvingly at my analysis.

'You'll be able to interrogate the Star Beast far more effectively after all this, you realize? You'll understand the nature of the problems better – the boundary between us and the rest of the universe, between our kind of consciousness, and the Star Beast's cosmic consciousness . . .'

I wander down to the Sutra Hall where the thousand-year-old helmet of King Sang Zan Gan Bu, builder of the Potala, is kept and I try it on, pretending it is a Bardo helmet linked by computer and radar networks to that Beast in the sky. It bears inscriptions in Manchu, Mongol and Tibetan: all messages to Heaven.

The golden helmet is too heavy, so I take it off and dust it with a rag instead.

Feng draws me into fervent conversations about the origin of life, and the universe – fervent on *his* part, that is. He maintains that the universe couldn't have been started 'from outside', by any outside agency, or it wouldn't be a *universe*. No more could life have been started from outside: or it wouldn't be *life*, but mere machinery. Activity must be its own agent, its own begetter, he says; and this self-arising of life reflects the self-arising of the universe itself. Each is inconceivable without the other. He seems to think these metaphysics will all fall on receptive ears, because I'm pregnant.

Does he mean to imply that my pregnancy is necessary to the universe? Or the universe necessary to my pregnancy? I *know* what made me pregnant: Ahmed Klimt, and the (forgivable) manoeuvrings of Bardo. Even so, it doesn't quite feel that way, any more. The sheer fact of pregnancy has taken over and become a free agent . . .

'Life's implausible, Lila, do you realize? Statistically, it's ridiculous that that there should be life. So many possible chemical combinations! It would take far longer than the whole history of the universe to run through a fraction of them at random. Yet life arises, almost as soon as it could.'

'If life's so necessary to the universe, why should the Star Beast try to wipe it out?'

'A fair question. Suppose this: suppose that a universe can't "know" its own nature, because it's "uni". Unique, a unit. It can't ever examine itself whole. To know itself, it might have to deny part of itself – the "knowing" part. It may have to disavow it. The Star Beast may be something of that sort, a disavowing aspect, a boundary-making aspect programmed into the structure of reality itself—'

Thus Feng preaches on about the Cosmos, like some crazy Nammk'a Dbyins. And I wonder if the world has gone mad already; if the Beast is slipping into our minds, through our defences.

Worse horror: if it has already slipped into *me*! Could Bardo's real plan be to extract and incarnate aspects of the phenomenon we call 'Star Beast' and give it a human body? I never did see into those crèches and nurseries of Virginia Beach. The image now haunts me of inhuman beings penned up there: beings with queer, twisted consciousnesses, half of the Earth and half of the alien universe. Beings which are just biological instruments for measuring the enigma of the universe in human terms.

'The timeless babies of Virginia Beach,' Maimouna murmurs when I tell her, fascinated by the horror of it. 'Babies who are half and half . . . babies who straddle the boundary . . . probes – is it possible?'

Is Feng leading me gently towards the realization that I'm likely to give birth to a monster?

One still day, as a treat, Dobdobs escort us up to the rooftop, in thick quilted coats. Mountain peaks are snow-rimmed and a light snowfall has blanched the whole roof. In the bright sunlight, under that indigo sky, it is blinding. More snow and rain has fallen on Lhasa in the last two centuries than in the previous thousand years, since a great reafforestation by the Chinese before the Star Beast came. Maimouna proudly informs me of this – as if it is her doing. It's still fairly dry. Windy, dusty. We sit in one of the gold-roofed pavilions, while the bitter air burns our teeth and nostrils, staring at the mountains, camped out in nowhere on the fringe of space, sipping luke-warm butter-tea. Giantesses of many races and mixtures of races squat upon a dazzling iceberg, their bodies watching themselves blindly, wondering whatever is within . . .

Sealed away from me, a strange being turns over and over within me in its own length. I am its universe of slimy tissue – heaving and undulating like a lung, flabbily panting for breath. My gas-cramped veins form lattices holding a mineral sea wherein the fattening fry flicks and somersaults.

I am Ocean, lately pierced by lightning. The white-hot tip of lightning struck and left a sweet pungency, a drip of candle wax in the water. My waters clotted round this soft fierce energy. Soon, a flimsy waxen stick sprouted fists and a head too big for it and began to batten up against my shores, its boundaries.

Presently, it comes ashore, enters the placental forest, to become a giant newt lurking in wait for any observer behind one of the cyads, which squat pineapple-like in the garrulous, throbbing greenery. Attempting to evade the gaze of this newt (whilst walking about in my universe, which is myself, like a God on the First Day of Creation) my foot parts a trembling green scum; there's no land underneath me. I sink through jelly waters to the mucous plug of creation. I would pull it out. I would empty myself, and once more be blue space on bare rock! I pull and tug. Through the pale bilious light of these waters, weed-cords come swirling out from the central bole. More and more tendrils take hold of me as the water thickens in my throat and lungs . . .

I wake up sick from dream thoughts. My ankles, swollen with fluid, will not grow thin again. My thighs press together. My lungs are crushed upwards from beneath. No deep breaths are to be taken any more – as my horizons squeeze together.

If only I could go up again, right now this moment, to that

gold tent pitched under the stars! Space enough up there, surely.

No, there couldn't be enough!

The whole mass of the universe would be pressing down in the form of the Horizon Beast that clamps round the Earth!

'Feng—'

'Yes?'

'I'm scared.'

'Don't worry, our Barefoot Midwives are the finest. No harm can come to a baby that's Bardo-born. Or to a Bardo mother.'

'It isn't *that*, Feng.'

'Well? You have to say, you know.'

Patient Feng. Not mad crazy Feng today. But Feng who is Master of the Great Wall that holds the Dragon back from devouring the Commune of Man. Feng who has such a perfect Potala wall of teeth; albeit something askew with the jaw. I trust you and distrust you at once. You're a man of great power. I know now; yet this isn't a society that brandishes its power. Instead, it conceals it carefully, erasing all hint of rank and hierarchy. Visible power corrupts a man and torments society. There can be no important men now, no politicians, presidents, kings or king-makers; only Humanity.

'I'm still listening, Lila.'

'I'm scared the baby won't be human,' I babble. 'I'm scared it'll have the Star Beast in it. Its thoughts will be all twisted up to tell you something about the Horizon Beast up there. That's what Bardo wants! Why is it always "medical supplies" that are flown around the world? What sort of supplies? Blood samples? No, genetic material! Samples of genetic codes, which only the big computers can unravel! What is it that makes someone a Bardo candidate? Something genetic! A potential – based on who was most vulnerable to the Star Beast illness. Something that will let us *potentials* make babies representing it. That's why we fly at prime time for conception. The Bardo fliers don't matter, only their babies! Babies are what Bardo is all about.'

'Babies are what the whole world is about, for the pregnant one,' he smiles.

'No, Feng! Don't make fun of me. That's why the silver

flows by the way of the gold. To manufacture mind-extensions of that thing up there. Because we can only understand it in human terms. These are the only human terms we dare work with – babies. No wonder the Miami crèche is secret! Why isn't it in the middle of the Sahara desert surrounded by atomic bombs?'

Feng shakes his head sympathetically.

'You couldn't be more wrong. You have my word. Bardo is a humane organization in the literal sense. It's dedicated to Humanity. The Miami crèche is secret for the sake of democracy, so that people won't feel there's any élite privileged group. Things mustn't be seen as even potentially divisive, Lila. We're all still individualistic, jealous apes at heart.'

'How can democracy be upheld by lies?'

'I don't see any lies. Information's controlled for the good of all. That isn't lying. How happy would it make everyone to know, and know *impotently*, about the Star Beast?'

His eyes roam that fresco of old Lhasa with its uniforms. We are talking in the Great Hall of the Sutras. Probably the uniforms were only a convention of the artist, like the stylized waves in the river, and the single visual plane the buildings are all drawn in. He taps a figure seated in a small boat upon the mulberry river. The fisherman is naked; his rose tunic lies ashore.

'It's a funny thing. Consciousness resides in the single individual. Yet the individual never can really comprehend what this thing, his consciousness, is. So it seems like a miracle: a "soul". Yet he desperately wants proof. Therefore he becomes a social animal.' His finger sketches in the praying monks, the prancing horsemen. 'Society seems like a larger consciousness which can know him. It isn't really. Not yet, at any rate. Since history began, society has only been the sum of the failure of all its separate parts to know themselves. Think of animals – how absorbed they are in nature! Then think of Man – how separated he is; how alienated. Yet that's *how* he can examine the world. Somehow Humanity must *re-enter* the world – the universe – with the consciousness it has acquired. When that happens, Humanity's whole history of alienation – Bardo's deceptions included – will be nothing. Once the ladder has been climbed, it can be pulled up safely behind you.'

He traces a route from a band of monks meditating in a courtyard to a roofed bridge crossing a stream.

'The water reflects. Did you know that the word "reflection" means "to bend again" – as light is bent back from a mirror? But how does a universe reflect on itself? Consider that word. "Universe" means "one turn". Not because light is bent back to its starting point around the curve of space. No, it means "one turn" because a universe is what might be seen by executing the mental leap of turning around so quickly that you see yourself whole! The dog chases its own tail; one day it takes itself by surprise and catches up with itself! That's the moment of enlightenment.'

He seems to be deliberately teasing me now – scattering clues to some great secret at the same time as he is hoodwinking and confusing me.

'Are you saying that the Star Beast is the spirit of the universe? That it's come to look at *itself*, in us – in Humanity?'

'The Universe-at-large manifesting itself?' says Feng, not answering, only echoing me. 'One wonders.' His teeth shine, predatory: an unbreachable barrier. Yes, a barrier can be predatory . . . If the Star Beast is, so is Feng.

Then the universe seems to pour down from the stone roof in a jelly glue upon my head, suffocating me.

Veins map my flesh: purple undercurrents flowing out from the sea within. My belly plumps with a stiff volume of liquid and limbs turning within themselves. Somehow gravity reverses and tugs the sea up against my lungs.

I'm cloven from my navel downwards by a jet black line, far blacker than my skin now. The line splits me in two, anticipating the way I shall soon softly split apart like an overripe fruit and force out from inside me the boundary-being that lurks there.

Cracked in two I am, like the coco-de-mer! Soft slabs of flesh face one another across a cleavage line. I am the Two-in-One from the Seychelles, and I'm stranded on my own shores.

I swelter in the entrails of this chilly stone palace, in my quilted clothes, waiting for Spring and Birth.

FIFTEEN

I came out of my trance in the first week of April. Out of my
womb-time.

Childbirth was a kind of orgasm of all the time that had
been suspended and stored up: a violent discharge of myself
back into the world again, and of my baby into her world.

By splitting apart we suddenly became two whole entities.

She had the bumpy, downy skull of a pod from a baobab
tree, and funny squashed features which I supposed would sort
themselves out in time into an approximation of myself and
Klimt. Her limbs were floppy and elastic. She would be a
tall woman. Her skin was a light milky coffee colour, mild,
smooth, with the only blemish on the back of her left thigh –
a little maroon trefoil. The Barefoot Midwife said it would
fade in a few weeks. Blue eyes stared up vaguely into mine.
The world was still One to her. Her separation from me had
hardly had time yet to be filtered through to her whole being.
So she squalled, she sucked at me, she slept. And I called her
Yungi. *Yungiyungi* is Swahili for water-lily. I thought of
her floating in that lake within me, growing, budding, expanding, flowering ...

I bathed her, and dabbed surgical spirit on the scab of
blood in her navel where the cord had been. But as I watched
her, sleeping with lightly flickering eyelids, I couldn't stop
myself wondering whether she would carry another deeper
stain, the stain of the alien which wouldn't fade as the weeks
went past ... Why did the Midwife take so many smears of
blood in the first three days, till the soles of Yungi's feet were
all pinpricks?

Feng came to congratulate me on the birth and tell me that
I would be recommencing training exercises for flights to the
'Rakshasa World', with a Tibetan partner, and that my
daughter would spend the day in the Palace crèche. Horror
welled up again.

'Your daughter's just busy dreaming,' said Feng, about her

flickering, closed eyes. 'Babies dream all the time during the first few days. They have to set the world in order. The blood tests are just routine precautions against jaundice. And we *do* need to be specially careful with lowland babies. The altitude, you know. Their bodies need to manufacture more red blood cells. Why didn't you *ask* the Midwife? Stop worrying. You've a fine baby. She's perfect. Be proud.'

'What about her mind!'

'Her mind is still only an idea of a mind.'

'Will it be human, Feng?'

He laughed. 'It ought to be! Seeing she's a human being. What else do you expect? Mind is a product of evolution as much as toes or teeth are.'

'If it's stained by the alien thing . . . if some of the Beast leaked down the radar web into her! Yungi was only a code for a human being when I flew. That was her most vulnerable time! My body-field was being manipulated while I flew, wasn't it? The genetic code is such a tiny thing, in the egg or the sperm.'

'I would say it is vast.'

'Vast, but so delicate.'

'Oh, very resilient, Lila! Or we wouldn't be here, would we? We would have mutated all over the place, long ago. She's an utterly normal human being. Can't you see that, you perverse girl? Perhaps it's *that* that disappoints you.'

'I don't see into her mind. Now I have to fly again, and become pregnant again. To make another "utterly normal" baby? Then another? How many years, how many babies? I feel like a cow!'

Feng looked exasperated. 'We're expanding Bardo as fast as we can, to save you this sort of thing.'

A Barefoot carried Yungi off to the crèche; while Feng took me to meet Kushog, my Tibetan lover.

Once more I practised the mental exercises I'd learnt in Miami. I reduced golden pagodas in the Funerary Halls to a line, then to a point. Wearing a Bardo helmet, I entered the yantra nest while the earphones *hummed* and *trammed* and *hrihed*. After a few weeks, I was ready to undertake the tantric yoga of love with Kushog . . .

What a fat unctuous overgrown child this Kushog was!

Seemingly composed of soft rubber, his bones included, he could master any love position. He spoke English quite fluently but utterly monotonously – chanting his sentences at me as though every sentence was a sacred incantation. All the words ran into each other. I could just imagine him five hundred years ago, the Chosen Blessed One from a community of yak-herders, drawing magic mandalas to ward off bloat and murrain from the herds, tussling with invisible demons, sweating himself into a self-induced terror as the imaginary devils nipped his folds of pampered flesh. Talkative as he was, it was worse communicating with him than it had been with the taciturn Klimt.

On and on he chanted at me about the perils to sanity from the Star Beast. Proudly and maniacally he demonstrated an old Tibetan ritual called *Chöd*, in which a lama persuaded himself that he's genuinely being devoured, flesh, blood and bones, by ravenous demons: crying out in sweaty terror that his bones were being cracked open and all the marrow sucked out, hooting as the wind whistled through the hollow bones, squealing as his skull was sawn open and his brains gnawed. After a while I understood only too well how the fat boy really *loved* the idea of the beastly thing behind the Rakshasa façade. That was more sexual to him than I was. He made love to *it*, turning our intercourse into a kind of vile *chöd* ceremony.

I met Maimouna again. She too was retraining for Bardo flight, having given birth to a son.

She'd called him Doudou, and didn't seem to think very much of him.

We were thrown together now by lectures on the 'Rakshasa world'. Maimouna complained about these at first, both in and out of class, on the grounds that they were a farce since all of us knew that the Rakshasa moon was just a programmed illusion, masking the horrid reality of the Star Beast.

The Dobdob Instructor, a patient but insistent Chinese called Chang, was lecturing a group of about a dozen of us, alternating from English to French to Chinese to cope with our different languages. Maimouna, who spoke all three languages fluently, found the triple repetition particularly galling; and said so.

'It's all very well for the ordinary people outside to be fed this pap about the Rakshasas,' she objected to Chang at the beginning of one session. 'It's a nice dummy for them to suck. It was all right for *us* at Miami Beach before we found out the truth. But must we carry on with it?'

'You need a mask,' said Chang. 'Just as a deep-sea diver needs a mask to protect him from the pressures of the deep. You need a filter. You simply can't stand the naked reality of what is up there. You need human thought-constructs to stand against the Star Beast and be able to investigate it. When you fly, you fly under light hypnosis – accepting this mask as the reality, right? How can you accept it if you don't know what it is? So it is your duty to get to know all the "contours" of this mask. I insist on it.'

Maimouna was still unconvinced.

'Put it another way. The Rakshasa façade bears the same relation to your real mission – which you now know! – as the art of archery bore to the notion of "enlightenment" in the Zen mystical system. You didn't study archery to become a perfect shot. You simply had to master the ritual perfectly so that you could achieve something else!'

'I can hardly avoid memorizing what's repeated so many times,' said Maimouna sulkily, in an aside to me; not aloud to Chang. 'What does he know about diving, anyway? A mask doesn't keep pressure out, does it? I thought it helped you see more clearly.'

'That's right,' I whispered. 'But surely you can see what he *means*. It's not his job to know about diving.'

'It seems to be nobody's job to know enough!'

So we added to our store of knowledge about a non-existent alien species. Curiously enough, I found the Rakshasa moon more inventive and ingenious and complex than hitherto – now that I knew it to be a lie!

Rakshasa was far below freezing point. A haze of hydrocarbon products, constantly formed by flash photolysis reaction in the lightning-torn, atmosphere-replenished skies had drenched the surface of the moon with a thick, ochreous tar of precipitated photolysis products and polymers, forming a shallow ocean of rich treacle-like organic compounds. In this ocean the ancient Rakshasas evolved, finally struggling out of the treacle on to land to colonize the spiring, porous mountains – expanding and contracting their bodies at will to flow through the honeycombed rock and, by inflating their flexible bodies with gas, flying through the clouds from spire to spire.

At first, communication and the pursuit of smaller food-beasts was a matter of scent as much as of sight for them. Rakshasa body chemistry was based on giant lipid molecules, Chang told us; and lipid oils had been an essential ingredient in the old human business of perfume making. As the Rakshasas developed and as they moved further from the treacle-ocean, vision became more important. The pyrotechnic gas-giant filled most of their sky like a great roof ablaze with lights floating overhead. Their 'daylight' almost all came from there; Barnard's Star itself was quite a dull penny besides. As they colonized higher and higher zones their eyes grew keener, till sight became dominant and phosphorescent signal patches on their 'faces' began to play an abstract, language role. Chemical secretions from their own bodies became the basis of an organic architecture as they etched and rearranged the porous mountains – easy enough in the low gravity – piling their homes higher and higher until finally the spires reached through the clouds into the fringes of space itself; whereupon they at last saw the gas-giant for what it truly was – another world, which their own moon was circling, just as both circled that orange penny of a star.

So out they floated into quasi-space itself: into that thin doughnut of atmosphere encircling the whole of the gas-giant, growing ever more alert to the radiations of space, the flux and tides of the cosmos, and eventually to the cosmic Action-at-a-Distance field.

Maimouna soon adjusted, and began to find the Rakshasa rigmarole intriguing too; or at least behaved as though she found it increasingly fascinating. The idea that our flying career would be one enormous façade from now on obviously appealed to the poseur in her. No doubt there was an element of currying favour, as well! She even began suggesting refinements and sophistications that could be added to the Rakshasa mask, which Chang politely declined, though in a commendatory sort of way.

Before long she was asking eager questions about the Yidags too, badgering Chang about how that particular world was put together.

'They fly to Yidag from *Russia,* Maimouna. We don't need to go into that in detail here.'

'It's so fascinating, Chang, the way the whole system is set up by Bardo. I really feel involved in it.'

'I'm glad to hear it.'

'Do the Russian flyers know that Yidag is a lie? Or are they as raw and innocent as we were in Miami?'

'It's not relevant.'

She hesitated. 'Or . . . do they know *something else,* which even we don't know?'

Chang looked completely baffled.

'What on Earth do you mean? Can you think of something worse than the Star Beast? You're letting this new-found enthusiasm of yours run away with you, Maimouna. Please concentrate on the task in hand. It's big enough.'

Maimouna protested. 'It's just because I admire how this war's been run so very much. The way the Earth is defended without there being any visible war at all. It's so clever. That's why I want to know everything. About Yidag too. I'm sure it'll make me a much better flier. Please, Chang! Do the Russian fliers know as much as we know?'

Chang sighed.

'They believe what you believed in Miami. Only they're busy flying to Yidag rather than Asura—'

'Won't you tell us just a little more about Yidag? It's so ingenious, the way Bardo put these worlds together to fight the war!'

Finally – flattered? – Chang gave in.

So we all learnt some more about how the fictitious Yidag 'bottle-beings' soaked up energy from the fierce sunlight of Epsilon Indi for six Earth weeks on end; how they had clusters of photoelectric receptor cells growing on their heads, and how their skin was criss-crossed by piezoelectric crystals. Piezoelectric crystals are crystals which generate an electric current when they're distorted; thus the heating by day and the freeze-contraction during the long nights generated power too. As well as analysing their sun's radiations and starlight through their photoelectric cells, this piezoelectric skin of theirs let the Yidags monitor gravity pulses. They could feel fluxes in the structure of space-time as intimately as we feel the pressure of a finger on our flesh, only far more minutely.

The Yidags developed a high-level technology of mobile cyborg units and quasi-machines, all linked to themselves by laser. With this they were busily recasting their mineral world into a crystalline-metallic network of machines and organisms. On account of their basic rootedness, society was non-competitive; nor were the Yidags destroying their environment by such large scale engineering. They were simply reorganizing it organically.

Maimouna smirked at her minor conquest of Chang.

'Have you noticed something about Dobdobs?' she asked me. 'I heard from one of the Chinese fliers, who heard it from way back, that in the old days the Chinese People's Army got rid of badges of rank and glossy officers' uniforms because they looked undemocratic. But they still had to tell who was who. So they used pens and pencils. The more pens or pencils a soldier had stuck in his breast pocket, the higher he ranked. Have you noticed how the Dobdobs who *didn't* know about the Star Beast always seemed to have only a couple of pencils in their top pocket – whereas Dobdobs like Chang who do know about the war have three?'

I can't say that I had noticed, but now that I thought about it, it did seem that she was right. Mentally, I reconstructed my original Bardo test . . . The merry Dobdob, Youngden, might have had a couple of pencils in his pocket – whereas Liu, whom Sam Shaw had radioed about the 'Defence Facts', certainly had three. That fretful airfield controller in Dar es Salaam? Two, perhaps. . . . And the same with all our instructors at Miami Beach, so far as I could recall – up until we were 'arrested'. Thereafter, three pencils definitely seemed to be the norm . . .

'Feng has *four* pencils in his pocket, hasn't he, Lila? So

what does he know that Chang doesn't? He seems to take a special interest in you,' she added, fishing jealously.

Obviously this was the real point at issue. Maimouna thought that I was closer to some seat of power. She didn't really care what Feng might *know*, any more than she cared a hoot about Yidags – only what extra power Feng might wield.

'He hasn't told me anything special. Except that Bardo is devoted to Humanity, and that my Yungi is a fine baby whom I should be proud of.' Unlike your own attitude to Doudou, I thought. No doubt she could read my expression easily enough.

Feng did seem to be *hinting* at something, though. All his talk about consciousness and the universe! Almost as though the Star Beast mightn't be such a bad thing after all . . .

'Feng's just . . . more in charge. He has to think about the Star Beast. Whereas the others have to fight it. Someone's got to work out *what* it is! If the defenders spent all their time theorizing about what's attacking us—' I shrugged.

'The system mightn't work so smoothly?'

'He's a senior administrator. And theorist, damn it! Busy working out ways to extract information about the Beast through human babies. That's the truth about his position. And the truth about yours and mine is that we'll both become pregnant again – when the silver flows by way of the gold! You can't escape by ingratiating yourself with Chang and asking about Russia. They're not going to send you there to help fool more Bardo fliers to keep the system running smoothly! The lousy thing is that if it doesn't run smoothly, we all go mad.'

Maimouna tapped her ear-globes archly. She wore them to lectures now, as though she wanted an opening to brag to Chang of how she'd guessed all along that there must be a Star Beast; but he took no notice of them.

'I'll become pregnant again, will I?'

'You'll be caught in the same old web.'

'I shan't.'

'Has your new partner promised to perform *mulabhanda* for you and keep his sperm to himself, then?'

'No chance of that. Very proud type. He boasts he's descended from a Siddha saint called Mular. That's his name too. I don't care. He still won't be fathering any little Mulars on Maimouna.'

'How can you stop him?'

She hesitated, then a cunning and braggartly look came over her face. She tapped her ears again.

'Oh, my spider and my fly will help me. But I'll scratch your eyes out if you tell anybody—!' And so at last she confessed her long-nursed secret – out of pride and arrogance, which had to have an audience. Or else she would have burst her top, like a bottle of banana beer that had stood too long. (I think she did genuinely need a confidante and friend. But she had to protect her own self-image too!)

'Once, in the Senegal bush, in a dirty little village, an old blacksmith made these little glass globes for me. He was a magic man. He could read the future in the palms of my hands. One day, he predicted, they'll take your contracap away from you, and you'll want it back again. You'll really want it! I'm giving you these two baubles to hang on your ears. They only look like baubles. If you unscrew the top of the spider globe and drink down all the juice inside, you'll never conceive. If you ever want to conceive again, you unscrew the other globe and drink the antidote. I had to spin a yarn about the globes being for meditating. That was all eyewash. Actually, dear, the spider and the fly are there to show *which is which*.'

'What's in them?'

'Juice from the roots of some scraggy sedgegrass. That's the contraceptive. It was an old folk medicine – lost now, except for that blacksmith. The old man was right about me needing it, wasn't he? He knew all about medicines too. He even knew they were taking genetic samples. So you see! He *knew*. He knew about purges too, and ice-caps. Or his father had told him. He was a hundred years old. He really doted on me, the old man. But he wouldn't speak out in public.'

'They're bound to find that you've got something in your blood, when you don't conceive. You'll end up visiting an ice-cap yourself. For *sabotage*. How do you know how this stuff will affect your body-field? You could let a streamer of the Star Beast sneak in!'

'An ice-cap?' she laughed. 'I'm going to find out what really runs Bardo – and I shan't find that out by being pregnant all the time. Who really rules the world? How do people graduate to a higher rung? Lhasa is just one step nearer to the truth – and that truth must be in Kazakhstan! Let's trust the benign intentions of Bardo. Sam Shaw was just scaring us with his little gun.' Her eyes shone greedily. 'I will be everything – or nothing. I'll take the risk. If they find out what's in my blood, that'll be very clever of them. My blacksmith said no one would ever know, once it's inside me.'

'Is there enough contraceptive juice for two people?'

She seemed amazed that I should even think about it.

'My dear, the whole dose was meant for *me*. Otherwise it won't work.'

'You utterly selfish bitch! I can think of a far better reason for not conceiving babies here! Maybe you don't care what your little Doudou is. Whether he's human or not. I care if my baby's mind is full of alien thoughts – even if they take her away from me. I care if she's only an animal-machine for spying on that thing up there!'

Maimouna hadn't thought of that! Full of her own schemes, she hadn't stopped to think *why* Bardo wanted babies out of us. She only wanted power in the dirty system.

'Why else do they want us pregnant?' I raged, under the gilded pagoda. 'What else do they want but baby biocomputers programmed with bits of that Star Beast!'

'I'll find that out, won't I?' She chuckled. 'You shan't. You'll be too busy with other things.' Twisting the spider globe open, she shoved it to her lips and sucked.

Nausea twisted her features as she drank her pickled spider. She didn't vomit it out, though. She composed herself. She smiled smugly, fervently, and superstitiously.

'You tell anyone, and I'll *hurt* you. I may be in a position to help you later on. I'll remember my friends.'

And off she stalked.

SIXTEEN

The view from the window of Feng's office was vast but narrow. It cut a deep oblong wedge into the Lhasa Valley and the flanking Tangla hills. The valley was patchily green with sprouting early crops. The plastered stone framing this view was at least two metres thick, and painted jet black; it seemed you were in a cave, looking out through a crack.

'We overheard your conversation with that silly girl, of course. There's a microphone hidden in the pagoda. A voice-activated one, linked to the Battle Computer. The whole surveillance system is, actually. The tapes get erased unless the system picks up key words like, say contracap or ice-cap—'

'So it's just like the telephones in our bedrooms!' I felt disgusted. It wasn't that I wanted privacy , , , it was just *so total.*

'No, no, those aren't rigged for special words. They record everything you say in the room. Because, you see, that would mean there was someone else with you.' Feng sounded so bland about it that his spying seemed the most natural thing in the world.

Why should *anything whatever* said in a bedroom be noteworthy? *Anything?* Only one answer really. If someone else was in your room, you could just conceivably be making love – freely and spontaneously. You could just possibly be making your own baby without your chosen Bardo partner. That mustn't ever happen. That would spoil Bardo's plans.

'Spying makes the military men feel more secure in their jobs,' Feng said. I think it was meant as an apology, this time. An excuse, anyway. 'Maimouna,' he went on, 'is not only venomously ambitious, but also rather stupid. Under that veneer of sophistication, she's as superstitious and gullible as ... oh, she really *believes* in magic – personally, for herself. Whereas you care. You think things through. Or try to.'

'What are you going to do about that medicine she took?'

'Nothing,' he smiled.

126

'She won't conceive! That'll spoil your whole plan – of babies for Bardo.'

'She'll conceive all right! We analysed the contents of those earglobes ages ago. The first time she was away from them in Miami. They're contraceptive and fertility drugs all right. Naturally occurring stuff – in sedgegrass and marshgrass roots – and highly effective. What the contracap releases into your system is a synthetic based on a similar sedgegrass, from Amazonia rather than Senegal. That old witch doctor must have been *good*, no doubt about it.' He leaned forward. 'We just switched the fly and spider round. Maimouna has simply guaranteed her own fertility!'

In spite of Maimouna's selfishness, I felt crestfallen on her behalf. Feng regarded me thoughtfully.

'I'll tell you something else, Lila, because I think you're ready for it and because, as I say, you *care*. As Maimouna recognized in her power-crazy way, we do need some people – people with the right motives to, what did she say? – ah, graduate to a higher rung. I think you're that sort of person. As it happens, you're quite right about babies for Bardo. We do want them born.'

'I knew it!'

'Though it's a shame you're right, *so soon*, because – not wishing to sound punitive – you can't innocently have any more babies now.'

'Feng,' I shouted. 'What is Yungi? What have you made me make?'

'There's no need to get annoyed. Maimouna was right about Bardo's benign intentions. Your daughter is the future. She's the way forward. She is hope. There are still the best reasons in the world for as few people as possible knowing *why* that is.'

'The Star Beast, I know!'

He shook his head, amused.

'There is no Star Beast. None at all.'

'That's as much of a fairy story as the friendly aliens are. In the present unevolved state of Humanity fairy stories are fairly essential. Even so, different fairy stories suit different people. The average paranoid mind which was running the world, gravitating to the top in politics and armies for hundreds of years, prefers Evil Giants to Kindly Spirits. It feeds on hostility and threats – imaginary if not real. It'll do its best to make them real! Those who penetrate the first mask of Bardo – the friendly alien worlds – are often of this sort. They're basically self-centred. Though they often dress this up as a sense of mission. They suspect conspiracies too. They want to beat them – or join them. Those are the Sam Shaws of this world. If Sam Shaw did know what the future actually has in store for us, he'd be its most malignant enemy, I promise you that. As it is, he's a courier of wisdom and change *without knowing it.*'

'All those Dobdobs in the war room downstairs in Miami—'

'—sincerely believe they're helping ward off a thing from the stars. It's a useful outlet for what you might call the perennial military mind; they're actually warding off their own aggression. Though God help us, if it *is* perennial, Bardo will have failed. I'm sorry Sam Shaw threatened you with his gun, by the way. Still, I'm sure it helped reinforce his faith in himself. Thus the real work gets done more smoothly.'

'What *work?* You just told me there isn't any Star Beast!'

'Nor is there. Let's think about evolution for a while, Lila. What does a species need to evolve successfully? An environment which is neither too poor nor too rich. For millions of years Earth was ideal: midway between poor and rich. Yet all this time immense energy resources lay buried in it. Oil, coal, gas: a treacherous abundance. So when we developed technology we took off too suddenly and too sharply. Social and particularly mental evolution lagged sadly.

'Technological evolution can easily become an end in itself: its own jurisdiction. It separates off from Humanity. It contains its own meaning. Technology *seems* like an adequate substitute for a proper system of knowledge because it dissects the world with its tools and it even includes Man in its dissections. Yet it's pernicious. Somehow Man has to learn to know himself more directly. He has to become more aware of the nature of his own thoughts, instead of simply thinking them like an automaton. The watchers in the cave – you know the myth? – have to swing round and *see.* There's so much light behind them; but they only see shadows of existence.'

The Potala Palace was all caves, I thought – a honeycomb of caves thrown up above ground by an upheaval of nature. Feng's room particularly was a cave. With *his* back persistently turned to the only source of light, he seemed to imagine that *I* was a shadow he was casting: his own projection, puppet and invention! Maimouna had been right after all, in her sly, suspicious way. If he could only execute one of those precious 'one full turns' of his and see himself as he actually was: a slavemaster of shadows, urging the shadows to know themselves while forever hiding the truth from them behind a whole series of screens – the Alien Worlds screen, the Star Beast screen – screens which would, needless to say, be lifted as soon as people's vision had improved! This wasn't any way to be wise and free. This wasn't any way to see anything. I knew it in my heart. Truth was open, not occult.

'What is it that lies within us waiting to emerge? What is it that will seem so inevitable once it has emerged: as obvious then as it was unimaginable beforehand? What is the next evolutionary stage, Lila?' he asked me.

The sun brightened the black paint of the window embrasure, a glossy gong of light. I laughed hysterically.

'Who cares? Monkeys didn't change into humans overnight! It took millions of years. It would have been a very miserable monkey indeed that sat around asking itself what sort of being the coming human would be! You live your life *now*.'

'Ah, that's where you're wrong. People got evolution equally wrong in the twentieth century when the technological hurricane was upon them, masquerading as salvation. They had such a puny span of recorded history to look back on that they had no real gut feeling for how alien – how essentially *different* – pre-humans, and pre-pre-humans before them, must have been. They just thought of them as more of themselves, minus tools and minus language. Nor could they conceive how *alien* future humans must be compared with them. Here again they just thought of themselves, this time with more tools; different, better tools, and their brains perhaps linked up to computers to speed their thoughts along. They blithely assumed that the future human must be much the same as themselves, too, because evolution obviously was such a very *slow* process.

'Evolution isn't necessarily slow, Lila! A huge change can

happen in a few hundred years, given the right conditions. Do you know why? A major change in a species doesn't depend on a single gene site or a single mutation – but on dozens! One mutation crops up here, another crops up there; this process goes on for thousands of years—'

'That sounds like a slow process to me.'

'Indeed it is, on the surface. Most mutations are recessive, which is why nothing appears on the surface. Nothing radically new is born. Yet the mutations are being submerged in the gene pool all the time. In reality, the whole gene pool is slowly being *pre-adapted* all this time for a new form of being. When the time is ripe this submerged new being can *rush* out. We've actually been submerging the future human in ourselves for thousands of years, and what could he be but a human being more fully conscious of himself? Humanity has been saturating itself throughout recorded history. Bardo's function is to be the seed crystal now!'

'You can foresee the future, like Maimouna's blacksmith, can you? What is this future human supposed to be like, then?'

Feng squinted at me shrewdly, balancing truth and falsehood in his mind, like a coin on a fingertip. A slight wobble either way . . . Lies – or the truth. What did it matter? I was sure that every truth would turn out to be a lie. There was no reaching truth. Full sunlight was pouring into the room, making it hard to read his face.

'If life is a random process, Lila, then life simply hasn't had time to occur yet. Yet life has happened – as fast as possible!'

'So you've said.'

'Is this only an outrageous accident? Or is there something in the physical structure of the universe itself which predisposes life to emerge? Bardo believe so. We believe that biology is "submerged" in physics. Likewise that there's a tendency in biological forms to generate consciousness. The present partial consciousness of Man . . . Or the whales and dolphins, perhaps. Within this present limited consciousness of ours, there must be – what else?'

'So that's what the Star Beast stands for? And all this mystique of boundaries and frontiers? Something within us, which we can't reach?' What if there was a final truth I could reach? What if I really could break through the frontier of lies? I was almost blinded by the sunlight behind him.

'Direct manipulation of the genes by surgery was another of the great technological illusions,' he mused. 'To create a race of superhumans using the laser-scalpel and the electron microscope . . . ridiculous!'

The sun couldn't really blind me. I had stared into the heart of yantras. I could fight it. The sun simply dissolved Feng; it made him as transparent as he deserved to be, as empty. I was more real than him.

'Your fears about Yungi are groundless. Bardo's machines couldn't possibly tailor your baby's genes. Or build new ones. We have to work with nature, not against her. How could one know *in advance* what Future Man would be? Automaton Man trying to predict and engineer Conscious Man would be like, oh, a computer trying to figure the workings of the mind that had programmed it.

'That's all I want to say, right now. Think about it. This is, if you like, your first real lesson *ever* about Bardo.'

The sun was a blazing toad now. It had crept out of the stonework to spit poison in my eyes.

Feng rose from behind his desk, swallowing the toad, eclipsing me, dismissing me.

I went back to my room, and soon they brought Yungi back from the crèche. Her eyes were questioning the world now. She was a whole world questioning itself. She was a world thinking itself into being as she formed the world around herself, in her mind.

She was hope? She was the Future?

But *what* future?

The pinpricks on her feet – scarcely distinguishable any more – reminded me of a strange story which a Barefoot Lama once told us children one Sunday in the former mosque. The story had sounded absurd at the time: a crazy joke and nothing more. It had stuck in my mind, perhaps on account of its absurdity. Now the story suddenly seemed mockingly true.

Once upon a time some king wanted to send a secret message through enemy territory to the king of another country. There was no particular hurry about the message, so what they did was to shave the messenger's head and tattoo the message on to his scalp. Then they waited till his hair grew back and sent him on his way. The man duly carried the message, hidden on his head – where, of course, he couldn't read what it said any more than the frontier guards could. He carried it with complete success, and when he reached his destination he explained to the second king how to read the message. The king ordered a bowl of hot water, soap and a razor to be brought.

When they shaved the messenger's head, what the secret message said was, 'Kill this man as soon as he arrives.' So they cut his throat, there and then, with the razor.

I thought about this story now, as I looked at Yungi's baby feet. That message from one king to another across alien territory was just like Feng's prediction about what Man must become – a message carried by a human, yet completely hidden from him. When the message *was* read, it spelt the end of Man, his death.

Alternatively, the story simply suggested that the less people knew about anything, the freer they were to live and be happy . . .

A Tibetan Dobdob, who spoke only Tibetan, was sitting patiently on a three-legged stool outside my room. There was no way that I could warn Maimouna that her medicine had been switched.

Three nights later, Kushog burst into my room, naked to the waist, wearing only his white draw-string trousers. He was deranged – with rage at me and a fearful frenzy directed at himself. He sweated and quivered like a jelly stimulated by a massive shot of adrenalin – posturing, exalted, fear-besotted, nihilistically ecstatic. His lips and cheeks flopped about in fishy suffocation. His eyes bulged like a bronze hyperthyroid god's. He carried a flickering, spooky candle half a metre tall. Whatever it was made of stank of charred flesh as though he'd torn off one of his own limbs and set fire to it for light. He waved it about like an arm, dashing hot wax in my face. I felt sparks of pain, then tightness as the wax dried and pulled. Great lunatic shapes danced around the walls. I thrust Yungi behind me, half-burying her in blankets. She flapped and mewed, but subsided safely.

'You left me! You won't fly with me any more! So I have to fly on my own, all alone,' he chanted at me in his usual rabid monotone. Shaking his enormous candle, he distributed more blobs of burning fat indiscriminately on me, on the bed, on himself. I succeeded in making a tent for Yungi with the blankets, a protective pocket of air. I was terrified, but the only thing to do was talk to him, calm him. Had he been sent to me deliberately? Was this some new torment of Feng's, some new trick? There was supposed to be a Dobdob on guard outside, segregating me. If he'd fallen asleep, surely the noise of Kushog's ranting would wake him up? Unless he'd been told to turn a blind eye, and a deaf ear! Were the microphones listening to all this?

'Did the Dobdob let you past him?'

'He is my brother!'

'What, he's actually your brother?'

'He is my brother in *nothingness*! I helped him trample down his False Self while he sat there meditating. I extended my brotherly love to him, to liberate him!'

'You mean, you killed him?' I was alone with him. Yungi too. No one was listening to Feng's microphones. If they were, then this was some sadistic test, either arranged with Kushog's full connivance, or else by playing upon his dementia, something easily aroused.

'My brother's dead to the world.' Kushog grinned hugely. His lips stretched in a flared red bow around a mouthful of blunt yellow teeth: the teeth of a horse. His mouth chomped shut. He could bite a half-moon out of my arm if he wanted.

Suppose this was a test? Suppose that I had to decide whether or not to save myself by betraying Feng's confidence and telling Kushog that his precious defence of the Earth was all eyewash? That was surely the way to deflate him and drive him away . . .

But what Kushog told me next bewildered me still further. For Kushog said that he had flown *alone*: to a new alien world more terrible than any of the three alien worlds so far 'discovered' – one which the Star Beast itself was responsible for inventing and throwing at the human psyche.

'Why fly without a partner?' I began. 'You couldn't possibly conceive a—' A baby. I shut my mouth. Private knowledge. Feng knowledge.

'They said I must fly alone to a new world the Star Beast has

133

woven, full of half-beasts it has made. A world which reels us in to it with the fiercest hook rays. I was chosen because my soul is strong – because I can fight devils that consume me alive, because I am a master of the Way of *Chöd*.'

'You really did fly without a woman?'

'You left me alone,' he jeered, spattering more blazing grease from that third arm of his.

'You wore the Bardo helmet? You still watched the yantra shapes? You heard the mantra, all alone?' I had to know what had happened to him. 'How did you get the power to fly? It takes a man and a woman together—'

'You left me. You weren't there. But I'm strong.'

'It wasn't my fault. However did you do it on your own?' If only I could flatter his vanity.

'I performed *chöd*, to fly! Difficult? Not for me! I burned my flesh and bones, my brains and blood into energy. The world I flew to was a *chöd* world. You couldn't have stood it, woman! Its hook rays yearned for such a one as me. The Star Beast has grown more cunning. It knows that we throw alien worlds of the mind at it, as masks from behind which to question it. We were safe behind the Rakshasa mask till now. Now there's a new world in the heavens. The Star Beast has made a mind world and peopled it with horror beings, and our radars read it back at us. It pushes the Rakshasa mask aside. It lures fliers to a ceremony of *chöd*, where those who aren't adepts will be eaten alive in body and mind. I had to fly. Who else?'

'I'm sure you were the right one, Kushog.'

He calmed a little as he chanted his story at me, beginning to look less like a pop-eyed fiend about to jump on me and tear my throat out with his great horse's teeth, and more like an utterly scared little fat boy telling the worst of nightmares.

While he was telling his story, I racked my brains to explain this new alien world. Where had it come from? Why? He seemed to be telling the truth – or at least telling what had happened to him. It began to seem that Bardo had revived the craziest, most savage kind of Shamanism in the bowels of the Palace as a sadistic experiment.

This was how he told it . . .

SEVENTEEN

A crisis in the War Room! Dobdobs crowded the desks, pushing buttons and twisting knobs, trying to douse red alarm lights. The great display screen showed the yantra nest around the planet being probed and feinted at by spikes of activity from outside, thrusting deeper and deeper. Occasional thin red lines of fire traversed the entire nest, stabbing right through the world. Earth's defences were being penetrated.

The Star Beast was attempting a breakthrough, said the Dobdob who had summoned Kushog at the double. Unless the frontiers could be firmed, insanity would roam the world. A single suicide flier had to investigate, using different techniques. Would Kushog volunteer to face madness, to save the world from it? Oh yes, he breathed fervently, full of the self-devouring spirit of *chöd*. Sole Guardian of Planet Earth against the mind plague, he was.

For the first time in history, a human mind must hang free. He would have to let the Star Beast programme whatever illusions it chose into him. He would have to accept whatever alien vision it threw at him. That vision was a vital message to Humankind. He would have to learn it through pain and horror, if pain and horror there was. Accept it! Equally, there might be inconceivable bliss. Accept that too! And overcome it! Kushog promised. Going into the Contact Room, he donned the helmet and squashed his rubber limbs into lotus position. He watched the yantra mandala, his brain rang with the *HUM!*, the *TRAM!*, the *HRIH!*, the *RAM!*, and the *OM!* – and all the while he tormented himself with his own Tibetan ritual *chöd* chants . . .

Already the gases of an alien atmosphere were beginning to percolate into his nostrils, enhancing colours and sensations, vastly distending time. (He was being drugged, obviously, by some psychedelic gas more powerful than the nutmeg essences used in my own training in Miami!) What rose up within him felt less like the familiar Kundalini serpent and more like a swollen python, digesting a goat – and the goat was himself.

'*Zab-chö shi-hto gong-pa rang-dol lay*,' he boomed ritually, making his lungs into gongs. '*Bar-doi thö-dol chen-mo chö-nyid bar-doi ngo-töd zhu-so* . . .' The opening of the *Book of the Dead.* 'Here we set ourselves face-to-face with the reality of the limbo state; and liberate ourselves on the After-Death plan by meditating upon peaceful and wrathful Gods . . .' So he recited to me.

Between pulses of mantra sound, he clearly heard the hooting of trumpets made of human femur bones and a tetchy skull-drum tapping out in his brain and body-field rhythms never so heavily accented before. Death-wish rhythms. Rhythms of cruelty and violence in the *Id.*

He flew.

The bindu point flared out around him, with all the stars of the galaxy in it. They pinched tight to a bottleneck behind him, and vomited him into another world . . .

Where there were red and blue mists, shifting lights, vague wet pastel hummocks and low domes like upside-down terracotta bowls.

I guessed that it might be the inside of Haleakala Crater on Maui he was seeing, projected into his helmet. However, I couldn't break in to his possessed sing-song candle-waving chant to tell him, any more than holding out your hand halts a waterfall. For him, this had to be a world built by the Star Beast from the mind-tattered remains of some alien people it had brushed by on its way to Earth and casually overwhelmed!

A landscape of mud, mist and clay. The Beings that inhabited it looked not far removed from wet clay, either: their features barely sketched in, contours unfirmed, unfired. Clay-people.

By way of speech, they only made one sound. A single glutinous slobbery bark. It never varied. It was the basic mantra of the death of meaning, the dissolution of language back into nature. It was at once all possible words, and no word at all. It was the sum total of inchoate sounds a baby babbles, thrashed into one noise, pronounced by a tongue of stiffening glue. One universal word, and no-word.

It was the sort of word a universe might speak, if it had a

136

mouth. A total word, affirming and denying everything at once. A paradox word.

An insane, useless word.

These Claypeople looked as if they were about to dissolve back into the primal clay. They were upright, bifurcate, walking slugs. Their bodies bounced about their dome village, stretching, contracting and undulating, never the same shape for very long. Pseudopod fingers at their wrist stumps, like snails' horns. Eyes like red fishes' gills, their mouths a slime-vent, opening and shutting all the time, barking their single word.

This was surely the seed-sound that contains all other sounds. This was the primal mantra from which all others sprang. It came before mantras, particles or atoms, before stars or lives or consciousness, this ur-*Om*, this proto-*Om* that they slobber-barked at one another, and at Kushog too – for he was one of them. He participated helplessly, hallucinatorily, in their life – if it could be called a life – though he could still think some Tibetan thoughts of his own about it. That word was the name of the boundary between Being and Non-Being. The first binding together of Being, which affirmed everything possible – and excluded, not 'everything else', but rather pure nothing. Pure nothing was still very close.

The Claypeople's village consisted of cone and cupola clay huts, arranged in a double circle around a central plaza, which was dominated by a large hearth equipped with a roasting spit. The single break in this double circle gave on to a perfectly straight avenue flanked by twin rows of circular clay statues: statues, apparently, of Claypeople bending over in a hoop to touch the soles of their own feet. This avenue disappeared into the lurid fog which wrapped the village round in all directions.

Apart from huts, statues, and the roasting-spit – made of stone, or a tangle of stalactites – all their world was soft and wet.

What did they cook on the spit? Hard to tell. No charred bones or shells lay near it. Were there any firm-bodied creatures on this world at all? Hardly, judging by the floppy, rubbery appearance of the Claypeople, who must represent the highest form of life here, but who seemed to have nothing stiffer than gristle in them. Yet they had mastered fire! Charcoal glowed perpetually beneath the spit, sputtering faintly in the thick wet air, kept alive by a rota of Claypeople who squatted and blew on it. Maybe the fire had fallen from the skies one day: a meteor, or a blob of lava.

Kushog never actually saw them eat or gather anything for eating. (Maybe the air was manna?) They also lacked any apparent genitals. This sort of creature could probably propagate by budding, or splitting. As he watched, the daylight dimmed, darkened, went black, then grey again, then diffusely milky, then a sombre purple, and even briefly a strident aching yellow. Impossible to say what suns or moons or auroras caused these unpredictable lights; everything was so diffused by the cloudy air. There were no fixed points in space and time apart from the double circle of clay stones, the spit, the avenues of statues. Kushog's consciousness felt an enormous pressure upon it to sink back into preconsciousness, his words into prewords, his thoughts into prethought.

Then came the dawn. It must have been a genuine sun-dawn. For the air blazed silver. The whole sky became the steel back-side of a mirror. At this signal the Claypeople galvanized themselves and rushed to blow the charcoal under the spit into a fiercer glow. Silver air and steel sky had no heat as such in them, only a light-beyond-heat, almost a spiritual light.

All the Claypeople, including Kushog, crowded round the cooking spit, blowing through their slime-vents, silent except for the hiss of the work. The stone spit was so firm. They were so shapeless and indeterminate. How could they ever have built it? They must have found it by a miracle.

Abruptly, they seized one of their number, and slung him over the spit. They wrapped him in a full circle around it, tying his feet to his head with some tough rubbery fibres. One Clay-person stuck long thin clay pipes in the victim's mouth and rectum. Others slapped wet clay on his body. A few cranked the spit handle – in silence. Not even a hiss of breath now. Their 'word' hadn't been uttered a single time since dawn, Kushog realized.

The fire glowed. They swung the spit. They slapped on fresh clay as the first coat baked.

What had been an inchoate slug-like alien being was slowly and methodically transformed on the spit into something far more alien and hideous. It became one of those curved-over statues which marched far out into the mists, marking the only road out from the village into the rest of the world.

At last, the cooked being screamed – breaking the silence. His nerves took over and cried out. The air rushed in and out of him in agony. Again and again came the cry. It was the same glutinous slobbery bark as the ur-*Om* noise. This was the sound that the fire forced out of him. This was the ultimate message, the final reality.

As the baking statue became firmer and more solid, and as the spit swung round, the Claypeople took up that slobbery bark of final pain in chorus and hooted it back at their world, gesticulating with their snail's horn fingers at every single object in sight, themselves included, naming everything with the same all-purpose word.

Kushog's slime-vent hooted it too . . .

By this time in his story Kushog was chanting, sweating and barking – and I really believed he was cooking his own flesh with that vast candle, passing it back and forth about his half-naked body till I could smell the char of flesh.

Yet what he chanted, however manic and staccato, was also strangely lucid – as though torture could produce not garbled feverish confessions, but on the contrary a perfect clarity of soul. He was making a huge noise by now – and nobody came. Yungi, muffled in her tent, twanged like a harp to his cries. I could do nothing for her or for myself. I could only hope that Feng would come before much longer – before Kushog decided to hold that candle flame to me, to teach me to see his vision for myself.

He knew now that these Claypeople, these Demon people, were reality itself – perpetually asserting itself in the midst of the ocean of becoming. Agreement on the nature of reality was astonishing to these Claypeople. All that they could say was that a thing *is,* not what it is. All that they could do was to fit a thing into itself and see how it fitted. Then *it was.* The fitting of a thing into its own shape formed the shape of their agreement on reality. That was how the universe fitted into itself, in order *to be*. The universe ached with being – therefore the stars *burned*.

'What is a universe?' cried Kushog. 'It is one thing. Yet it isn't One, it's Everything. But if there's nothing to compare it with, how can it have Laws? What is *Law*?'

All that his Claypeople could do was to put the thing into itself again and again, and see that it fitted. Putting oneself *into* oneself made sense, made thought.

The baking of the statue was finished, and the fire died back to a glow again. The mantra of existence had been confirmed for another day. The universe still existed. It still fitted into itself. It had given itself its own law. It had existed for as many days as there were statues leading from the village: their chronometer – and their compass as to the direction of reality.

When the new statue had cooled sufficiently for clayflesh to touch it, a band of the Claypeople, Kushog among them, hoisted the artefact and bore it out at a chanting run through the gap in the double circle, down the roadway.

Purple and rose mist swirled around. The only firm ground seemed to be where the roadway led, in a narrow-straight line of pure geometry. To right and left, glimpsed between the walls of old statues, was vague glue – mere binding material midway between gas and mud. Where the road terminated, this gaseous muddy binding glue swirled ahead too. For the road led nowhere. Only out, into chaos.

This wasn't a highway. It was a rule. A series. A proof of natural law.

These statues weren't statues; they were definitions – enunciated in a vocabulary of pain. And the language of law was pain – because law always punished; it tortured into categories.

The road appeared longer now. More chaos had been firmed by the time they placed the new statue at the end of the series, and trooped back, barking the sound-that-contained-all-sounds at the earlier statues.

Different kinds of daylight, and dusk, and day or moonlight followed one another seemingly at random in the Claypeople's world, till once more a silver-and-steel 'dawn' held its polished mirror back above them. This time it was Kushog himself whom the other Claypeople seized, draped over the spit, and bound head to toe – so that he performed one full turn, rejoining his own being like a snake swallowing itself.

(While he was telling this, he rippled the molten candle underneath his throat and armpits, as though solidifying wax would transform his own human body into a Claypeople hoop.)

The world went dark when they slapped wet clay on his eyes. At first, the turning over and over of the hoop of his body afforded brief bouts of relief from the mounting pain and even the warm breeze sighing through his body from mouth-pipe to anus-pipe was strangely soothing. Then it became a hurricane of burning air, baking his entrails too, inside – tearing from him that One Word of Pain. No need to fear mispronunciation. No risk of getting it wrong. The geometry of his own body, bent over on itself, formed the trumpet proclaiming the single sound that fitted him most perfectly. Pain halted the world, in a cry. Pain was the only reality that absolutely must articulate itself *to stop itself*. His cry was the picture of pain, the pain pictured the world.

The universe, Kushog knew in his delirium, seeks non-existence, nirvana. The universe, God, whatever the name of the total sum of everything might be, exists in a tragic agony, yearning not to be, never to have been. All its stars and galaxies, every particle of matter, every wave of radiation sears it. It has to fit itself into itself to articulate this pain, and the more fiercely it articulates this, the more persistently it exists, and creates itself. For it has wrapped time and matter round themselves, tying a knot in the midst of absolute nothing so that its end generates its beginning; so that its primal explosion and its final collapse wrap around each other too, eternally and simultaneously, now and always. Immense compassion overcame Kushog in the final moments of his agony, as his bent-around body screamed the root sound.

Squeezed to an hourglass of burning, dripping wax, the candle finally burst between his fingers. Flame splattered, and extinguished. In the darkness of my cell, Kushog moaned a single sound which, having no change or variety, was like a very loud silence, the song of the vacuum of space.

Snatching Yungi from her tent of blankets, I fled from the room, banging my shoulder into Kushog, then into the door, which I slammed shut behind me.

The Dobdob guard was sitting on his stool – as motionless

as a statue. He heard nothing. He saw nothing. He thought nothing.

I tried to shake him by the shoulder. He was immovable, infinitely massive — an axle of the universe, holding tight all the cords of gravity for everywhere else. Being the pivot for everywhere else, he dared not move so much as an eyebrow. Dared not think one thought. Or else the world would crumble from his inattention.

He was hypnotized. Obviously, Kushog had done it, with his flickering candle flame. Kushog was cunning. He hadn't tried to resist the Dobdob's urge to guard the corridor. He had magnified it into a paralysing obsession. His fantasy visit to this new alien world had given him insight: at the cost of burning him out! So consumed by his alien *chöd* encounter was he, indeed, that he had no human body left with which to beat or rape or punish me — as might have been his original plan. His quivering fat was all melted and insubstantial. The Dobdob's body, on the other hand, had grown as dense as matter at the core of a star. No wonder Kushog had claimed that the guard was his brother. Kushog had exchanged his substance with the guard; exchanged it for the guard's own soul. Together, the two Tibetans had reached a hideous mad nirvana, respectively of flame and stone.

I fled on, till some Dobdobs found me and took me back to my cell, which was empty now — and took Yungi for observation, to the crèche. The Dobdobs seemed almost as puzzled and confused as I was by what had happened.

A new guard sat on the stool, fresh and innocent. I might have imagined it all.

Except that my face was tight with wax. I scraped it off with my fingernail. It was real, all right.

EIGHTEEN

Feng seemed genuinely embarrassed by the incident – and I was sure that he didn't quite understand it himself. Kushog's experience certainly had nothing to do with making babies!

'Children sometimes pull the wings off flies,' he muttered. 'What can one do? They grow up . . . No, there are only Rakshasa flights from here. You're right. It was to be a man and a woman flying. What happened? An experimental mind-training programme got switched on-line by the computer, that was all. The Dobdobs down below acted on it. It shouldn't have been fed into the main system.'

'Down below?'

'Down in the old shelters where the War Room is.'

'I suppose this was a trial run for the crater on Maiu? The mists and everything—'

He smiled gratefully. The smile of someone who's glad that you've furnished a satisfactory explanation of your own accord. A smile of absolution.

He also gave me a cup of tea. He had taken me up to one of the golden pavilions on the roof. By now, no longer pregnant, I thoroughly enjoyed the buttery salted taste of the Tibetan tea.

I realized that I wasn't going to learn any more about Kushog's flight from him. Instead, to distract me from one horror, he told me about another . . .

He had an envelope full of photographs with him. I'd already seen prints of them in Miami. The 'Star Beast victims'. I took one look and sneered.

'They're all genuine, Lila. People really did sit down by the millions and die, starting in 1995. It wasn't a Star Beast, of course. It was a kind of encephalitis. Sleeping sickness.'

It had appeared suddenly, and simultaneously, all over the world, Feng said. The same thing happened on a smaller scale eighty years earlier, during the First Global War. An inexplicable epidemic. It was as though part of the human race seemed bent on locking itself away from an impossible world. As though the patterns of life had become hopelessly tangled.

The First War was terrible enough, yet in many ways the situation was much worse in the nineteen-nineties. Ceaseless brushfire wars all over the world, rampant sabotage, terrorism, revolution and counter-revolution, coup and bloodbath, collapse of government . . . As the world money system fell to pieces world trade increasingly became a matter of barter and blackmail. Land and sea were polluted; there was drought and famine. Always there was the threat of a final nuclear war, tightening its psychological screw. And television screens and radios connected at least half of the world's people permanently to the ongoing horrors like a set of ever-dripping taps, so that this was what swam before people's eyes and buzzed in their ears day in and day out even when they weren't being burnt or blackmailed, starved or terrorized themselves. It was overload – and the only circuit-breaker to disconnect people was illness: physical illness, mental illness. In the rich countries that still had reasonable medical services, from thirty to sixty per cent of the population had to be treated for mental illness at least once in their lives. The 'infection' even began spreading to the biggest of the collective socialist states, China, which had tried to isolate itself. Finally there came the big epidemic. Millions of people would rather go into a coma than live in such a world. There had been sudden technological evolution; but no corresponding mental evolution.

'The epidemic's victims couldn't see the patterns of life any more. They saw nothing. They froze. In mid-sentence. In mid-gesture – as you see. Their brain waves were very curious. New, complex patterns seemed to be trying to emerge – then breaking down from their own complexity. The higher brain functions were simply stalling, as a result. There was a drug called L-Dopa – Laevo-Dihydroxyphenylalanine, to the chemists – which could unfreeze these people for a while so that they could explain what they felt was happening to them. They said it felt as though they were being forced, for sheer survival, to grasp too huge a pattern of knowledge. Because they couldn't integrate it all, they froze, they went dark, vanished to a point: from the sheer mental "gravity" of too much to perceive, too much forced upon them by a chaotic world.'

'They couldn't cope—'

'Oh no!' Feng leaned forward urgently, spilling a blob of tea: which spread out greasily. 'This was the paradox. They were the ones who were trying to cope! They were the ones whose nature made them try. They said they felt the capacity in them *struggling to emerge*. But they failed, and illness swallowed them. The ones with hope were the uniquely vulnerable ones.'

A yoga class had come out to exercise on a distant roof. Their Bardo uniforms were red and white flags, semaphors. I examined the red horses galloping around my cup.

'I suppose those were the first Bardo fliers?' I queried finally.

Feng almost sighed with relief, so glad that I'd understood.

'You said they were frozen!' I accused. 'You said they died like flies. How could such people breed and have any babies?'

'The L-Dopa drug unfroze them for long enough. And in sufficient numbers. Believe me, they weren't reluctant. On the contrary! Randy as rabbits. It seemed to be an offspin of the illness – though perhaps this was a simple biological survival urge. At any rate, those *were* the most genetically "saturated" people on the planet, Lila – precursors of the more fully conscious individual. The tragedy was that the awful pressures of twentieth century life were forcing them to act out a potential that was still only *dormant* in themselves. Forcing them to develop it prematurely in their own lives, instead of it being expressed in their children's or their children's children's. It seemed like a cruel trick of Nature. Those who promised most, must die.'

'So there *was* a Star Beast, within—' The image hit me of revived zombies copulating, then being tossed aside as soon as they had mated and borne fruit . . .

'The sickness acted as a pointer to who should be brought together. The epidemic showed us how to cast our net into the gene pool. Of course, we've refined our technique since then.'

'It's horrible.' I remembered the tale of a Zulu king, when the whites first invaded Africa. He set up his finest warriors for the whites to fire their bullets at, simply to test their range and accuracy by where his warriors fell . . .

'We could only save a number temporarily. After childbirth,

145

we had to let them relapse . . . But the epidemic spread for a long time. The human race had *almost* been ready to evolve a new, more conscious sort of being. Naturally, an epidemic of this scale – along with the sheer pandemic panic it was causing – was the last straw on the camel's back so far as the world's sagging governments were concerned. And, naturally, the most important international organization was a World Health Organization, voted emergency powers by the world's governments to try to explain and stem the epidemic *at all costs*. Bardo was born out of this – guided by individuals of real vision who had been waiting in the wings while mediocrities and madmen ran the world.'

Feng gestured grandiosely at the Tangla hills, just like that Zulu king setting out his warriors. The range might have been a genetic, not a geological formation.

'World security was so weak and torn apart now, it was actually possible to impose a new form of society upon the world – one which wouldn't stress people to their breaking point, too soon.' (As Kushog had been stressed to his breaking point?) 'And to make it stick, worldwide. With blanket control of communications as a first major step – and the lie about the Star Beast as the cause of sickness to fool the high commands in the stronger nations into acquiescence and collaboration. This was the most magnificent forgery. It took a lot of scientist sympathizers to pull it off – a real brotherhood of those who were fed up with having politicians, generals and bureaucrats as bosses.

'But – beyond stabilizing the world – the real point of Bardo is human evolution. Humanity could have evolved safely and spontaneously over a longer period of time but for the damned technological take-off! This isn't an area of free choice, any more than breathing is. It's an inbuilt biological plan, programmed by the sort of universe we're in.'

He peered at me.

'You've a rare capacity for organizing *patterns*, Lila. It's a Bardo characteristic. Actually, you'd be the perfect casualty, if the world was still as complex and chaotic as it used to be, because you'd drive yourself to see *too much* – and you're not a future human yourself, you're just a forerunner.'

'I suppose my Yungi is the one who'll know,' I mumbled

miserably, utterly cut off from her, not caring that she was away from me in the crèche.

'She might be. We're positive that the physical universe is structured to evolve life and consciousness. You might say that life is the universe's message to itself, about itself. Yungi might be it, yes. We're able to set up suitable physical circumstances for a higher consciousness to emerge. But I can't say yes or no. It may be her sons and daughters, or theirs.' Feng's eyes shone, his head swayed with a cobra-like absorption. 'What happened at the close of the twentieth century was the make-or-break of conscious life on this particular world. We already passed that hurdle successfully, through the most awful chaos and suffering. Maybe, perversely, *because* of it. It did show us the way ahead. It did let Bardo gain power—'

Blue space was pressing down upon my brain, and upon the ring of barren mountains. Was I only ignorance and unconsciousness? Was I not awake at all?

'Pain. And chaos. That was Kushog's trip the other night. Was that a blessing in disguise? Did that wake him up and make him more conscious?'

'It was a mistake. I told you.'

I went to the crèche the next day to see what they were doing to my Yungi to make her into a woman of the future. The fresh-faced replacement Dobdob trailed after me uncertainly. He apparently hadn't any instructions to stop me going in that direction, *away* from Maimouna and other Bardo fliers whom I might contaminate; though as soon as I reached the crèche, he made a telephone call to report where I was.

The babies' cots were all wired for sound. Delicate feather-weight earphones were clipped to their skulls. The softest murmur of music hummed through the room. Slipping Yungi's earphones off, I held them to my ear while the Barefoot on duty looked on: patiently, or apprehensively, I'm not sure which.

The music was an Indian *raga*: a rippling river of bright, rapid, metallic sounds, a wire spider's web shining with beads of sun-soldered dew, reverberating in a complicated pattern. Where was the harm in such lovely music? I let the Barefoot take the earphones away from me and clip them back gently on Yungi's skull. She slept, enmeshed in *ragas*, eyelids flickering.

Summoned by the telephone call, Feng arrived as I was leaving.

He led me towards his office, holding my elbow in a stilted crablike grip. 'Music is both sensuously appealing and mathematically exacting,' he remarked primly as we walked along. 'Music reflects on itself. Its form is its content. That's what's unique about it, as an art. It helps, at a time when the infant brain is still patterning itself, programming its own gestalts of the world.'

When we arrived in that now familiar cave, he poured more butter tea from a big thermos bottle with an orange dragon chasing its tail around it.

'That's really what the Asuran business of exclusions and inclusions and horizons is all about, Lila. How to bring the horizon of Man's knowledge inside Man, so that Man can understand *how* he thinks, instead of simply thinking automatically. How to wake up from the hypnotic slumber of ordinary consciousness, and learn to perceive what perceiving *is*! Because, really, most people spend all their lives in a light hypnotic trance. *You do too,* though you probably don't believe it.'

'What will we know then, Feng? What's the use of it? Why can't people just live and *be*?'

'You sound like a prehistoric animal asking, "Why should I evolve? What can I possibly evolve into? What's in it for me?" I'll tell you what I felt when I first discovered the true plan of Bardo. I was a Bardo flier once, as well. I fathered some children, I suppose. Then I got suspicious. I started asking questions; and when they were finally answered – it was a moment of absolute wonder for me! A revelation. Because the universe "out there" stopped being an alien thing, right then! There was no external enemy Nature to be fought by Humanity and tamed. It had never been "out there"! That was only a hypnotic illusion. Nature was here in every atom of my being, in every moment of thought, all along – submerged in me. I'm made from its very texture. Future Humanity will know all this directly, in ordinary daily life.' His eyes shone. Surely

I must see this too, they pleaded. 'Not only that, but the cosmos actually *makes itself* out of the various consciousnesses in it which are evolving to understand it. Life isn't a chance event in the universe. Life is an integrated part. So is thought. The universe generates life, Lila, so that ultimately consciousness will generate the universe!'

I saw nothing. I was inside a mouth; and the mouth was shutting on me.

'When I saw, I lost all doubts. I knew I had to work towards this. In the midst of the horrors of the nineteen-nineties, the human race was dragged upwards into greatness by something that had been within us all along. That's the really wonderful thing. You *must* see this and help the work. If only because you're directly a part of that future now, through Yungi. She's a lifeline to that future. I told you, she is Hope. But that future has to come about peacefully. The human race, as we know it now, has to be absorbed *upwards*. There mustn't be any conflict or venom between the Old and the New. There could so easily be – even now. The infuriating thing is that people are still quite capable of rising against Bardo – even the War Room Dobdobs! – to try to kill your Yungi and all the other Bardo offspring. Bardo has to work with subterfuge to save itself. That's why the real plan has to be hidden away.'

'You mean to say that Bardo would declare war on the world if necessary? Then Bardo is a real Star Beast!'

'Oh no. The moment we're forced to fight, we lose. So does the whole human race. All its hopes, lost. Because the hands and feet would have declared war on the head, and strangled it, leaving a senseless body with no judgement, no higher consciousness. That's why islands are being made ready—'

'Such as Maui?'

'No, much bigger than that. Ceylon is being cleared, and New Zealand and Cuba, in preparation. People are being re-settled from those areas. It all has to be done so discreetly. You really have to help us. We need organizers. People to run the system. Not your Sam Shaws, who would shoot us dead if they knew – or your Maimounas either, whose motives are all wrong—'

'Help you to drive people from their homes?'

'The whole world's our home. The whole *universe* is. Madagascar has already been cleared without any trouble – as a retirement zone for ex-Bardo fliers.'

'For worn-out breeding stock?'

'Hardly! Bardo is the most *humane* system possible. We need senior administrators who understand the real problems, with feeling. I've chosen you as one. It's Yungi's future you're protecting.'

'But Yungi's an alien!' I shouted, rising.

'*And* your child. Who do you suppose that Asuran was you talked to in Miami?'

'A programmed illusion. Probable responses to questions about barriers and things. Garbage in, garbage out,' I sneered, shrugging back into the seat.

'Not at all,' he smiled courteously. 'It's the Bardo children themselves who operate the flights. Do you think we keep them locked up underground? They know what's going on much better than you do. They use some highly sophisticated games equipment, hooked in to the Bardo helmets and the phoney Star Beast displays. The game is to keep up the alien masquerade – with all the debate about mind and numbers and the cosmos – impeccably, and mesh this in perfectly with the body-field events of the flight. All this, mark you, on three simultaneous levels: the level of the friendly alien worlds, the level of the Star Beast war, and lastly and most importantly the human biology level. Of course, the debate with friendly aliens and the Star Beast war both really represent the same thing – only, in inverted terms! – the expansion of consciousness beyond its present boundaries . . .'

'But babies are conceived during these flights! Are you saying that it's all just a game played with living human beings?'

'Exactly! A game. A completely serious game. And children are conceived in the process. That's the whole point to it: to get the flier's body-field tuned for the critical period of conception. To harmonize the body-field "signature" of the Bardo child actually operating the game with the two adult lovers who carry submerged genes *for* such a child. To imprint this signature upon the mother's own body-field – already well trained to respond! – at a time when egg and sperm are coming together so that the chromosomes will link up in a positive pattern with the Bardo genes dominant. It's perfectly possible to beat the supposed randomness of heredity, this way!

'Don't forget what a sensitive receiver of body-field information a single sperm or an egg, or even a single cell, is. Evolutionarily, this plasma of ionized particles that we call the body-field forms the primary patterning system for organizing life. It's the earliest message device of living matter, Lila. Why, even inanimate crystals are brought into being by "preforms" – energy fields that anticipate the solid matter! The system exists even before life – for life to build upon. Here, this force is brought to bear upon the message of life itself, locked up in the DNA codes, acting as a selective electromagnetic filter – right down at the germ-cell level – to attract the right combination out in the resulting zygote – the fertilized egg. An early follower of Backster's called Marcel Vogel was the first to show how people could think and feel their way down into the very DNA molecules in a cell, using the body-field, and influence them.

'The second flight, a week later, is to reinforce the field that's been imprinted, just in case the mother's womb aborts the slightly alien "wavelength" of the blastula – that's the pre-embryo stage, attached to the wall of the womb by now, with its future "map" determined, but still amorphous so far as the organization of the cells goes . . .

'This is how Future Humanity presides over its own conception, Lila. Almost by its own bootstraps! Obviously the Bardo children have to operate the game. How else? They show us the way – towards themselves. They've been being born and growing up for a long time now, in increasing numbers, with their own adults supervising them. It's down to a fine art now. And in the process of imprinting the pattern they educate and strengthen their own body-fields—'

'They programme the flights? Then they programmed Kushog's flight – to drive him mad!'

Feng shook his head impatiently. 'I already told you that was an accident! A mistake! Listen to me. Maimouna set wicked traps for you, that one did. Well, she's flying at noon – to get herself fertilized.' He chuckled. 'It's funny how people always imagine they get pregnant on the second flight, just because there are always two flights in succession . . . Come along and see for yourself, Lila. You'll understand the process better.'

'Do you think I want to see her making love? You sound like a *brothel* manager!'

'No, it's abstract. Schematic – you'll see. No one-way mirrors. For the hundredth time, we *respect* human beings. What are we doing, otherwise?'

My rage at Feng was by now so icy cold that it had frozen tight inside me. It couldn't function any more; it only sat inside me like a block doing nothing. And curiosity did draw me; I *had* to know.

I nodded dumbly.

He escorted me down to the Hinge Room at the bottom of the palace; thence down by the elevator to the huge cavern, where a jeep and a truck were parked, driverless and empty. He pushed a button by the elevator door to illuminate the cave temporarily, and led me across to one of the great steel tunnel doors, where he pushed his 'credit' card into a slot and punched out a code on a little panel of numbered buttons.

The door slid smoothly back into the cavern wall. Far behind, in the other direction, gleamed a distant penny of daylight where the exit road led out into Lhasa city.

NINETEEN

We eventually reached a room duplicating the War Room underneath the Procyon Embassy in Miami. With the same rows of desk consoles. The same display screens. The yantra nest. The Star Beast looming. Twenty or thirty Dobdobs, each with three pencils, sat at the consoles monitoring the situation.

'The men of war,' Feng murmured to me, as we passed by. 'The Rakshasa Embassy is always on a war footing, of course, but there was a genuine surprise alert not so long ago – as you know from poor Kushog's experience – so they're doubly on their toes during Maimouna's flight. These people are fighting a war. I hate to think who they would be fighting, if it weren't for the Star Beast.'

I felt sympathy for these obsessed fanatics who all, now that I looked more closely, had something of a Sam Shaw about them – Chinese, Koreans, Mongols, Arabs or whatever race they were.

'They'd be fighting your future human.'

'Fighting our own future, yes. What a criminal prospect. Still, this way, even the potential criminals have a positive role to play. So they aren't criminals at all. They're saved. Put them in a War Room with nuclear missiles to fire and a human enemy to hate, though! Then they'd be real criminals.'

We walked along a circuitous corridor lit by dim yellow lights. I had the impression that we came round almost a full circle in the end, bringing us nearly backing up against the War Room.

Feng unlocked a bright, merry little room with a single large, kaleidoscopic machine in it, curving round a swivel chair, and looking like a computer keyboard mated to an organ in the most baroque, fantastic style. Over it, to left, right and centre, were three illuminated display screens. It was the machine itself that made the room seem merry, compared with the rest of this underground complex, where dour military purpose prevailed. This might have been a machine for playing music to all the senses at once – a scent and colour and taste organ, if such a thing existed! A machine for enchanting the whole human body-field. Dials and switches, pedals, buttons and pistons were all the colours of the rainbow.

The machine was functioning of its own accord, though no one was sitting in the seat. Switches flipped, dials turned, pedals sank and rose fast and fluently. And the screen displays pulsed accordingly. It was quite a small machine, really. The swivel seat was deceptive – almost too small for most adults to sit at ... A child's seat.

On the left-hand screen floated the Star Beast, throbbing about the bindu point of planet Earth. As for the right-hand screen ... Red clouds drifting past tall spires. A blazing, colour-drenched sky resting on spires ... I saw a stingray swimming up out of the mists to meet me: and swelling out – till it had almost the same contours as the Star Beast. This must be an illusory 'Rakshasa' – and the landscape an illusion of the moon of Barnard's Star.

The middle screen mystified me, though. A curious, soft skull swayed and trembled towards me, never still, never quite the same shape either. A great ram's skull. Its horns splayed out into soft buds at the tips. It had a single long nostril, with two minor cul-de-sacs near the top of it. And a great triangular lowered brow, from which pink tubes led out along the insides of the horns, away from the red bone of the brow. Away towards the end of one of these horns glowed a tiny star of light: a bindu dot. For symmetry, this little star should have been on the forehead of the beast; perhaps it was moving towards that position, ever so slowly – then it would perfectly correspond with that star of light which was Earth, cocooned in its web of yantra forces. Ram's skull, Rakshasa and Star Beast were all basically the same shape. Unlike the Rakshasa illusion and the abstract Star Beast, though, the ram's skull looked more alive, more real, as it flexed and throbbed. The top of a 'spine' seemed to enter the base of the single 'nostril' of the skull from below, too, pushing up and sinking down again, in a slow piston action.

'Can you identify the middle screen, Lila?'

'I don't know. It looks alive. Real.'

'Indeed it is! That's a human womb, during love-making. It's Maimouna's womb, scanned through the belly-pad. She's flying, right now.'

'That dot of light. See? It's the egg coming along the Fallopian tube. When she flies again in eight days' time, it'll be fertilized and stuck fast in the womb, growing rapidly . . .'

The star on the forehead, in place!

The nostril was the vagina. The pink shield above – the lowered brow – was the uterus. The horns branching away were the Fallopian tubes. Of course!

Switches flipped and pedals moved in and out spontaneously. On the screens, Star Beast and Rakshasa pulsed in patterns related to the events in Maimouna's body, the physical joining of her and her lover and the intersection of her own body-field with her lover's; Mular, yes, that was his name. Star Beast and Rakshasa copied the changes in field configurations; copied – and modulated too, influencing the body-field events presiding over the egg's journey to conception. Lines of force rippled along the ram's horns, created a cradle of interference patterns, and the womb boomed faintly – a triangular drum with curved sides, held taut between two Fallopian tubes and a vagina.

'This is just a slave unit, to record the moves. So we can supervise, if necessary. A back-up system. The machine actually being used is in a monastery on top of Mount Ga Dan some way east of here. That's your Tibetan equivalent of Virginia beach. For the Bardo born. A beautiful, isolated place.'

The controls moved with a zombie life of their own, as though possessed. Somewhere, kilometres east of Lhasa, fingers were flickering over these pedals, playing body-field music. Childish feet were dancing on the pedals. One of the Bardo-born was playing with creation, right inside Maimouna's womb.

And with this toy he, or she, imprinted a pattern on the earliest moments of life – before life, even.

With this toy a child was making a baby be *something else*.

A baby such as my own Yungi!

Enthralled, and horrified, I was only vaguely paying attention to Feng's words.

'. . . How do you persuade submerged genes to express themselves, if you don't know exactly which ones they are? What

155

you *can* do is to provide the egg with the body-field environment that will draw them out, if they're there, from the moment of conception. The subtle body of old Taoist medicine is no figment of the imagination. It can certainly be brought to bear, this way, on something as delicate as the genome, as I said to you before.'

Lights flickered, pedals moved. Somewhere upstairs, in a slow trance, Maimouna made love to her Indian, bewitched by false sights, false sounds, and hypnosis.

'You must realize that the very physical elements themselves, such as sodium and potassium, of which our bodies and our brains are made exist *because* there are already forms — configurations — corresponding to them in the universe. Geometric entities of enormous power. Our brains exist, and function as they do, because these entities exist! And our brains are structured to evolve towards a knowledge of these underlying forms. Our ordinary body-field already represents them in a primitive way. The more integrated body-field of the Bardo-born represents them much better—'

Some alien brat was playing music on her body: just as it had been played on mine, and hers, in Miami!

'. . . Now, these forms aren't passive. They pull the wavefront of Being towards them. They act as *attractors*. That's how we draw Future Man into being. We collaborate with the geometry of the universe itself. The form of game we play on a machine like this, is the game of life unfolding to understand itself—'

The idea of the whole world of living, working, breathing, loving human beings deliberately run as a biological *game,* for some warped ideal of an alien superhumanity, sickened me. Feng was a traitor to the human race that already existed here and now. What existed was what mattered! Living *now* made a person — or a fish, for that matter — *real*. Worshipping the future was a sickness. An arrogance. A deceit. When Man tried to take control of his own evolution, he obviously became — inhuman. The proof was before my eyes — and burned into Kushog's brain. Inhumanity!

'Attractor lines,' recited Feng. 'Canalized trajectories . . . spontaneous emergence . . . chreodic channels . . . levels of consciousness . . . embryo . . . body-field . . .' He gabbled his biological gospel at me.

Maimouna would have sold herself to him at the drop of a hat for a taste of this sort of power.

But *I* threw myself at the machine that was making an alien of her baby.

I tore at the dials and switches. They wouldn't move. They were locked rigid – except when they moved of their own accord; then they forced my hands away, bruising and hurting them. I might as well have stuck my fingers into a running engine.

I fought the machine in some accelerated moment of time – leaving Feng wallowing behind me in slow motion. Then he caught up with me and pulled me away roughly, anxiously hovering over his precious machine in case it was hurt.

'Fool!' he said.

And I hit him.

My hand snatched a fire extinguisher from its bracket. It wasn't a fire extinguisher just then; I only knew what it was afterwards. It was a club of red steel, the colour of pain and blood. My hand caught it and hit him with it.

He slumped across his Body-field Organ. There was a little blood on the back of his skull, but not much, and he was still breathing; his pulse felt strong.

He hadn't expected anyone could be angry enough to hit him, in the world that Bardo had brainwashed. Because he only thought about people as abstract things. Not as humans. Not as individuals. That was an oversight.

Suddenly, I knew where I had to go. I pulled my own Bardo uniform off, then Feng's. Naked, his limbs were thin and straw-coloured, with ridges and creases. He was a big crumpled spider. One of his pencils had fallen out of his pocket. I kicked it under the machine. Three pencils was quite enough spurious rank for me. I dressed in his clothes, then tied his wrists and ankles with my own torn-up tunic, gagged him, and stuffed the remains under his head to support it. He would be waking up. I tore out the telephone cable, then locked the door on him with his own key and raced back round the corridor in the direction of the War Room. The noise of my sandals slapped back from the walls like startled bats. I was perversely happy. I was shivering with happiness now.

I ducked past the War Room, where those fools were betraying their world without knowing it. Arriving at last at the steel door, I pushed Feng's credit card into the slot and punched the same pattern of buttons as I'd seen him do. Intellectually, Feng might have known I have a good visual memory; he didn't take precautions against it.

The door rolled back quietly. The parking space still held the jeep, though someone had moved the truck out in the meanwhile.

But I'd never driven anything in my life.

And what about the checkpoint at the tunnel mouth? Would they really believe I was a Dobdob? I thought back. Was there a steel bar blocking the road, the same as at the Miami checkpoint?

No, there wasn't. Because massive steel doors could block the tunnel entrance in a few seconds – so a simple pole wasn't necessary! I could drive straight out into the open.

If I could drive. Shifting over into the passenger seat, I inspected the controls from that angle; from where I'd been sitting when Feng drove me here, with Maimouna in the rear. Concentrating, I tried to recall the pattern of movements of Feng's hands and feet when starting the vehicle and driving it; then I slid back into the driver's seat and turned the key. The engine sprang to life.

The jeep promptly jumped forward a few paces and the engine died. At the same time the cavern lights, on their time-switch, blacked out, plunging me into darkness.

I fumbled the jeep's headlights on and the rock wall lit up in front of me; also the speed-clock, but there was still precious little light in the jeep itself.

And I thought. How once, long ago, in a shuttered room in Bagamoyo, a Chinese man had measured my skull with his fingers, in light almost as dim as this, with his eyes closed. His fingers had moved across my head by touch alone. To look with the eyes would have been to fail to see.

So, calmly, I sat in the darkness, breathing in and out. After a while, I let my own body do what it chose to do, of its own accord. My hands and feet found that they knew what to do with the gear-stick and the three pedals on the floor. Pushing my foot down I pulled the stick into a nowhere-place, then backwards. My fingers switched the engine on again; my foot rose from the floor. The jeep backed out as I swung the wheel, and we were pointing the right way.

The jeep bounded out of the cave, into the tunnel – bucking and lurching a little, since my body didn't know how to drive it all that well. Once it scraped the wall. But it drove; it drove. And fast.

I passed the checkpoint at speed, waving a non-committal hand at the Dobdobs. One of them ran out into the road (in my mirror) and shouted after me; but I was already turning on to the long road with the archway and dodging cyclists, goats, a bullock.

As soon as I was at least a kilometre from the palace I braked the jeep beside a group of boys in quilted jackets with long sleeves doubled at the cuffs. There was a chain of mountains to the east, and the road was heading almost due east; but which mountain was Mount Ga Dan?

I repeated the name half a dozen times to the boys, miming 'Where?' One of them giggled helplessly, perhaps at my pronunciation; perhaps he had never met a black woman before. Another boy cuffed him reprovingly. A third boy laid his hand on mine, however, and pointed away down the road. Away and away.

'Ga dan si,' he confirmed. 'Ga dan si.'

How far was it? I tried to gesture. The boy who had cuffed the giggler frowned at me and the other boy. When I tapped the pencils in my pocket, he only frowned more, and looked more suspicious. Why did I not know where it was, if I wanted to go there, even if I was wearing a Dobdob's uniform? He pursed his lips, then questioned me, politely but firmly in Tibetan; then in Chinese. I ignored him. Fortunately, so did the boy who was pointing my way to me. He ran round the front of the jeep and scrambled into the passenger seat, gesturing me to drive on. I had a guide.

The other boy ran round the back of the jeep and plucked

at his friend's sleeve sternly; but by then I was already driving off – with my guide laughing in the other boy's face.

In the mirror, I saw the boys running back along the road in the direction of the Potala. I drove faster, killing a hen in a spate of brown feathers.

TWENTY

Eastwards out of Lhasa the road was wide and empty. I had more feel of the jeep by now and drove easily, looking around at the landscape, free and in the open for the first time in nearly two years.

Thin copses of poplars separated green wheat fields from apple orchards. A caterpillar tractor, with wood smoke puffing from its funnel, was dragging a wide disc harrow through a vast field of soil. Riders on roan ponies were cutting over it, rifles with curved double bayonets over their shoulders. I guessed the double bayonets must be used for spearing any game they shot, at the gallop, without dismounting. A cement works was half hidden behind windbreaks of willows whose cascading foliage was white with dust . . .

My guide sat silent, realizing that we couldn't communicate. Did *he* think I was a proper Dobdob? Or was he a little rebel, off on an adventure? He had characteristically huge Tibetan features: strong nose and jaw, slabs of cheeks, and broadly-set eyes. However, an impish curiosity speckled his countenance, like gold in butter.

The journey took the best part of an hour, I estimated. Mount Ga Dan must have been at least sixty kilometres from Lhasa. For thirty of these we were driving through tall pines and firs and spruces – product of the great reafforestation of which Maimouna boasted. Then at last we emerged on to a broad strip of waste land, fallow and unused, a sort of barren zone, a no-man's land; and the boy was pointing up, and nodding.

Ga Dan was only properly a foothill to the stark, rocky giants behind it. Still, it looked big enough to me. Staring up into the sky, I could just make out large buildings clambering up one another to the summit like a flight of stairs. However, what lay lower down its flanks was hidden by steep forest. It looked as though the carpet of trees had been torn apart here and the end dragged up around the mountain in a cloak. Indeed, tonnes of topsoil must have been hauled back up the slopes at one time and bound with grass and bushes. Other neighbouring hills remained as sterile and stony as was Ga Dan nearer its summit.

We drove across this no-man's land into the first dense foliage of the slopes. And here, in the woods, we came to a halt – firstly because the road took a sharp uphill turn, stalling the engine; but also because a large board by the roadside bore a red warning swastika, with lines of Tibetan and Chinese script. Through the foliage, coming to meet the road around the very next bend I caught sight of a high wire fence, no doubt converging on a checkpoint. I pulled the hand brake on.

The boy jerked a thumb inquiringly at my uniform, then up the road, urging me on. He wanted to see what was round the bend, beyond that fence. That was why he'd come. This was his adventure, his ambition. When I shook my head, he looked disappointed, then confused and alarmed – as though I was some demon he was caught in the woods with. Black Kali, who stamps on graves, no less! Deep down, he was probably as superstitious as Kushog.

A cloud happened to pass over the sun just then. Its shadow swooped down through the woods, drinking the daylight. The boy uttered a cry and scrambled out of the jeep. He fled off as fast as his felt boots would carry him down the road – not, thank God, the other way.

It was just as well to be rid of him. I ought to have dropped him off on the other side of the waste land. Abandoning the jeep myself, I cut away from the road through the trees.

The woods were pleasantly scented and buzzy with insects, the ground underfoot softly crunchy with years of fallen pine needles.

The fence, however, was high, sharply-barbed, and in good repair. Red swastika plaques dangled from it every hundred metres or so. A rabbit's bones and fur lay crumpled up against the wire. This might have been pure coincidence, but I didn't dare touch the fence now, in case it was electrified. It might well be. Fences around the eland parks inland from Bagamoyo were electrified to keep the beasts in.

I followed the fence through the woods, right away from the road, till I came to a stream that had undercut its banks, washing out sufficient space to wriggle through safely, at the cost of getting my uniform a bit wet and muddy. Then I really started to climb Mount Ga Dan, while the early afternoon sun intermittently stewed my neck through the branches. I paused frequently, not so much out of breath as to avoid an attack of giddiness at this height.

The first sign of life I came to, after maybe twenty minutes, was an orange and white pagoda rising through the trees. Four zigzag storeys perched on top of each other with doors opening out on to each succeeding rooftop. On top of these four storeys squatted a round bastion with a doorway set into a splendid peacock's tail mosaic. This in turn supported a cubic room with a dome, from which rose the final, stubby cone of a minaret. A low doorway leading from the cube room on to the bastion roof was flanked by huge painted eyes: wavy and elongated under the flared brows of roof guttering.

I walked around to the building's northern side, keeping to the trees.

There, on the round bastion roof, a naked youth stood staring down at me. *The youth had wings.*

The wings were white-feathered, tipped with red; each with a large black spot, like the mock eyes on a butterfly's wings.

He walked closer to the edge. The wings stayed where they were. They weren't wings at all . . . but *eyes* – another pair of those undulating painted eyes. The black spots were the pupils of the eyes. Yet the shock junction of his naked body with the ornamented doorway behind him (and perhaps a touch of sunlight in my eyes) had really made me *see* a winged youth – till he moved. The illusion still lingered, even so! His bare shoulders looked strangely deprived now – with the eye-wings floating disembodied behind him – as though the illusion wasn't exactly an accident, but that he had stood there deliberately to take advantage of it. His nude body looked as puce and stringy with muscle as a skinned rabbit's. Black hair was knotted behind his head. His face was sharply avian, with an eagle's beak of a nose.

By now he was virtually standing over empty space, since

there was nothing underneath the lip of tiles supporting him but a ten metre fall to the zigzag roof below. He poised himself, then suddenly squatted with a fluid motion. He lowered his legs over this thin rim and flipped his body forward and sideways. His arms twisted lithely upwards, so that his fingers caught the tile rim. This held him motionless for an instant. Then he dropped the rest of the way to the roof below. It was three or four times his own height that he dropped. Impact rolled him up into a ball. But he bounced up promptly, stepped to the edge of this next roof and dropped himelf off it too, using the same technique of catch and fall. And so on, down the other giant steps of the pagoda, to the ground – watching me all the time as though his gymnastics took no special concentration.

He looked several years younger than me. Fourteen or fifteen. Hard to tell for sure, since the pagoda dwarfed him – yet equally *he* dwarfed *it* when he dismounted from it so casually. Since he was still staring at me intently, I parted the branches and stepped into the small clearing surrounding the pagoda.

'I am Strider-Over-Buildings,' he told me (in Chinese first – I supposed – and then in English, when I looked blank).

'Oh yes. And why do you stride over buildings? What's inside that building, anyway?' I could see how his nose had been badly broken by a fall once. Which was why it looked so hooked. He hadn't always been so inhumanly agile.

He seemed surprised by the questions.

'Buildings enclose human beings, don't they? Right! So, a Strider-Over-Buildings encloses these enclosures. Buildings are boundaries, consequently I bound over them.' He laughed. (Cackled?) 'Do you see the plan of this building? A yantra mandala in three dimensions—'

'I see it.'

'Yantras are simple mental maps. Therefore this building is a thought machine. A sort of brain.'

'It contains a computer? One of your baby-making machines?'

'You don't understand. This pagoda is a *model* of a brain. How is it a brain? Well, the lower floors are the ancient hindbrain, obviously. The round floor above is the midbrain. The floor of the Eyes, that's the forebrain. Man is a monkey riding on a lizard's back, which was once a fish. Look out of any window on the way up; a different view appears. The windows construct the views. Without the building, there would be no views. So how do you grasp the entire building, and all its views at once? Simple! My body strides over it, then the building is memorized inside my muscles. My body has mapped it. My movements become *ideas*. The muscles think too, you know. The pagoda is a mental exercise – for the body!

'Come inside the building. Once inside it, you're inside *me*. We'll understand each other better in the building.'

'What's in it? I haven't time to waste!' It was mid-afternoon already. 'Is there anything in there?'

'What is in there,' he retorted, 'is simply the chance of seeing what is outside. Of course, this chance couldn't exist, were it not for the building. The building contains *itself*, that's all!'

'It's empty.'

'Are you stupid? I just told you what is in it.'

'Where are the machines Bardo uses? Further up the mountain?'

'What is a machine, girl? Obviously this building is a machine. Depending on how you see it. A thinking-machine.'

'I mean the machine for playing the Rakshasa game. Tell me the way, will you? You must know what a Rakshasa is?'

'I was a Rakshasa. Any child is. That's before I became a Strider-Over-Buildings. Before I gave the problems to my own body to solve physically. How could I have found out anything about the *meaning* of this building, except by climbing it both inside and out?'

'Damn you!' I swore, and ran on past him into the trees, uphill.

A hundred metres higher, I looked back. The youth was still on the same level as me, watching me. He must have raced up inside the pagoda. He was back on the round roof, with 'wings' outstretched. Apparently hovering, levitating.

I climbed for another half an hour after leaving this infuriating boy, and passed many other buildings, and structures resembling buildings, buried away in the woods. There were ancient Tibetan pavilions with verandahs and swooping golden roofs. There were blank oblong towers. Later, tucked away among the trees, were constructions quite alien in appearance, which seemed to belong to no human place or time, but rather to some zone of pure geometry.

I circled a featureless, milky white sphere fifty metres high, made of glass or pottery, fitting into the lap of a dell like a huge egg in an eggcup. An impatient, finger-drumming music pulsed from inside it, as though it was getting ready to hatch.

I came upon clusters of ten-metre-tall coloured crystals which were squeezing aside the trees, as though they'd sprouted of their own accord rather than been put there by anyone. Or, if they had been 'seeded' there, they were continuing to grow spontaneously. Among them were all kinds of polyhedra, from the simplest to the most complicated, with colours hovering between pure shades: colours at the visual borderlines where blue blends into green, or purple into violet, or even red into infra-red. For an instant I imagined I was actually seeing infra-red light from one of them with my own eyes. Light was astray in these groves of crystals; time too. Shining in the heart of one great diamond-shape was the white midday sun – though the real sun was sinking by now. A ruby shape held the swollen red ellipsoid of the dawn sun in it. A looming amethyst held night – velvet dark, with a galaxy of star-flecks, silver flakes suspended in black oil.

Further on, inside a transparent golden crystal flask, apparently full of liquid, a girl's nude body hung. Upright and motionless. She had small breasts, long trailing legs, all the gawkiness of adolescence. Her toes didn't touch the base of the crystal flask, nor her head its top, which had a silver metal cap. A trailing mosquito of a girl, trapped in amber, she hung there. Alive; with her eyes wide open; but not a finger twitched, not a bubble rose from her lips.

Whatever was she floating in? It wasn't water, or she would have drifted upwards – unless, perhaps, she had learned to breathe water and her lungs were full of it!

Pressing up against the golden wall, I thought I could make out a thin membrane covering her body like a second skin. Maybe she took what oxygen she needed in her trance from the jelly-like fluid, through this second 'skin'.

Whatever was she studying by floating daylong in a vat of golden fluid, staring at the same point in space while the sun rose and set? Was she drugged, or was she there voluntarily? I had a vague feeling that she registered my presence, after a while. Just a feeling. I went away.

Of the many other crystals I saw in this part of the woods, half a dozen held adolescent bodies floating in them.

Yidags! I realized. That's what these crystals were. Some of them, anyway. A muzzy TV picture would show Yidags where the crystals stood – with human beings apparently reflected in them. The majority of Yidags must be in Kazakhstan but they were here too – great crystal bottles. With human bodies floating in them, in a trance.

These crystals made the woods hum and purr around them, as though signals or resonances were passing between them. At first I thought I was just hearing the hum of bees and grasshoppers. But – *chirr! chirr!* – there it was, off in the infra-red of sound.

Next, a wet devastation opened out among the trees. A great scab of flattened, muddy slope, with a double circle of clay huts built in the midst of it and a lane of clay hoops leading out across the mud.

Water trickled constantly down the incline, like lymph from ruptured tissues, spreading ooze and slime ankle-deep. And in this mess was built the village that Kushog had seen – with the same stone spit at the heart of all. The same Claypeople were moving about. I recognized them as human children in disguise only because the floppy black hooded coveralls they all wore had the hoods down at the moment. Fair tousled Caucasian heads, frizzled African heads, glossy Polynesian heads poked out. With heads fully hooded, I'd have seen a herd of slithering seals or walking worms – just as Kushog had. To move about at all through that tilted morass involved wriggling, sliding and undulating. All this water – source of the stream that had gained me access, and several other streams no doubt, nourishing the rich vegetation – must be pumped up Ga Dan, prodigally, all the way from the Kyi or Yalutsangpo . . .

Overshadowing the village hung a long grey balloon tethered by cables – with banks of lights visible inside the skin which I guessed must change its present dank grey to silver 'dawn' or whatever else they chose to floodlight the village with. Aerials and other paraphernalia jutted out of a nacelle in its fat snout, some pointing at the ground and others westwards in the direction of Lhasa. While I watched, a spidery ladder uncoiled from the nacelle, letting a swaying black worm scramble down towards the mud.

Did the Rakshasa world – wherever its stage-set was – have a similar balloon tethered overhead, as an imitation 'gas-giant'? Very likely!

I certainly had no intention of getting caught up in any cooking games. I carefully skirted this sodden scab of open land, and headed on up through the trees.

Till I came to the Prism.

I'll call it that. That's what it looked like. A five-metre-high wedge of solid glass, or rock crystal, in the middle of a small clearing. It cast a fan of rainbow light across the earth; and the earth itself, hard and smooth as a china plate, had a mandala of thick silver wires or rods embedded in it like a complicated, life-size printed circuit. A schematic city with four gates at the four points of the compass, and as large as the foundations of a small house, this mandala seemed like the ground plan for a yet unbuilt building of considerable complexity, collapsed into two-dimensional space. Where the traditional mandala design places lotus blossoms and sacred umbrellas, there shone metal mirrors – discharging the prismatic light falling on that unreal, magic city out into the trees, the leaves flickering with rainbow colours like humming birds. A feather of violet sat on my shoulder. A wing of topaz danced on my palm. I felt the hot rush of living colour on my cheek.

It was so enchanting; that tall translucent prism, the map of silver on the ground, the chromatic scattering. A detached, logical part of me recorded that in point of fact the prism wasn't planted at all deeply in the soil. On the contrary, it was resting right on the surface, upon a slightly concave base – like one of those rocking stones one hears about, deposited by glaciers upon mountains, which look massively heavy, which a finger's touch can sway, yet which no force can topple. Indeed the breeze, gentle as it was, seemed to be swaying this prism as I watched, giving wings to light.

As I stepped out of the foliage into the clearing, the walls and pathways of the mandala came even more alive with light.

They became a living mind-city before my eyes, a maze of consciousness. My feet walked forward of their own accord. Helplessly, not wishing to help myself, I entered the east gate of the mandala. All my life seemed to lead to this moment.

And I was trapped.

I was an abstract entity, made up of beams of light alone. All my thoughts and sensations were pure shapes of light. Yet I knew that I had a black, surly *matter* existence, really. What *was* matter, though? Matter was only energy bound up so tightly that it couldn't escape back into energy again – back into light. Yet there had to be matter (my solid black body) or what could light illuminate? There had to be matter, or light was unfulfilled. Without it, there would be no light. Was a ray of light 'light' while it was passing through space from its source to its destination? No, it was pure potential. It was pre-light. Light shines *on* something. The energy of light needed the dark energy locked up in matter, to fulfil itself. Yet the instant of seeing light extinguished light. Light was like the 'present moment' of time. It hardly existed at all. It ceased to exist as soon as it came into being. Yet at the same time it was everything, the whole of everything there was, right now. And at the same time it was *nothing*: it had already ceased to exist. Energy was only a message from itself to itself, saying nothing except: I am! That was the whole message of light and life. Such an idiot message. Such an idiot universe – that simply *is*! The Star Beast – this entity which existed in a total present that spanned all of time, and which represented the universe as a single instant . . . whereby the universe hardly existed at all, but merely floated as a tendency, a ripple in a void and a nothingness infinitely denser than any material cosmos! – this Star Beast which was pure Consciousness without any object but itself, swam out at me from the mandala. And swallowed me.

TWENTY-ONE

I woke up in a small stone room with a thin window showing (morning?) sky with huge puffs of cloud ... It was so bright.

Where was my Yungi? Had she been born yet? Of course, or she wouldn't have a name! Where was she then?

I remembered fat Kushog bursting into my room, after which they took my Yungi away in case he had injured her ... But how could he have harmed her? With what? His own body had already been cooked, his feet stuffed in his mouth, till he evaporated – leaving only his mind running round in circles, in a hoop of clay! Claychildren had done this to him: Claychildren on a mountainside. Yungi had been taken from me to become one of them ...

Maimouna would be taken off too, to hang in golden fluid in a globe which the purring forest would wear in its ear ...!

And I'd been taken too – from Africa, from the magic of finding a coco-de-mer, from flame trees, from humpbacked cattle grazing on the beach, from the beauty of life buoyed up forever by our faith in our Alien Friends.

Now I lay in a stone balloon in the sky ... As clouds unmasked the sun, light poured through the window slit, drenching the room. The bed fluoresced. Mandalas flared and spangled at me from the buckling, glowing stones of the walls; and I was thrown back into a clearing on a hillside, where I was entering the gate of the Mandala of Exalted Consciousness – wherein the Star Beast hides, with its monstrous knowledge of everything and nothing!

'No!' I screamed, pressing my hands over my eyes. (There was light behind my eyelids, though! As if my eyelids had been cut off.)

Someone walked into the room. Someone shuttered the window with a bang. I felt someone sit at the foot of my bed.

As the light behind my eyelids dimmed, I opened my eyes

again, a little way. The room was dimming too, its multiple images of itself sorting themselves out into one single stone cell.

The someone who sat on my bed was Feng, with a bandaged head.

'Where's my Yungi, Feng?'

'In the Potala. In the crèche. Being looked after, while you run away.' (Said quite gently, though.)

'Where am I?'

'You're in the Ga Dan monastery – right at the top of the mountain. That's where you wanted to get to, isn't it?'

The room was fairly calm now, almost dim. A soothing stone cave, a burrow. I knew how mice must feel when they've escaped a hawk in the sun and dived deep down a hole. But while I thought how safe it was, the room rippled again!

'Everything's floating, Feng! Nothing's holding it up, but itself!'

'The building you're in, my dear, is quite solid, I assure you. It was put up in the year 1409 by a certain Zong Ka-pa, founder of the so-called Yellow Cap sect—'

'Feng, I'm scared. The room came alive. No, my mind came alive. More alive, I mean. My mind was all mirrors for my thoughts. The mirrors were there to show me them, but all that I could *think* was mirror beyond mirror, with nothing in them. Feng, the universe doesn't mean anything, it just is. There's no meaning. Life is just *being alive.* I hit you, didn't I? I'm sorry. I had to—'

'To see for yourself. Now you've seen. That's to say, you've seen a *little.* It overloaded you. Because you aren't ready to look at reality. Don't forget what a nest of separate sub-systems, often mutually deaf and dumb, your own mind is! How you drift from one phase of consciousness to another, buoyed up by the blithe illusion that the same "I" is always present. What a constant, repetitive chatter of noise goes on in your head, just to reassure you of your own identity and wisdom. Yungi may be able to see what you can't, when she's older. You'd better get some rest. Restore your equilibrium.'

A bell jangled in the next room, or the one beyond. Feng excused himself.

171

Though the room rocked and glowed, I got up after half a minute and followed him. The room immediately next to mine was empty, apart from a carved wooden chair crawling with dragons, a large golden oil lamp, and a television. Out of curiosity, I switched the set on – and the familiar, throbbing ram's head swam into being. A Rakshasa – *alias* somebody's womb. The spawning ground for aliens, whose minds could match this Star Beast of a universe. Maybe in this very building sat a child as devilish as a Claything, playing biological music, luring humanity towards inhumanity.

Feng's voice came from the room beyond. I glanced round the door. It was a largish hall, with a dazzling woven mandala of a carpet, and a few flat tasselled cushions to sit on, on the far side. The carpet wriggled and leered at me. It flowed forward to trap my feet. Each strand of dyed wool was a live sticky tendril beaded with bright attractive saliva to wrap round my legs and drag me down into its pattern to make more sticky poisonous threads.

Slipping back into the darker anteroom, I listened to the two people who were sitting calmly on cushions on that awful, devouring carpet. One, of course, was Feng. The other was a pregnant young woman, with a round apricot face and black hair swept back in a pigtail which reached all the way to the carpet, where it warred with the weave, flicking and teasing it as she moved her head. A prehensile tail sprouting from the back of her head.

Feng seemed angry. 'It isn't a pleasant or an easy task to rebuke your superiors,' he was saying tightly. 'However, I really should advise you that our "Men of War" in the Embassy were quite upset by the escapade. Whose idea was it? Remember that ordinary human beings are still in the majority. Bardo has to concern itself with breeding out of them for at least another two centuries.'

'But Feng, we've never tested the chrysalis procedure in interaction with old humans.'

'And now that boy Kushog's in a catatonic trance.'

'His hypnosis of the guard showed a high degree of mental control. He may be in a chrysalis state of his own right now. When he comes out of it in another few weeks—'

'No, he's showing the same brain pattern as for the encephalitis. The failure pattern. You ruined him.'

'The experiment has to be tried. If we could force the chrysalis transition on the best of the old humans—'

'Listen to me. The wasps' nest still has enough potential sting to destroy Bardo. If events took the wrong turn—'

The woman interrupted. 'The Council think we should reduce the birth quota per head of population to zero point nine per couple. This will phase out the old population a little faster, but still quite gently. Over a period of, say, five hundred years, instead of seven. At the same time, it means we have progressively less genetic pool to draw on, to attain our own optimum population level. If we could induce change in the normal population, the whole process could be speeded up. That's the main reason for the recent interference. To see if it can be done. We know a lot more about the mental structures involved than in the beginning.'

'There's still a good argument for maintaining a large co-existing old population, you know! How many High Adepts can Nature afford? You have to have farmers and technicians. You have to have administrators and social scientists.'

'Like yourself, Feng, yes. But that isn't a stable solution. Not when the chrysalis phase is a general biological crisis for Humanity, as surely as puberty is. After a while you're going to find that the gene pool is fished dry, don't you see? The recessive characteristics will be far too diluted, in the residue. There'll be nothing left to emerge from Old Man. There'll be that huge residue.'

'Who'll still form a majority, numerically.'

'Exactly. That's why it will be marvellous if the Change could be induced in anyone with a promising body-field.'

'What about the discrepancy between *ourselves* after the Change? We still understand so little about this. Are we all eventually supposed to become High Adepts, after another thousand years? Or will there always be the Low Adepts too? Or will they be phased out as well?'

'Time and the High Adepts will tell us that. We really should press ahead with the Kushog sort of thing, for everyone's benefit.'

I stepped out into the hall, defying the shimmering carpet and all its sticky tendrils, stared straight into that bland apricot face and demanded:

'*What are High Adepts? What is this about reducing the population to nothing? What are you talking about?*'

'Ah, Lila!' said the woman, unperturbed. 'That's your name, isn't it? You blundered into one of the Teaching Machines on your way up the mountain? But you're still upright and sane. Congratulations. It encourages us to press ahead.'

'Your carpet is trying to eat me, but I won't let it!'

'Don't!' She laughed, smacking the floor, sending woven waves rippling towards me. 'Impertinent carpet. You'll have to walk across it, if you want an answer to your question.' She cocked her head on one side and waited, while the trailing end of her pigtail twitched from side to side like the tip of a cat's tail.

'I don't know *your* name.' I stamped my foot on the carpet's edge. The carpet subsided and behaved like a carpet wherever I walked, though distant parts of it continued to surge and heave and open chasms.

'It's Fatumeh.'

As soon as I reached the centre of the carpet – guarded by blue elephants flourishing umbrellas in their curly trunks – and stamped these down flat, Fatumeh uncoiled herself smoothly from the cushion and held out her hand to pull me to safety. Briefly she held my hand to her belly, to emphasize that she was pregnant. Her gesture both blessed me and cautioned me. She seemed utterly innocent of any vileness in what had happened to Kushog or in what she was so casually discussing with Feng.

'What people never actually realized, even when the theory of evolution was accepted,' she said gaily to me, as though continuing a conversation begun long ago – as indeed it had been, by Feng, 'is that Humanity didn't stand outside it as an observer. On the contrary! Humanity would obviously have to pass away, as surely as the hominid pre-humans passed away. A new form of being was going to take its place. But how many people felt this in their guts? How many of the old biologists, anthropologists or philosophers? Not many at all.'

'If I was a prehistoric fish and if there was any way you could really make me *see* my billionth descendant . . . I'd throw myself ashore in despair at being where I was. I'd lose the whole wonder of living the life I actually had!'

'Or you might just discover that you could breathe air, if you chucked yourself ashore like that!' She grinned. 'Even to be part of a long slow process of change and to know about it is surely exhilarating. Don't you think so? Just imagine how much more thrilling it must be actually to feel yourself evolve *in this present life.*'

'Individuals can't evolve. The Star Beast epidemic proved that. If there ever was a Star Beast epidemic!'

'Did it prove that? Man is a neotenous animal, Lila. Once upon a time we would have defined this by saying that Man stays in a juvenile form for many years, up till adulthood. So there's plenty of time for a highly co-ordinated being to mature. But neoteny's quite common in nature, in another sense. Tadpoles and caterpillars are the neotenous forms of frog and butterfly. There's a chrysalis stage in between. During it, feeding and locomotion come to a full stop, while great developmental changes are taking place inside. Afterwards a new, different sort of being emerges.

'Imagine the contrast in world-outlook, puny as their minds still are, between the caterpillar and the butterfly! Try to conceive the sheer reorganization of the nervous system which goes on at the same time as grosser physical changes – such as the sprouting of wings – are taking place! Let me tell you that up until now a human being has been neotenous all his life! A larva from birth to death.

'Bardo brings together the submerged genes which allow a new human being to emerge from the Old Human. And it happens through a chrysalis stage – a puberty phase of the nervous system and body-field.'

'Providing that it's properly prepared for,' added Feng. 'Even the Bardo-born might pass unawares through the critical stage if they weren't primed for it – if they weren't able to go into stasis in the Yidag bottles or the clay hoops. We need to blank out the noisy chattering input of irrelevancies before the mind can turn round and examine itself and make new internal connections. The human caterpillar has got to have chewed on the business of life for a few years first, though. Its mind has to carry enough material for the metamorphosis to work upon.'

'A change in the pattern of the body-field tells us when the time is ripe,' nodded Fatumeh. 'But Feng's right. The change still has to be triggered, and insulated – by blanking out in the Yidag bottle or the clay hoop. They're more than just ceremonial rites of passage; though they're that *too*. They're an environment for radical change – a physical chrysalis to wear while the mind turns inwards and the nerve-cells rewire themselves. I know. I've hung in the dazzling tank, and come out new.'

'You don't look much like a butterfly to me. You haven't sprouted wings. You look like an ordinary human being.'

'The mind changes form, the brain pathways forge new links; the limbs don't change. Still, if you filmed my body-field by the Kirlian high-voltage method you'd see wings, if wings are what you need to see. Body-field wings! Wings of energy which I couldn't have grown except in the chrysalis of a Yidag. Yidag's far more than just a fantasy world that your comrades in Russia fly to. What are those supposed Yidag aliens? Superb data analysts! And they breed new Yidags.'

'By laser beam interference patterns. I've heard.'

'By being consciously aware of genetic data. They communicate genetic data openly, instead of its being hidden away in a coded sperm or egg package as it is with us. The information *structure*, you see, is revealed in the process of passing information, when two Yidags "mate". So the Yidag is the perfect emblem for the mind examining its own workings, and producing a new being as a consequence. Just as the Yidag game focuses the body-field properly during Bardo flights for the Russian fliers, so it prepares *our* children for the perfect chrysalis package. Do you see how neatly the "myth" and the *facts* of Bardo combine?'

'There's nothing arbitrary about our alien worlds,' said Feng. 'Each in its own way is very thoughtfully designed to bring the Bardo stamp to bear upon the conception of a new child – yanking the new pattern out of the Old Human pattern that submerges it! – at the very same time as it trains the child actually operating the game for the coming change in his own life.'

I shivered. 'The "Old Human"? You're saying that there never have been any "full" humans in this world – till now?'

'Exactly!' exclaimed Fatumeh. 'Only larval humans. Overgrown children whose capacity for the chrysalis change was just slowly building up, under the surface. No wonder the species acted so stupidly half the time! If the capacity ever did emerge accidentally in the past – and I suppose it must have done, by the laws of chance – any hope of going into stasis would be completely swamped by normalizing, brainwashing feedback from Old Humanity. Encephalitis? Sleeping sickness?' She laughed. 'Those epidemics were just foreshadowings of what might be possible – but gone askew, before their time. The coma, in its mature form, is a positive not a negative event. Naturally, we're sorry about Kushog's accident . . . It may be that only the Bardo-born minority have brains "wired" to accept this sort of complex change. Still, we'll keep on trying. Our High Adepts may find a way—'

'So Kushog's accident was an experiment to force the change upon what you call an "Old Human"!'

'Indeed it was. I'm not ashamed of it. He was switched online to an edited recording of the body-field and brain-wave functions of one of the Bardo-born undergoing the change – in a filmed location which I believe you've already seen.'

'That filthy scab of mud—'

'I still disagree with the experiment,' Feng said quietly.

'Maybe the error was in feeding him a High Adept experience instead of a Low Adept one,' allowed Fatumeh. 'We ought to repeat the experiment with another flier, using a Low Adept recording this time. And the bottle instead of the clay hoop.'

'For goodness' sake do it in Russia, then! In the normal Yidag context. Just so long as my Dobdobs in the Potala aren't ever thrown into a panic like that again! I really must insist. You simply can't risk sowing doubts about the Star Beast. Or you'll be *dead*. The old human race will cut its own head off.'

'High Adepts, Low Adepts!' I cried. 'Are there differences among you super-people, too? Are some not "super" enough?'

Fatumeh frowned briefly.

'Low Adepts don't emerge from the chrysalis quite so deeply

changed. The geometrical entities that draw life out of non-life – and consciousness out of living matter, and a higher consciousness still out of that! – aren't able to express themselves so fully. We can pretty well forecast from the body-fields of the growing children who will make the full leap, to High Adept – and who will only make half the leap. I'm only Low, myself.'

'Does that upset you?'

'Of course not. We stand between the High Adepts and the old humans, such as Feng – or yourself, who in turn stand between us and the mass of old humanity. Ours is a pivotal role. And we *have* made a leap, make no mistake.'

'Made half a leap!'

'Don't sneer. It only degrades you, Lila. Come! This is a matter for joy and celebration, not frowns and protests. Come down and see the emergence of an Adept. Today, as every day, we celebrate the smashing of another clay hoop or the decanting of another crystal bottle. To be a Low Adept is fine enough, believe me. I've gazed in that glass prism for hours, seeing the way things are.' She smiled dazzlingly.

'Anybody can hallucinate. It's just a hallucination producer, that prism.'

'Not hallucinating, *seeing*.'

'I saw the planet Asura once, but it was all lies and illusion.'

'I saw the young girl I had been,' she recounted raptly, 'the larva born of Bardo before I was a human being, and I saw the old woman I will be long after, my skin mummified yet stretching to contain this growing girl! For eternal moments I lived my whole life simultaneously, backward and forward, just as the universe itself exists. I lived my whole life through from beginning to end – not the exact details, but the general texture of my whole life – and it was *good*, even though it was terrifying too. It took a high indifference to overcome the terror, and profit from it.'

'Yes, your high indifference for human beings!'

'No, not that sort of indifference at all. A higher state of mind – accepting, existing. I was a simulation of God, pure consciousness, pure space, creating my life out of myself on a ripple of probabilities. I was the young person winding into the old, the old person woven around the young. The Prism held me tight and spun me within myself, like the "strangeness spin" of an atomic particle. My hundred years' probable life were pared to a point and dragged like wire through all my nerves, rewiring me to Universe-Time: time that *is* and *isn't* simultaneously – because the end of the universe, its highest co-ordination level, will form its own beginning. I live a little in Absolute Time now, Lila. Death means nothing to me. I always am. Can you understand this?'

The horror of my entrapment in the Prism!

'This universe is just a light bulb switching on and burning out a moment later,' I said. 'And there's not even a light bulb or a switch or a power source! There's just a kind of knot tied in nothingness that got pulled too tight and became something by accident for an instant. Is that what you saw? Is that wonderful?'

'I saw it. And I stayed with it. It is wonderful. Because God is the void this knot is tied in – and I reached that void. Though what the nature of the void is remains for others, for Higher Adepts, to see . . . one day.'

The carpet writhed and reared again. Molten gold flowed around the rivers of the mandala, bearing rabid energies along.

Fatumeh tossed her pigtail. 'What is the point of the Old Human – now that we have seen this? He has succeeded. He is fulfilled. Let him pass.'

'What is the point of *you* – if you only want to be a void! What sort of existence is that?'

'When we are one with the void behind the world one day, we will be able to tie that knot in the void ourselves. We will be God. We will be able to create out of nothing – maybe *this* universe, maybe another universe. Or universes. One day, together.'

She began weaving shapes in the air, copying the warp and woof of the carpet with her hands. The tips of her fingers caught the sun. Her nails were mirrors. Where they moved, they still remained – as light-tracks burned into my retinas. They left indelible traces which the air retained. The mandala of the carpet wove itself into light, entire before my very eyes.

'I always am, this moment always it,' Fatumeh sang. 'The boat goes round and round. Round these golden rivers of light! Nothing is lost that ever has been. There is nothing to mourn. I can halt time a little to show you this. I can lead you into the same river twice.'

She wove till the carpet was complete, hanging there, glowing. Then, with a sweep of her hand, she erased it.

At that instant, the sun jumped out of sight, behind the window frame. It moved in a leap – like the hand of a clock leaping forward from one minute to the next.

My heart jerked with the shock. She had only mesmerized me with those flashing hands of hers! Hypnotized me. Made me dream my own picture of the carpet in mid-air. It was just a conjuring trick. My mind was so vulnerable, still.

She'd not proved *anything* special. Anything!

'When the dervishes danced themselves into a trance,' she said gaily, 'how much time passed for them? Didn't they too dance to stop time? I can weave a shape that will halt time for myself for a whole day. For *you*, I can stop time for a few minutes. The mind weaves a chrysalis for itself. One learns, inside it. About the knot tied in nothingness.'

I don't know what Feng had seen. But he begged me, 'Come and see. A man, a woman. Two Adepts will be coming out today. One from clay, one from liquid.'

I went numbly, with him and Fatumeh.

A crowd of children and youths tagged along with us, prancing and banging finger drums and cymbals, and blowing trumpets made of bone – human bone? To welcome the emerging Adepts, Feng said. Naturally! It was plain enough to me that being drowned in a crystal of liquid or baked into a clay statue were *initiation rites* – to prove the power holders strong. A way of electing and perpetuating a private, secret ruling class, which seemed to have decided now that it could eventually do without any class of ordinary men to rule. Which, of course, was the surest, if maddest way of holding on to power forever! With what gusto Maimouna would have thrown herself into this routine!

My vision was still playing tricks, and the top part of Mount Ga Dan seemed a very unreal town indeed as I stumbled down through the monastery buildings, the buildings flowing and twisting elastically like dream buildings; but I did note one blank tower equipped with huge horns and antennas which might have been the actual place where some brat was playing womb-music for transmission to Lhasa.

But . . . had the glass Prism *really* been such a false experience? Such a phoney mystery? And only that?

No! That wasn't true. I'd seen the Great Nothing, the Great Darkness at the root of all Light and Being. It had been a genuine vision – of horror.

Yes! It was a lie. I'd just been dazzled into a fit, like an epileptic by flickering lights. In any case, either way there was nothing to be got out of it. No enhancement of life. No humanity.

'The Asuran Intermix,' Fatumeh was saying, 'is a fine training for the young children in losing oneself and gaining access to a new and larger self—'

'You don't fly to Asura from *Lhasa*!'

She indicated the huge aerials of buildings, blithely.

'We're in contact with Miami and Kazakhstan all the time. We can fly to anywhere, from anywhere. You see, all three alien worlds are important teaching games, as well as genetic optimizers. Asura teaches the higher and lower mental states. Yidag prepares for the mental "puberty" change – the chrysalis shift – and lays the groundwork for teaching machines like the Prism. We have to have access to all of them. And, of course the High Adepts are busy designing new alien worlds, to incorporate new insights and techniques . . . It amuses our children richly that the outsiders take their mind games for actual realities—'

'I bet it does!'

The lowest of the old monastery buildings was the terminal for a funicular ratchet railway. A single line descended steeply into the upper reaches of the woods from here. We boarded a carriage (built like a flight of steps inside) and rode down. Off to the south I saw a lake of broken glass tilted on its side, the solar energy panels for the Ga Dan community. Trees flickered in front of these, so I stared down at the wooden floor to keep my mind and my eyesight clear.

'Why do you put some Adepts through the hoop, and others in a bottle?' I asked quietly.

Fatumeh replied, 'It's simply a question of which chrysalis seems more appropriate. As I said, we monitor the body-field and watch how well each child performs on the machines—'

I felt sick.

'—the Yidag bottle is a bit more outward-looking and connected to the world, if only because it lets the light in. Immersion in the liquid completely blurs any actual "view", of course. There's just sheer *glow*, rising with the dawn then dimming with the dusk like a very long sine wave – in a simple harmonic motion of light. So it's still a very cut-off experience. But the hoop cuts outside input right down to zero. It wraps the child up utterly in its own mind. Cuts it off as completely as a spaceman floating in a void where no stars are. Its own mind is all that it can confront.'

'Isn't there some sense of touch? Some heat? Some pressure? The hoops must be a lot more painful than floating in a bottle. Kushog was *tortured*!'

'No, the clothing protects. It insulates and isolates. It evens out temperature and pressure. In the initial stage, till the trance is deep enough, it actually cuts down sensation. You see, it's smeared inside with an anaesthetic gell. That's to begin with. Later, it dries out.'

'Kushog—'

'—wasn't ready for the experience. His imagination ran away with him.'

'*Why put him through it, then?*'

'He might have been ready. His obsession with *chöd* . . . It would be nice to recruit directly from Old Humanity too. More continuity, if you like—'

'Less guilt!'

'There's no guilt. None at all.'

We quitted the train in a small clearing, where several woodland paths converged on an ancient carved slab a couple of metres high. Most of the old slab had been scratched and raked into illegibility, though not recently.

'Peasants scraped the words off in the old days,' explained Feng. 'They thought they were magic. They brewed medicines with the powder.'

Fatumeh grinned at human naïveté. 'Taking their medicine the hard way!'

To my mind, she and Feng belonged to a world of wild superstition too. Simply a higher version of it: more technical, more powerful. Reason and humanity had been tossed aside in a monstrous conspiracy, which had somehow seized control of the world in the midst of whatever troubles had actually brought down the previous rational, technological civilization which we'd all so cleverly been taught to loathe. How long had these worshippers of Future Man been infiltrating the world, till they succeeded? For centuries? I would probably never know the real historical facts. History had been so cleverly warped, or erased. The most I could do was keep my eyes open and learn as much as I could in their stronghold . . . Somewhere, somehow, some truth could still be restored. There was still time enough, if their plan for erasing Humanity was to take several centuries, and if their servants, such as Feng, still felt insecure, afraid of the wasps' nest of all the ordinary human beings in the world.

We walked through a glade, and came to the great golden crystal with the naked girl suspended in it. We squatted on our haunches in a circle with the others and waited. Minutes passed. More minutes. Everybody was quiet now.

'Soon,' Fatumeh whispered, draping her pigtail over her belly. 'It will be soon.'

We watched for long minutes while sunshine flooded the crystal and insects buzzed loudly round it.

'How do you know?' I forced myself to ask. 'Is there a time-switch or something?'

'No, nothing mechanical. You can tell by her height in the fluid. Ah. See?'

A thin line of golden bubbles rose from the girl's lips. Quite suddenly she floated up till her head vanished from sight in the crystal's metal cap, which now began to rotate slowly. A dozen youngsters pressed forward to form a human pyramid up the side of the crystal, as the cap sprang loose and hung by a wire. The girl's head emerged, her eyes blinking. Her shoulders and arms pushed up, fluid rolling back down her skin into the vat as if it was all one single substance that could be infinitely stretched but never snapped. The sheer loyalty of its molecules was the reason for the membrane that I thought I'd seen protecting the girl's body.

She swung her legs over the lip and perched there, flexing her body for a while, drawing deep breaths. Then swiftly she shinned down the backs of the human pyramid, which collapsed back to the ground around her. She stood there radiantly.

'How long has she been in that—?'

'—Polywater,' added Feng.

'Hush. Listen,' said Fatumeh.

The girl spoke to everyone in the clearing, but it wasn't any language I knew. Syllables stuck together in blobs that became sentences, which themselves were blobs that formed larger blobs – Many-in-One. It was a language of flow like a whirl-pool, a language of encirclement. It was a language that flowed like spilt mercury, bouncing, splitting, clustering, absorbing, in bright liquid blobs that all ran together finally into one, yet carelessly handled could split into a thousand particles and be lost. That's how it sounded to me. It was a memorized mumbo-jumbo. It was a magic ritual, such as the Old Magicians must have used to call down Storm Gods and Sun Gods, Gods of the Hunt, Gods of Power. A cryptic succession of nonsense syllables that made her seem a more primitive, not a superior form of human being at all!

'She's been in the vat twenty days, this one,' remarked Fatumeh when the girl's recitation was at an end and she was leaving the glade accompanied by one of the adults. 'Her mind has been composing this . . . well, praise song, you could call it, while she was in there. She has a higher co-ordination brain capacity now. Her speech shows it. Important physical changes take place in the brain during the chrysalis phase, you see. The topology of thought grows more complex, more self-analytical. We all have an inborn programme for learning human speech. But the channel width of language is still very narrow – even though there are a vast number of unused simple sounds, in every language, that could widen it. For example, the whole of the English vocabulary can be reduced to one-syllable words without robbing it of any subtlety – there are *so very many* unused combinations! The chrysalis phase takes the speech programme one step further, by generating a potential for far denser, richer structures – with the language patterns of old as a sort of simpler, larval form. There's feedback-training from the evolved Adepts nowadays, to the time before she enters the chrysalis, of course. Now she'll have to refine her new speech among them. What we're devising – and *using*, thanks to the chrysalis "re-wiring" – are higher order languages that can express vastly more, tersely. Actually describe the appearance of faces – or the activity of swimming, say – instead of just naming them with a crude label . . .

'Can a butterfly still crawl, after it has ceased to be a caterpillar? Of course, if it chooses to. Just as I am speaking to you – and Feng – now, in a way that you'll understand! But it's still crawling. It's clipping my wings for you. She's a Low Adept, like myself. The High Adepts, though . . . they can't clip their wings and be prehuman again so easily. Their concept environment is so different – their whole *umwelt*, their perceived environment. They represent the full chrysalis leap. That girl and I are still only partial leaps, midway between old and new – winged caterpillars, if you like. Actually, we hope to proceed to their level before the end of our lives. Far-Future Man – as opposed to merely Future Man – may very well have more chrysalis stages in store for him than we realize yet!' Her voice rose into a hymn of thanksgiving, a song of triumph. 'Including, perhaps, eventual disembodiment into a free psi-plasma state, a liberated body-field – without a body, able to draw energy from the sun, even from the fabric of space in ways we can't yet dream – till the stars are reached, that way! We will be angels, one day. Not I myself, but my children's children a hundred generations ahead. Though I live with them already, in Absolute Time. I am not lost; any more than Old Humanity is lost!

'We may never die then, unless we choose. Perhaps we can embody ourselves temporarily then, in other animals on this and other worlds, even in trees, in anything alive – and *be* the tiger, or the giant saguaro cactus in the desert, or the whale in the sea, or even a beetle or a snail. These embodiments will only be games. It will be out in space – when we really learn to read the universe – that we shall meet other great minds that are equals or superiors, and learn with them, or perhaps learn on our own, how it is that we will become God and bring into being the universe which brought us into being! The gene pool will have to resaturate itself for generations, before this happens. That's the work, from now on.'

She calmed down. We left the glade of the golden crystal, with the remaining celebrants, to hike through the woods towards the artificially wet scar of the Claypeople village.

TWENTY-TWO

To walk down that avenue of statues, knowing that there were human beings fastened up in some of them, made my skin crawl. The girl floating in golden liquid at least looked serene. The acceptable face of this inhuman, alien cult. But the baking of human flesh in clay to make a mental pupa revolted me and I flinched from contact with any of the vile objects – in as much as anyone could flinch without sliding through thick slime into another of them!

The balloon was tethered low, forming a long grey roof. Bright sunlight couldn't play tricks with my eyesight, and I saw how foul, dank and mistaken all this was. This was the ultimate place where children were brought to pull the wings off flies.

Half-way along the avenue, a crowd gathered round one of the statues. The majority were 'Claychildren' – their suits flopping about amorphously and their hoods pulled up over their heads. They stared out through red goggles, like a band of mad lizard priests.

The hoops were not so hooplike, after all. The human spine could hardly have stood so much abuse. They were more of a rounded triangle, with the body – hunched in a foetal position – forming the bent hypotenuse. In the village plaza, cane and spit baskets of the same shape – which Kushog, in his delirium, had failed to notice, or which had been edited out, somehow, for him – lay piled up waiting to be used as frames for new statues – banana-shaped boats for holding the body.

Something wearing black shinned up the rope ladder to the nacelle of the balloon. Shortly after he or she entered it, intolerably bright blue light drenched the village, as the whole underside of the balloon lit up with powerful, yet diffused lamps. The lamps dimmed out, leaving the avenues haunted by ghostly images of the clay statues as wriggling spirits.

More mystification – bright lights to blind you in the daytime!

The clay on top of 'our' statue began cracking and crazing,

shortly afterwards. It burst apart in a spray of dirty potsherds and splintered cane; a dried, black, leathery hand forced its way out, then a second wrinkled hand. Mummified hands. Baked, dried meat hands. What a horror – a body mummified alive, and still alive after it.

The hands swung together in a swimming thrust, and forced framework and clay apart. A featureless, withered head emerged. Followed by a shrivelled body.

However, the dry black skin was already beginning to peel and shed itself. It was one of those slug-suits they wore, bone dry, ready for sloughing. One of those null-sensation suits, slowly dried out and crisped, by body heat mainly I suppose, after the initial turning over the fire, till its tightening pull awoke the victim from his trance . . .

Wearing it was a youth: unharmed, undamaged – his skin blanched white. His buttocks wriggled free. His feet kicked the remnants of the suit and clay away as he climbed down to the ground by himself, unassisted; a lesser distance than from the crystal's top. He tore the last black crêpe fabric free from his eyes and mouth; and he spoke, too . . .

Mumbo-jumbo!

'His body speaks too, in concern with his mind,' whispered Fatumeh. 'See how his whole body speaks!'

As he spoke, the youth began oscillating. With immense concentration, he nodded his head, flexed his arms, bent his legs, and waggled his fingers – all in separate, contradictory rhythms, as though he was trying to suggest new axes to three-dimensional space, trying with his own body to map out different dimensions at right angles to each other: each with its own particular frequency, yet all within this here-and-now space of ours. He looked . . . so distorted, so disjointed. Yet as he danced, and as he spoke on, in messages of the body – messages which his body seemed to communicate directly to my own muscles, and thus into my mind underneath my conscious awareness, without my *knowing* the content of what he was saying – the world itself began to distort, to fragment. I felt myself drawn inexorably in to his crazy multi-dimensional dance.

'A High Adept,' breathed Fatumeh. 'He will scale the heights.'

A master hypnotist, she meant! I felt myself flying apart –

as though at the Dusk intermix on Asura; as though I'd actually made the bird fly from the tree – and Klimt's threatened calamity had followed. What happened then is hard for me to say – for this 'me' labelled Lila Makindi – because I flew apart into many separate selves. I had no *self* as such, for a long while. I remember now; but it wasn't the same as the experience. I was a hundred separate personalities, a hundred separate states of mind simply conspiring to think they had an identity together. I remember; but it isn't the experience – any more than the name 'swimming' shows the integrated complex motions of the body on the water. I was experiencing the *disintegration* of my phantom 'self' named *Lila*, into the separate coexisting spheres that underlay the 'field of Self' . . .

I was: a Brain That Dreams . . . a wraith of fantasies concerning the remembered world, seeing them all with an internal eye that had no consciousness of time, and hardly even knew how to focus. Any effort to focus it made it slide away, like a rolling socketless eyeball under the pressure of a finger, to refocus just as indefinitely on something else. If only I could wake this eye from its endless, rolling dream, I could tie a knot in this chaos of fantasies. Each knot I tied was a bow, that slipped free even as I tied it. I was only a Brain That Dreams.

I was: A Brain That Works. That turns the head, that takes steps, plants the foot down, clenches fingers in a fist, opens the mouth to speak; a Brain that pumps lungs, beats the heart, swivels the eyeballs, flinches from fire, holds urine in the bladder, too. However, the Brain That Works was only the *doing* of these things, an automaton. It could not help my Brain That Dreams to tie that simple knot.

I was: a Brain that Searches and Perceives. Even this state of mind swiftly flew apart into a Brain that Perceives, and a separate Brain That Searches, each ignorant of the other. I perceived: a chaos of lights and colours that had no breadth, no depth, no height – a swirling blur without meaning, without dimensions. It made no sense. I *searched* – with all kinds of shapes and patterns, to fit on the world, to give it a form and make sense of it – but there was nothing to fit these on to, no communion with the Perceiving Brain, even though I perceived, and searched the very same scene (where a boy dictator's limbs were disjointing rhythmically in a host of separate, private dances) ...

I was: a Brain That Remembers; a Brain That Records. I remembered *and lived again* my love-making with Rajit on Sinda Beach. His hair hung down in a black, water-twisted rope; my mouth was sweet and drunken with his palm-wine flavoured kisses. My Brain That Times and Locates raced away from the vividness of such total, resurrected memory – for this Brain That Remembers obeyed the same stasis of time as my Brain That Dreams; only, it dealt with What Was, rather than with What Might Be. With events not permutations.

Somewhere between these brains, between dream and memory, there must be a Brain That *Wills*: a brain that turned all the possibilities of the world into one particular set of events, one reality; a brain that knotted the probable into the real ... I couldn't find it! For there was no 'I' to do the finding! The idea of 'I' was only a conspiracy, an illusion. All possibilities existed. Everything – and nothing. And so my thought-states flew apart into lesser and lesser states: into cube, then line, then point, each along its own personal axis, of dreaming, working, perceiving, forming and searching, remembering – as the dancer bent each hand separately, in his dance, each finger of each hand, and each joint of each finger, in a semaphore performed with huge attention, that spoke directly to this flock of minds. The box of my skull and the scaffold of my body was the only agreement they had on who 'I' was.

If this was so for me, then indeed no human being really existed – yet! How I recoiled from this non-existence of myself, of all mankind, *afterwards*! At the time it happened, though, there was no 'I' to will me to recoil ...

Finally the world returned; and so did 'I'. The naked youth, his dance done, stalked intently out of the clay village – white as a worm hatched in human flesh, white as the droppings of a distempered dog!

'You *knew* there, Lila,' insisted Feng.

'I knew nothing,' I moaned. 'Hypnotism ... hallucination ... what do I know? Only that I'm always manipulated. Every human being is manipulated. But to be human is all there is for human beings. Just living in this world is wonderful. Loving.

Tasting palm-wine on the lips. Swimming. Working, growing plants to eat—'

'Being "human" in your terms,' sighed Fatumeh, '*is* a state of hypnosis. "Just living" is just that! You couldn't hold yourself together there, could you? That's because there isn't really any coherent *you* to hold together. You're just a cluster of different states of mind, bound together in one large atom like so many electrons orbiting it. The electrons are leaping from orbit to orbit all the time, knocking each other out and excluding each other!'

'Bardo is about the ⁚⁚⁚ genocide of man, woman, human beings. Your Future Man will never exist. There'll always be something *beyond*, and beyond again. A dog never catches its tail. You're so wrong.' I tore a lump of jagged clay from the ruptured statue and pitched it high at the balloon. It fell short. It fell nowhere special.

'Just because a more conscious human being is emerging out of Old Humanity, is that murder? So the butterfly murders the caterpillar?' said Fatumeh mockingly.

I tore another lump free, bristling with needles of splintered cane, and I slashed at Feng and at pregnant Fatumeh. At least I was able to will that petty little attack – of my own free will!

Not that I hurt Fatumeh; though I may have caught Feng. She waggled her hands in the air before my face; and time stuck fast for a moment, till she walked aside. She was a very adept hypnotist. And I was three times vulnerable – from my first trapping in the Prism light; from Fatumeh's carpet-weaving trick; and now from the boy's mind-wrenching dance which made me doubt whether I was 'I', a person at all. I was just a subject under her control. A puppet. An automaton.

Fatumeh shook her head sympathetically.

'Anybody can be hypnotized,' I cried.

'No, Adepts can't be. Unless they want to be. But ordinary humans do hypnotize themselves almost all the time. That's quite true. Lightly or deeply. Your Old Human is still a pre-conscious creature, with brief gleams of true consciousness, fading almost as soon as they dawn. He's asleep. The lifelong dream is enticing and magnetic. Your Old Human can get very angry in his dreams. Like you, just now. He lashes out, to stay asleep. You must realize you've been shown something important today – woken up a little – not just fooled.'

'I don't blame you for the shock reaction, Lila,' said Feng, touching his cheek, perhaps to hide a cut I'd made. Perhaps not, for I saw no blood. 'You can take a week to think about this. You'll have to decide then. That's long enough. We do need administrators. Enthusiastic go-betweens. We'll certainly know whether you're telling the truth, when you say yes. As I sincerely hope you will. You're quite a transparent person, you know. We do *know* people.'

Was I indeed? Who did Feng mean by 'we'? Grandeur by contamination!

'Anyway, a simple Backster test can tell us if your **yes** is genuine. Any plant hooked up to a galvanometer will do.'

'Otherwise,' said Fatumeh, 'you do realize that there's only one place left for you?'

I remembered a red hen walking down a tyre track in Baga-moyo village, hypnotized by the regular line. Walking – until a dog raced out barking to break its trance ...

'Doesn't a dog fully exist then? Doesn't a hen fully exist?' I pleaded. 'Should we get rid of all the dogs and hens just because they're living in a dream?'

TWENTY-THREE

So I had a week to think things over, back in the Potala, by myself. A tough Mongol or Tartar drove me back to the Palace, alone. My door wasn't kept locked; but another patient, incommunicative guard sat in the corridor outside.

Perhaps alien 'Adepts', far out in space, had indeed influenced the human mind. There must be other advanced thinking beings out there somewhere. So perhaps Bardo's lie was in some queer distorted sense the *truth*, to be discovered eventually by those 'disembodied' Adepts who would leave the Earth one day? Perhaps Bardo was even an alien experiment with *Humanity*, carried out so subtly and over so long a period that even Bardo didn't know about it! Carried out by intelligences so advanced that you would have to call them 'gods'! Does one argue with a God? Does one go against God's will?

Like that hen in Bagamoyo, I brooded down this track, then down another; and always I was shocked away by a bark, in me: of *anger*.

Yungi had been removed permanently to the custody of the crèche. I didn't mind. She wasn't mine . . . Besides, Bardo had quite successfully taught the world for long enough to rein in the personal self! All for the sake of a healthy human society, they said. It was really because they didn't think that the mass of people had any 'selves' to bother with!

Anger again. Fury at them.

Bibi Mwezi had poured boiling water over her arm, to express *her* self! Maimouna had drunk a pickled spider down!

It was nonsense about 'alien gods' guiding us. Faith in the Beyond used to be a fine excuse for ravaging this world with a clear conscience. There was just a different faith, now – in a different Beyond. Which let Bardo, with an equally clear conscience, pronounce sentence: Man is Past.

All this time Feng left me alone.

On the sixth day I demanded to see Yungi. I had to leave my room. It had become like one of their clay hoops fastened around me, cooking me into something I refused to be. The stone walls were mirrors, thrusting me back in upon myself. Until I gave up my anger. Until I submitted. *Believed.*

Suddenly I found I longed to see Yungi. Yet I was scared to see her, too. Did I only want to see her so that I could recoil from her? If I didn't recoil from her, but loved her and believed in her instead, why then I must clearly foresee the day when a gangling milk-coffee girl drifted down into a golden Yidag bottle, dangling there for days till finally she floated back up to the surface with a praise-song on her lips that I could only hear, not comprehend – a butterfly with wings invisible to me. Was I to love that strange, altered being, who could only feel a wry compassion for me?

To know, I had to see her. It was she herself who must tell me how. My body said so.

Opening the door, I said Feng's name to the Dobdob and pointed at the telephone nearby on the wall. He dialled and handed me the receiver.

'Feng? Is that you? I must see Yungi. Only she can make my mind up for me. She's the part of me that's still outside of me. The part that I still can't reach. Can you understand that?'

'Certainly. Pass the phone back to the Dobdob. I'll tell him to take you there.'

When the Dobdob cradled the phone, he gestured me along the corridor with him in the direction of the crèche.

It was early evening now. A bright July evening. When we arrived in the crèche the Sun was shining right through the window embrasures, illuminating the mandalas on the walls. The room hummed with that murmur of earphone music like the drone of bees. Most of the babies were asleep. Over some of their cots hung large polyhedral mobiles of plastic or glass, turning slowly with shapes moving about inside them as they turned: kaleidoscope mobiles. The Dobdob greeted the Barefoot Nurse, who joined him by the door to chat softly.

I found Yungi asleep, her head turned on one side, the eyelids like grey porcelain seashells. Her hands were bunched up by her head, near the humming earphones, the palms half open.

One of those mobiles turned above her cot, presenting one transparent face after another so that she could watch the changing, scurrying shimmer inside it whenever she was awake.

Kneeling beside her, I gazed up into it from her viewpoint. I saw a series of different illusion-mazes with a little red dragon running through each of them. The constant rotation of the mobile created the illusion that the little dragon was running this way and that, searching for a way through. At the same time, a multitude of small, cunningly arranged mirrors and sections of polarized glass altered the apparent layout of the maze while the polyhedron turned, so that the dragon image had to run a different way each time. An illusion chasing through illusions.

Getting up, I twirled the mobile faster and Yungi's eyes opened. Her hands flapped against the mattress as though she was about to cry. On the cheek where she'd been sleeping was a pressure mark. I watched it slowly fading. Like the tiny handprint of a slap.

Golden sunlight caught every dust mote in the air: the yolk of day, sieved from the white. I spun the maze mobile very fast, and Yungi burped. A curd-like drool dribbled out of one side of her mouth. It smelt so faint, yet so penetrating. As if it could not to be washed away. If I as much as touched the curd with my fingertip the smell would sink into my skin forever.

Kneeling down again, with the smell of the curd growing sickly strong; I stared up along with her at the vastly speeded-up series of races through the many possible different mazes.

Dragon raced up one path. Which became another path. Which Dragon was already racing up again. Which became another path. Flash, flash, flash. The separate, alternative mazes fused into each other – till they were all happening at once. Till all options were equal, and Time got cancelled out by the inpouring of extra, co-existing Spaces. Till Time became Space. And glueing all these multiple Spaces together was that same intimate, nauseating stink of curd . . .

Red dragon ran away into the distance, looking like a scuttling hen. Already he was setting out in pursuit of that same hen. For red hen, red dragon were the same beast – at different points!

Dragon was a tiny Star Beast – the Star Beast of Yungi's mind, growing up. The beast that would feed on the hens of Humanity, scattering their feathers to the wind – though it *was them* all along. Yungi was watching *me* scuttle up and down in there, to left and right.

Her curd stank of dragon's breath. My baby dragon! Where was the innocence of a dragon?

Again she burped and drooled as she blinked into the many whirling mazes, which were all one . . .

'Lila!'

A familiar voice. Silky and sly. Maimouna's. I straightened up dizzily.

'What are you up to? Doting?' She laughed softly. My Dobdob guard looked doubtful but apparently the nurse reassured him. Maimouna must have been busy ingratiating herself. He didn't stop her coming in to speak to me.

'You dropped out of sight. I haven't seen you for ages. Have you flown yet? I have, of course. I just finished my second flight.' She smiled confidently. 'I imagine I shall be flying again in another few weeks.'

'Do you really? Well, which is your baby?'

'Doudou? Who cares! I think he's down at the other end, unless they've moved him.'

'Why visit him if you don't care?'

'I'm finding my way about, Lila dear. Feeling out the ground. Setting precedents. Discovering things.'

'Insinuating yourself; I see. Tell me, do you still have that other ear-globe of yours? The one with the fly in it.'

For a moment she looked horrified. She must know that the nurse spoke no English, but she glanced at the Dobdob anxiously.

'Don't worry, he doesn't understand either—' Still, there were always Feng's microphones to beware of. Maybe there were some hidden in the crèche . . .

Yungi's eyes were closing sleepily now that the mobile was slowing down to normal speed again.

I murmured, 'Farewell, dragon daughter. And if you don't grow up – and if your life gets cut short – please remember that you've *been* alive. Which means that you've *always* been alive. You came into being. That must be better than not having ever been at all. Nothing's ever lost, my Star Beast daughter, isn't that so?'

'What are you mumbling about?'

'I want you to hug me, Maimouna. I want you to look as though you really love me like a sister.'

She approached me – rather as though I had a knife hidden up my sleeve.

'Hug me,' I pleaded.

And she did indeed become ingratiatingly loving then – connivingly so, like a child trying to gain a present. She put her arms around me. I held her too, and whispered.

'You're pregnant, Maimouna. Truly! They switched the spider and the fly around back in Miami. Feng told me. You drank the fertility drug instead. I saw your little egg drifting out along your Fallopian tube to meet Mular's sperm. Feng showed me it all on a scanner while you two lovers were flying. He was quite amused. You're going to have more babies. Till they retire you to Madagascar – yes, that's where they send you. You didn't know that – and that's just *one* thing—!'

Briefly, all too briefly, I tried to explain about the true aim of Bardo; to convey a little, just a little, of what I had seen.

'They don't want *you* for a helper. If you still want power, there's only one way to get it. You'll have to tell the Dobdobs running the war what the Star Beast really is! And where to find it! On Earth, not sixty kilometres from here. Even here, in the crèche—'

I broke down; I cried in her arms. Because I was telling her to turn those men of war downstairs into warmongers once again. I was telling her the way to revive the devil in Man ...

'But they needn't become baby-killers! The Bardo-born can easily miss the change in their lives if they aren't geared up for it. I could still take my Yungi away and raise her normally—'

Did I really believe it? Weren't the Dobdobs all too likely to use their guns murderously and indiscriminately, in rage at the conspiracy they'd been so unwittingly protecting?

Maybe not. Humanity might still rise against Bardo with a compassionate anger. There'd been one and a half centuries of Social Ecology – a blessing in itself, even if its foundations were a lie! We might still be able to keep the spirit of the society that Bardo had created, even in the midst of cutting off its head . . . It mightn't happen too bloodily.

'Make the ordinary Dobdobs understand what the Kushog emergency was really about! Lead them down the corridors to the room behind their War Room! Drink your other drug so that you can lose the baby, then you'll have to fly again and go down there, won't you? You'll become their queen, their liberator. Fate threw us together so that you could have this chance.'

She pulled away from me, frowning.

'You really must hate me, mustn't you, Lila?' She lowered her voice with exaggerated caution. 'Just because I couldn't give you any of the drug! When I even took the trouble to explain how there was only enough for one dose! When I went out of my way to tell you!'

'But . . . don't you believe . . . anything I said? I thought you wanted to find out what Feng really knew!' I stared at her, and I realized that actually she was looking utterly crafty. Oh yes, she *had* taken it in. She was just faking – while she thought about it!

'If I did believe all that, my dear, would I run back to my room and drink that fly-juice just on your say-so?'

'Wait till the end of the month. You'll know you've been tricked by then. And not by me.'

'Obviously I shall wait till the end of the month.'

'If it's too late by then—'

'You see, there's a world of difference between a contraceptive – and an abortion drug! So you couldn't trick me, if that was the idea.'

'—you'll have to find some other way. Oh!' I realized what she had just said. Of course! Why else would they have left the fly-globe with her, if it was anything more than a mere toy *during* her pregnancy? No wonder I was puzzling her, as I grasped frantically at any straw. 'You must get down there somehow, Maimouna. If you're so clever at finding your way about!'

'I'm sure I could.'

'You must wake the Dobdobs up. Maybe you can work through Chang? But that's dangerous – just telling one Dobdob. You must tell them all! I can't manage it. You're still practically a free agent compared with me. You have to be their liberator. And everybody's!'

'Maimouna shall make up her own mind what's best to believe,' she said with an oblique smile, detaching herself still further, veering towards the door. 'And what's best to do. Speaking as a free agent, I shall bear it all in mind, my dear, I promise you.'

Yes she would. She must. Feng must see his contempt for fallible, human Maimouna rebound. I'd planted the seed. Even though it was the power, not the truth, she cared about!

With a wink, she took her leave of me. Not as someone mocking me – but as my accomplice, I hoped.

But what about me, *now*? My own time had run out. Feng had said they would know if I was telling the truth if I said yes and didn't really mean it. And if they were in any doubt, a mere plant hooked up to a galvanometer could tell them! I had to believe it. But if I said no, and my Dobdob guard reported me talking to Maimouna – she would never be able to act, in my absence.

Something had to distract him completely. Something that closed my case forever in Feng's mind too – leaving Maimouna free.

Yungi lay naked in the cot except for the nappy tied round her middle. No pillow, of course. And too warm for a blanket this July night.

A few clean nappy towels lay on a shelf. I snatched hold of these. My Dobdob was still looking vaguely out along the corridor, where Maimouna had departed. The nurse, then . . . ! She would have to see me.

I tugged the earphones off Yungi's head, waking her up with a little grunt of surprise. It took a while before she actually started crying at the disturbance. Such a while.

Then I pressed the soft heap down upon her upturned, noisy face.

I pressed gently. As ineffectively as I could.

At last the nurse cried out in Tibetan.

The Dobdob reached me first – pulling me away violently and quickly towards the door. It had surely only taken seconds but I couldn't be sure that Yungi was still alive. I couldn't see her! She might have breathed in strands of towel or vomited and choked on that.

Neither could I hear her crying. I tried to hear her, how I tried. I cried out myself, involuntarily, as the Dobdob twisted my arms to rush me along the corridor. And by then I was too far away to hear.

EPILOGUE

It's winter and the wind rages like a wall of ice, up top. There's so much hail and snow in it, it may as well be ice: a stiff block scraping across the ice-cap from end to end. Nothing moves; everything is locked up tight. Even the wind is solid. Life stands still, transfixed.

This place is called K 22. K stands for *Karma*: the Indian word for what a person's deeds in life produce. Geographically, it's between West Ice Shelf and Shackleton Ice Shelf on the Antarctic coast. In summer I have to wear wooden spectacles with slits in them, to stop myself from going blind; the clothes I wear even then make me waddle like a penguin. In winter the storms force everyone underground for months on end.

Elsewhere in the world, for the next few hundred years or maybe for the next few thousand years, they are busily upgrading the human race; that's to say phasing it out of existence. We don't discuss this too often, we prisoners. By now it seems incredible. We must have been sent here for some reason. Perhaps we were saboteurs? Agents of the Star Beast? A certain woman called Maimouna obviously had no wish to be a saboteur. I waited and waited for us to be set free. Nothing happened. Maybe she had no chance, or failed.

There are no permanent guards. We're left to ourselves, guarded by the environment. From time to time, Dobdobs who can't speak any of our languages inspect us and bring us more supplies. Bardo is a humane organization. Even if not human? We're set tasks, too, by printed instructions, which we perform out of boredom, even when they're dangerous. Some long-lived radioactive waste still lies buried in the ice, here and there; so we keep a watch on the level of radio-activity with geiger counters. Or we drill down through the ice to discover what the world's climate was like thousands of years ago. I think they're afraid of a new ice age cramping their world. Or maybe hoping for it – to speed up events. Or else we do other chores.

Karma 22 holds some five hundred people. The oldest is seventy; he has been here more than half his life. We Antarcticans will be extinct before the human race itself. Fewer prisoners arrive every year. Conceivably Bardo is filling fresh camps elsewhere round the rim of the ice-cap, not wishing to overcrowd us? Who knows? Our nearest neighbours, K 21 and K 23, are three hundred kilometres away to east and west; we have no contact.

From time to time some of us still discuss the situation. On the whole despondently; old rebels have lost heart . . .

The oldest prisoner spoke of someone called Hitler and his 'Nazi Party' who had waged open war on the world two centuries ago under the swastika banner, having mesmerized a whole nation into zombie soldiers. That group too had wanted to create a master race of superhumans. They too were sorcerers, mediums, who believed they were in touch with higher powers.

An old woman corroborated. She'd read all this in some suppressed antique book too. However, she disagreed that the present state of the world was similar. Her anger had mellowed with age.

'That man Hitler and his crew butchered millions of people and looted and burnt the world. Bardo is benign.' It would be nicer to die believing that.

'Maybe this is just a more successful second attempt we're living through!' I said, knowing next to nothing of the history they talked about. 'How can extermination ever be benign?'

A negro from Southern Africa joined in. 'No one *is* exterminated. The world *is* a happy place.' He too used to think as I did – or he wouldn't be here.

'Oh yes, for a few hundred years – till it's empty, except for *them*!"

'Maybe Man as we know him has always been a precarious compromise,' suggested the old woman. 'Not the highest sort of life at all, but only something perched midway between the beasts—'

'—And that Star Beast they worship!'

'They don't worship it. They . . . aspire to it. You make them sound like Devil worshippers. I know it seems beastly, negative

202

and terrifying to us – their sort of vision. I just don't happen to
be Bardo-born. I don't understand what it might seem like to
them.' We had all had more or less the same final experience, in
Lhasa or whatever. Some people's spirit had been broken by
it, even though they kept their sanity.

'You're weak. You're old. I won't call you a traitor.'

'We all have to live together, till we die,' nodded the old
man. 'I still think that Evil – no, damn it, let's say a Power;
an Alien Power, since it's very alien to us – has taken over the
world, and we're locked up in a sort of human Hell because of
it. The damned thing is, we can't be sure!'

'I can,' I said to the old man. He supported me, some way
at least.

'Did you see any actual evil?' the woman pressed.

'What about manipulation, lies, genocide? Isn't that
enough?'

'But it isn't genocide,' protested the negro.

'As for lies,' the old woman grieved, 'they're right. If we're
honest, our brains are lying nearly all the time, spinning fantasy
after fantasy. Bardo has woven a coherent, peaceful fantasy
of alien worlds, so that people won't start fantasizing hatreds
and differences. Those who can't stop themselves from doing
this have the Star Beast war to run. Whoever really wants truth
– unless they're told it's something they haven't got? Then
they only want it for the wrong reason, from resentment. And
they can't have it anyway, because they aren't coherent – because they fluctuate from one moment to the next, from personal fantasy to personal fantasy.'

'I'm talking about the *facts*,' I insisted. 'Not about this vision
of the universe, which is just a horror, anyway.'

The Prism! The knot tied in nothingness, by the turning
around on itself of something unimaginable in a void so complete that it was denser than matter, denser than stars! The
'destiny' of the living fibres in the cord from which this knot
was tied, to become conscious, then to become conscious of becoming conscious – so that this Cord of Being could learn how
to knot itself! (At the same time there was *no* cord, except
for the knot tied in it – even though that knot comprised a
whole universe of galaxies and stars and atoms!) A knot tied
in nothingness, only held together by the shaping of that knot

itself, by the relatedness of itself *to itself,* by the reflection of itself within itself! Horrible!

'I mean the *facts* about Bardo. I mean the fact that the human race – the wonderfulness of human life – is being reduced by Bardo year by year to a plane, then a line, then a point, so that it can disappear without a trace, while they "evolve" to chase this Nothing-Truth! Shall Man not even have the dignity of knowing he's being made to die out?'

'We're just mourners, here on the ice, mourning Man, Lila,' the old woman said gently. 'We have lived. We have loved. We have burned bright. Now we're burning out. Nothing that ever existed is really lost. Who has actually been killed? Nobody!'

'That's the appalling, clever evil of it, compared with your Hitler or whatever he was called, without his cardboard super-race! They've brainwashed you too.'

Next summer, I shall set off westwards across the ice shelf towards K23, muffled up like a penguin, with packs of dried fish on my back. I may not arrive there. Probably I won't. When I do arrive, it may be just like here: another identical karma-prison. Who knows, I may even find a woman called Maimouna there? A woman who tried. If only I could believe *that*! Maybe the sheer fact of my arriving, of my leaping the gap, may shock them out of their apathy and acceptance over there.

If I arrive, may I be the spark that leaps the gap! May I be the spark that sets the ice on fire!

Hearts, Hands and Voices

IAN McDONALD

A lyrical science fiction novel with haunting echoes of contemporary Ireland and Ulster from the 1992 Philip K. Dick Award-winning author.

'He is one of the finest writers of his generation, who chooses to write science fiction, because that is how he can best illuminate our world' – *New Statesman*

'At once disturbing and beautiful: superbly realised' – *The Times*

£4.99   ISBN 0 575 05373 9

Casablanca

MICHAEL MOORCOCK

For the first time in paperback: a fascinating miscellany of articles and a long novella form a collection by the ever-controversial Michael Moorcock.

'There are times when he reads like a strange hybrid of William Burroughs and Edgar Rice Burroughs: and there are times when he writes better than either' – Peter Ackroyd, *The Times*

£4.99   ISBN 0 575 05445 X

Wulfsyarn

PHILLIP MANN

On its maiden voyage, the *Nightingale*, the most advanced craft in the entire fleet of Mercy ships belonging to the Gentle Order of St Francis, vanished into deep space with its life bays packed with refugees.

Almost a year to the day later, heralded by a distress signal, the *Nightingale* reappeared, damaged in ways that meant its very survival in space was a miracle. Only one survivor walked from that partly mineral, partly sentient craft – its Captain, Jon Wilberfoss.

This is his story, as told by Wulf, the autoscribe.

'A *tour de force* . . . and . . . revelation . . . that haunts the mind long after the book is finished' – *The Times*

£3.99   ISBN 0 575 05162 0

The Martian Inca

IAN WATSON

Julio and his friends had salvaged a space capsule that had crashed on a remote Bolivian mountainside. They had inhaled the strange red dust that the pod contained, and fallen into comas. Only Julio and his beloved Angelina survived. But now these two view their world in a new light, believing that they have been reborn as terrible, powerful Godlike creatures – the Inca and his Queen.

Meanwhile in Space, a manned mission to Mars is also about to discover the devastating effects of the deadly soil.

What is the mysterious constituent that makes this dust so literally mind-blowing? And can it really increase Man's evolutionary potential?

'This book contains a new, near-poetic dimension. The most formidable fiction [Ian Watson] has yet written, and also one of the most compulsive' – *The Times*

£3.99   ISBN 0 575 05558 8

Aztec Century

CHRISTOPHER EVANS

In her dreams, Princess Catherine could still see London burning, and the luminous golden warships of her enemies, the Aztecs, as they added yet another conquest to their mighty Empire. Sweeping from occupied Britain to the horrors of the Russian front and the savage splendour of Mexico, *Aztec Century* is a magnificent novel of war, politics, intrigue and romance, set in a world that is both familiar – and terrifyingly alien.

'Intelligent, finely written, and towards the end, absolutely nail-biting' – Iain M. Banks

'A sacrificial *feast* of a story – highly original sf from the first page onwards, an intriguing and compelling thriller to the end' – Robert Holdstock

'Christopher Evans is particularly brilliant at mixing a cocktail of the everyday and the wonderful to make a magical alternative history' – Garry Kilworth

£8.99   ISBN 0 575 05540 5

The BSFA takes you beyond your imagination